OSTRICH C

David Nobbs was born in Orpington, educated at
Cambridge and in the Royal Corps of Signals, worked as a
reporter on the *Sheffield Star*, and his first break as a comedy writer
came on the iconic satire show *That Was The Week, That Was*, hosted
by David Frost. Later he wrote for *The Frost Report* and *The Two
Ronnies* and provided material for many top comedians including Les
Dawson, Ken Dodd, Tommy Cooper, Frankie Howerd and Dick
Emery. David is best known for his two TV hit series *A Bit of a Do*
and for *The Fall and Rise of Reginald Perrin*, now revived in a contem-
porary version, starring Martin Clunes. He lives in North Yorkshire
with his second wife, Susan. He has four stepchildren, eight grand-
stepchildren and one great-grand-stepchild.

Praise for David Nobbs's novels:

'Painfully hilarious, wonderfully observed and slight sour at the
same time'   *Guardian*

'Thank goodness for David Nobbs! He carries on the comic tradition
of P G Wodehouse with this marvellous new book; a sweet and
touching love story written with his trademark sly and subversive
humour. A perfect antidote to these dark times'   JOANNE HARRIS

'Probably our finest post-war comic novelist'   JONATHAN COE

'A marvellously comic novel'   *Sunday Times*

'One of the most noisily funny books I have ever read' MICHAEL PALIN

'Very funny sketches of provincial newspaper life'   SUE TOWNSEND

'The most satisfying novel I have read in years'   *Express*

DAVID NOBBS

Ostrich Country

HARPER

Harper
An imprint of HarperCollins*Publishers*
77–85 Fulham Palace Road,
Hammersmith, London w6 8jb

www.harpercollins.co.uk

This paperback edition 2010

First published in Great Britain by
Methuen & Co Ltd 1968

Copyright © David Nobbs 1968

David Nobbs asserts the moral right to
be identified as the author of this work

A catalogue record for this book is
available from the British Library

ISBN: 978 0 00 742786 4

Typeset in Garamond by Palimpsest Book Production Limited,
Falkirk, Stirlingshire

Printed and bound in Great Britain by
Clays Ltd, St Ives plc

I

'A change of environment will bring you new business and personal interests,' said Cousin Percy.

Pegasus was glad to hear this. He fancied a change of environment. He could do with some new business and personal interests.

'Thanks,' he said.

Pegasus cherished a secret ambition – to be a chef in a country inn. He'd never told anyone, not even Paula, for fear they'd laugh. It had become, over the years, something almost shameful. Several times he'd been on the point of taking action, but always this fear of ridicule had held him back. Now, with Cousin Percy's prediction to urge him on, it would be different.

'You will star in a new musical,' said Cousin Percy to Pamela Blossom, actress, singer, pin-up of the Atlantic weather ship S.S. *Hailstone*.

'I could do with the money,' said Miss Blossom.

He wanted to leave, to start his new life straight away, to go down to Kensington Gardens, to the seat, and say good-bye to Paula. He accepted another glass of the red wine and willed Cousin Percy to hurry up.

'You will win a vast new export order in the Middle East,' said Cousin Percy to Thomas Windham, the industrialist.

'That would certainly be just the fillip we need, and I'm sure everyone at Articulated Tubes and Cartons, on both sides, will do their level best to make your prophecy come true,' commented Thomas Windham.

Fifteen celebrities sitting in a circle, waiting for their predictions, waiting for the photographer to catch their modest smiles,

5

all invited because they were tipped to be the big names in their chosen fields during the next decade. All except Pegasus, who was there because he was family.

'You will operate on a royal personage,' said Cousin Percy to Tarragon Clump, the kidney surgeon.

'Well well,' said Tarragon Clump, who wasn't used to giving quotes.

Why had they all come? Vanity? Curiosity? Dipsomania? Agoraphobia? And why did Cousin Percy do it? Aged thirty-four. Ordained 1959. Suddenly lost his faith during the 1961 Cup Final, in the fifty-third minute. Became a free-lance journalist and designer. Pegasus had seen a play he'd designed – strong, spiky scenery. What had made him become the horoscopist for *Clang* and give this repulsive prediction party?

'Will I do the double this year?' said Edward Forrest, the cricketer, whom Pegasus had once seen bowled first ball at Lords.

'It will be a rewarding time emotionally, and a plan will bear fruit,' said Cousin Percy.

'Stuff the bloody emotions,' said Edwin Forrest. 'Stuff a plan bearing fruit. Will I do the double?'

He would leave London, the dreary institute off the North Circular Road, the bad dreams, his Hampstead flatlet where an old woman died upstairs and three months later he found out.

There'd be no more dreams, not in the country. Dreamless sleep.

'You will compere a new quiz programme between members of the dry-cleaning trade.'

At last the predictions were over. The circle broke up, conversation began. He could leave now.

He took a last glass of wine and drank it rapidly. Behind him someone said: 'I suppose royalty would be much the same as everyone else as regards vital organs, would they, Mr Clump?' but he didn't stop to hear the reply. He said: 'Good-bye. I must be off,' and Cousin Percy said 'Oh, are you off?' and then the voices faded and he was breathing the cold, clammy February air and he was on his way to Kensington Gardens.

He must get away from his old haunts and his memories of Paula. He must stop hanging around the National Film Theatre on Jean-Luc Godard nights in the hope of seeing her. He must cease these visits to Kensington Gardens.

His heart quickened as he approached the seat – the fifth seat on the left of the Broad Walk going towards Bayswater. It was on this seat that he had first kissed her, and it had been there that they had usually met.

He sat on the seat now and thought about her. He thought about the smell of her flesh, that faint, earthy, rubbery emanation of warmth.

She had light fair hair and her eyes . . . he couldn't remember the colour of her eyes.

His parents would be upset. They had made sacrifices. Weather forecasting wasn't all that well paid. They saw him as a famous biologist. His mother had visions of the Nobel Prize. Stockholm. Steady, sincere, unemotional applause. It would be hard to tell them, especially after all these years, especially after it had grown into such a secret ambition.

A new leaf, blown on warm zephyrs. A new life. A new Pegasus. New business and personal interests. A limitless prospect. You're going to miss out on all this, Paula.

The sky was heavy and colourless. Night would creep up unobserved. Pegasus sat on the seat, rather drunk, rather cold, thinking about Paula.

He closed his eyes and tried to remember her legs, slightly on the short side. She was a little round-shouldered but very desirable, unless his memory was playing him false. He thought of his lips flecking the inside of her arm just below the armpit, and of licking her left ear, in Academy One, during the Czech cartoon.

Soon his eyes filled with tears and his lips moved a little as he appealed to her.

Paula, Paula, how could you do it? I would have adored you for ever. Any impression you may have received to the contrary was caused by the tension which is inseparable from an intimate relationship between two tender and passionate souls. How could you leave me for anyone, let alone a man who translates Ogden Nash into Latin as a hobby? How could you make such a nonsense of my life, my darling rubbery lovely utterly . . .

Hell! A light silent rain was beginning to fall from the still, grey February sky. He was getting wet, because he had brought no raincoat, because his father had told him that the fine weather would continue.

2

Some of the slides had a man in them, and when one of these was shown the pigeons would find food. Some of them had no man in them. This meant that the pigeons would find only buttons and hard objects in the bowls.

When this pattern had been fully established, when man in slide equalled goodies even to the most retarded pigeon, Cummings would insert the algae. Some untreated, some flavoured, some mixed with pesticides, some from the outflow of nuclear power stations. Then Bradley and Pegasus would correlate the results.

Pegasus was merely a cog in all this. Miss Besant brought him his instructions from Mr Colthorpe, he got his results, Miss Besant took his results back to Mr Colthorpe. His little piece of work was fitted into someone else's grand design.

Bradley passed through now.

'Fantastic,' said Bradley.

'Yes?'

'The cats given the fish-flavoured weed from the Yorkshire Ouse are doing fantastically well. Twelve per cent heavier than the cats fed on normal cat food.'

'Fantastic.'

This was progress. Vast immovable growths of weed-guzzling cat. Must make the break today, while Cousin Percy's prediction is fresh in my mind.

Pegasus had often alleviated the boredom and distastefulness of his work by trying to convince himself that it was in the national interest, that he was a dedicated man, patriotically resisting the brain drain.

At other times, when he was wanting to persuade himself to give up and become a chef, he'd tried to convince himself that it wasn't in the national interest, or that the national interest wasn't in the world interest, or something, anything helpful.

He had never yet convinced himself of anything.

He began to go through the arguments again, the same old arguments, so familiar that he thought of them in note form nowadays.

He thought: Food, research into new sources of. For: increased use of earth's resources. Elimination of starvation. Against: increased depletion of earth's resources. Elimination of starvation could lead to even worse population problems, hence to even worse starvation.

Conclusion as regards value for mankind of nutritional experiments: no conclusion.

Miss Besant was typing – smoothly, lightly, efficiently, by way of contrast with her plump figure and red legs. She lodged in Willesden with two friends, kept her personality in the bank and only withdrew it at week-ends.

The coffee came round. Have one on me, Miss Besant. Nice momentarily to feel generous. Vile coffee. Niceness gone. No air. Stifling. Poor old pigeons. Dancing helplessly to man's absurd tune. Slides in one of the cages not coming through. Sort that out. Coffee now cold. Resume arguments.

To hell with the arguments. Make the break now.

'Miss Besant?'

The clacking stopped.

9

'Yes?'

'Will you do me a favour? Go and get me a copy of the *Caterer and Hotel Keeper*, if you can find one.'

The decision had been made at last.

It was National Pig Week, and a display of pig products had been laid out in Reception. A double track model railway wended its way among the scenic gammon, and two pork pies rode slowly round and round, one in each direction, from nine till five-thirty.

Mr Prestwick, personnel manager of Wine and Dine Ltd, averted his gaze from this exhibit as he made his way back to his tiny, hot office high above the Euston Road.

'Send Mr Baines in, Miss Purkiss,' he said into the intercom.

His ulcer was playing him up, his rise hadn't materialized, his wife had sent a van for all her furniture, he was living alone in half-empty rooms, he had never felt less like managing personnel.

Baines entered, with all the absurd hopes of youth. A tall, slim, quite good-looking young man with slightly stick-out ears and a surprisingly solid face.

'So you want to work for us?'

'Yes, sir,' said Baines, and Mr Prestwick envied him his steady unaffected middle-class voice. Something was going wrong with Mr Prestwick's voice. It didn't always stay tuned in quite right. Sometimes there was a low whistle, or a hum, or a crackle.

'One or two questions, just make sure you know your French irregular herbs,' said Mr Prestwick.

Baines managed some kind of a smile. They usually managed some kind of a smile.

'Are you familiar with our organization?'

'Not really.'

'You're aware that we're synonymous with quality?'

'I imagine you would be.'

'Do you want bouillabaise in Barnsley or moussaka in Macclesfield? Then dine and wine at your nearest Wine and Dine house. Doesn't that mean anything to you?'

'I'm afraid not, sir.'

'Visit the Golden Galleon, Aylesbury, and enjoy the best of British Duck?'

'No sir.'

Those idiots in 117 had been wasting their time. Mr Prestwick laughed inwardly, hurting his ulcer.

'I want to work in the country, sir.'

'You're a graduate, Baines. Arts graduates . . .' My God, I whined. I went off my wavelength. He hasn't shown he's noticed. 'Arts graduates go either into management or to our scenic department at Hatfield, where all our décor and costumes are made. Science graduates go to our research department at Staines. You are a science graduate. You would be sent to Staines.'

'But I thought I made it clear, sir. I want to be a chef.'

'We sent a chap like you to Staines two years ago, and already he's our chief macaroon consistency supervisor.'

'But sir . . .'

'You have a science degree. I don't think the organization would let you waste your talents by becoming a chef.'

'Well, if you can't give me this job as chef in a country hotel, sir, I honestly think I'd better look elsewhere.'

Mr Prestwick followed Baines's back as he walked away down the Euston Road. His own son had been a disappointment.

'Miss Purkiss?'

Miss Purkiss entered with her long legs and notebook.

'Take a letter, Miss Purkiss. Reference AB/47/32E. Dear Mrs Prestwick. Further to my letter of the twenty-sixth ult. I must report that the nest of tables was mine. It was left to me by Aunt . . . Miss Purkiss?'

'Yes, Mr Prestwick?'

'Is there anything at all odd about my voice?'

'No, Mr Prestwick.'

'My voice seems completely normal to you, does it?'

'Oh yes, Mr Prestwick.'

Why did they all think he wasn't capable of facing up to the truth?

He must seize the moment. If he waited until he'd got a job, he might never leave.

But ought he to leave? Wasn't his true work here, with Bradley and Cummings?

Pegasus thought: Two. Will knowledge gained in methods of conditioning minds of living beings prove beneficial or harmful to mankind?

Disturbing thought: What can be done by Cummings to a pigeon can be done by a dictator to Cummings.

Unclassified thought: Scientific enquiry in itself neither good nor bad. A process.

Question: Can we ignore future applications?

Answer: No. Therefore we must ask ourselves the

Further Question: Is man good or bad?

Answer: No.

Supplementary Question: Is . . .

Bradley came through, looking rather sad.

'Can't understand it,' he said.

'No?'

'All the Dungeness rats have died.'

Bradley's sadness lay not in the ending of animal life but in the refusal of the rats to fulfil man's predictions.

He must act now.

'May I use your typewriter for a moment, Miss Besant?'

He began to type his notice. Then he hesitated.

He thought: Three. In favour of experiments with minds of birds and animals. Could help fight against mental illness. By helping to understand animal mind, could help to liberate human mind.

Against. Could be used by fascists, dictators, power-mad school prefects (Murdoch!) etc. By helping to understand animal mind, could help to enslave human mind.

Conclusion: no conclusion.

Always the same. It was impossible to decide anything by means of reason, either because he had an inferior mind or because it really was impossible to decide anything by means of reason.

The Dungeness rats had all died, poor sods. Life would be easier if he could hate rats, but he didn't. He never wished anything any harm, rats, Paula, spiders, anything.

He resumed his typing. As he typed he could see Cummings, cooing to the pigeons, rapidly becoming one himself, inflated Cummings going through his courtship display. Coo coo. Conditioning himself when he thought he was conditioning others.

He finished typing his notice. He put it in an envelope. He addressed the envelope to Mr Colthorpe. He dropped the envelope into the internal mail tray. He felt wonderful.

'Miss Besant?'

'Yes.'

'If your boy friend told you that he knew a place where you could get the best algae in the Home Counties, what would you say?'

'I haven't got a boy friend, Mr Baines.'

He had only thought of Paula once during the last hour. He was on the mend.

'Why not, Miss Besant?'

'Why not what, Mr Baines?'

'Why haven't you got a boy friend?'

'What a question, Mr Baines.'

It was not Pegasus's nature to be referred to as 'Mr Baines' by young women. He wanted Miss Besant to call him 'Pegasus'. He wanted to share his happiness with someone, so he asked her out that evening. She wasn't beautiful or intelligent, but she was nice, and wasn't it selfish always to go for the beautiful and intelligent? He would choose this nice lonely Miss Besant, whom no one else had chosen.

As the evening wore on he grew terrified that Paula would see

13

him with Miss Besant. He took her to the Classic, Tooting, in order to avoid being seen by anyone he knew.

His old head prefect Murdoch was sitting two rows behind them. What did it matter? Why on earth did he mind?

That night he dreamt that he was in a cage, being fed on seaweed and Cummings's droppings. Twelve school prefects were waiting for him to do his sample. An electric recording device had been fitted to his head. Some of the slides showed traffic accidents. The others showed Miss Besant. Sometimes there was blood in the accident, and sometimes there was blood on Miss Besant. When there was blood he got an electric shock. It was hot, stifling. The sweat poured off him.

3

Easter Saturday, an early Easter in March. A cool strong wind buffeting the windows of the Goat and Thistle. The buds vulnerable on the trees round the fine Suffolk church. The village spreading away down all the lanes, out of the church's grasp. Nearby the sea, the estuary, the bird sanctuary, the nuclear power station, and all the secret research establishments which are such a feature of the unspoilt East Anglian countryside. Peace and quiet, except for the traffic, the planes screaming overhead, a radio blaring in a garden. Manchester City's greater attacking flair will just about see them through. This could be the year when they hit the proverbial jackpot. Saturday. Easter Saturday.

In the bar of the Goat and Thistle Jane Hassett was serving beer to two early bird-watchers and Mr Thomas, the milkman. In the dining-room people were lunching in undertones. From the windows you could see the marsh and the sea, but the power station was hidden by heathland. It was a backwater.

Tarragon Clump, the amateur naturalist, keen dinghy sailor, virgin and kidney surgeon, sat at a window table in the stark dining-room with its white tablecloths and clinical white walls. Its spirit of non-conformism weighed on him, and he ordered a half bottle of wine instead of a full one. He chewed his tiny piece of lukewarm sole in parsley sauce morosely. Vulgarians, thought Tarragon, the English, thinking of them as if they were foreigners, his own family even, the Clumps of Gloucestershire. He looked out over the marsh and tried to make out a bird that wheeled indolently over the distant woods. Too far. Binoculars not yet unpacked.

He turned his head to gaze greedily at Patsy's legs as she bore inexpertly towards him a plate of devilled kidneys and five veg, all watery.

'I wonder if I could have some mustard,' said Tarragon, and he shifted in his seat, the better to look up Patsy's legs as she leant over to reach the mustard.

I wonder if there'll be any pochard on the marsh, he thought, to take his mind off Patsy's saignant legs as she reached for the mustard.

'You already have mustard,' she said, blushing as she saw the mustard pot on Tarragon's table.

'So I have, Patsy.' He smiled at her. Patsy with her country ways. Patsy, the potential haystack tumbler. Patsy and the other waitress, Brenda, trim like an air hostess.

Unmarried at thirty-seven, Tarragon had come to feel for the Goat and Thistle the sort of affection married men look for in mistresses – secret, temporal, understanding, no need to book in advance. His modest, domestic Jacobean mistress, plastered, three gables, thin wisps of pargetting. Unchanging.

And now once again it was under new management. Once again it had to be established that Tarragon Clump was a regular here, a popular figure with his ready money and manly binoculars, his thick pullovers and square-jawed, wide-nosed, narrow-foreheaded face. It had to be hinted that in London he was a success. A leading man in his field. A man who would one day operate on a royal personage.

He attacked his meal aggressively, trying not to gaze at Patsy or Brenda, feeling the excitement of the impending marsh, glad to be back. Four whole days, four gumbooted forceps-free days of bliss. A little sailing in his dinghy. A lot of bird-watching. A steady movement of his big, strong legs over squelching paths. Oh, Clump, there is health in you yet.

When this vile meal was over he would introduce himself to this new woman in the bar, he would sum her up over a brandy. Young, surprisingly young. Good thing too.

Over his brandy he said: 'Well it's nice to be back.'

'You're one of our regulars, are you?'

'I manage the occasional weekend. Plus the odd week here and there. Odd's the operative word.'

I must stop saying that, thought Tarragon. Odd's the operative word. It doesn't mean anything.

'I'm Jane Hassett,' said Mrs Hassett.

'Clump,' said Tarragon. 'Tarragon Clump.'

'Back again, then, Mr Clump,' said Mr Crabbe the storekeeper.

She couldn't be more than thirty. Long neck, bony white shoulders, curved nostrils, green eyes, one thing after another, several of his favourites among them. Cut it out, Clump.

Two young men entered the bar. One of them was vaguely familiar. They ordered pints.

'Frankly, you want to do something about the cooking,' said Tarragon.

'I know,' said Mrs Hassett. 'We've got a man coming next month. A Frenchman.'

'Ah, a Frenchman,' said Tarragon.

'I hope you won't mind my asking,' said the vaguely familiar young man. 'But you don't happen to have a vacancy, do you? In the kitchen, I mean.'

'Well, we do need a vegetable chef,' said Mrs Hassett.

The whole thing was fixed up in no time, and the vaguely familiar young man bought drinks all round.

'You're Tarragon Clump, the kidney surgeon, aren't you?' he said.

'We call ourselves renal surgeons, but yes, I am.'

'I met you at my cousin's prediction party. I'm Pegasus Baines.'

'I thought you were vaguely familiar.'

'He's never even been vaguely familiar with me,' said the other young man.

'This is my friend Mervyn,' said Pegasus.

The tall, familiar one had apparently been driving around from hotel to hotel, begging for work.

Tarragon fixed his eyes on Mrs Hassett's neck and said: 'His cousin writes a horoscope. Old friend of mine.'

'I never read them,' she said. 'Afraid, perhaps.'

'Any operations on royalty yet?' said Pegasus.

'Not yet,' said Tarragon.

'A good year for kidneys, is it?' said Mervyn.

'The beer's good,' said Pegasus.

Tarragon felt annoyed. These people had come between him and Mrs Hassett. They had disturbed his afternoon.

'Well,' he said, 'I think I'll be off down the marsh. See if I can see the odd bird or two. Odd's the operative word.'

Damn!

4

Pegasus sat with Morley and Diana on the back lawn of twenty-three Grimsdike Crescent, Uxbridge, waiting for Sunday lunch. Blackbirds sang, planes flew overhead, and the world stood still, waiting for Sunday lunch.

A faint breeze blew snatches of radio towards them, Two Way Family Favourites, the Critics. We've been to see the exhibition of Private Bob Norris of B.A.O.R. 17. I loved the way he captured the, the as it were, the at once transitory and yet eternal beauty of Mavis Bungstock, who lives at ninety-seven, Cratchett Lane, Axminster. She hopes to see you soon, Bob, and could well develop into the Francis Bacon of the 1970s.

They read the *Sunday Times,* each a different section, having nothing much to say to each other now. Diana was sixteen, still at school and too young for conversation. Morley was twenty-eight, a prematurely elder brother, serious, with slow movements and long anecdotes, a leader writer on a Yorkshire daily, a future pundit.

Pegasus felt nervous. He hadn't told the family yet, and it would be hard. He was firmly expected to bring Grimsdike Crescent its first Nobel Prize. He wanted to tell Morley and Diana, but couldn't begin.

'Come and get it,' said their father at the french windows.

They went and got it, Pegasus immediately, Morley gradually, Diana deliberately the last of all. There was wine – a rare treat.

'After all,' said his father, 'it's not often we're all together.'

Pegasus was irritated by this apology. If the Shah of Persia had been there, what would he have thought? And he was irritated by his own irritation. A bottle of wine was an extravagance.

It had meant financial sacrifices bringing up the children. It had meant frayed carpets, a rusty lawn-mower, *Radio Times* but no *T.V. Times,* an old decrepit car. Pegasus felt that it was his irritation, not his father's apology, of which the Shah of Persia would disapprove. And even now Paula was making love to a man who translated Ogden Nash into Latin. At this moment while Pegasus was chewing Yorkshire pudding she was biting gently at the thick dark hairs on that odious young man's revoltingly hairy arms, while he mouthed sweet hexameters into her ear.

'What's wrong, Pegasus, aren't you hungry?'

'I was thinking.'

'I hope you aren't sickening for something.'

'No, mother, I'm not sickening for anything.'

'Well, anyway,' said his mother, 'it is nice, all being together like this.'

'Quite a family,' said his father.

'I think Morley's gone a lot more dour since he went up North,' said Diana.

'My library book's set in the North,' said his mother. 'I can't get into it. I don't like sordid books.' (Murmurs of dissent.)

'There's nothing sordid about the North,' said Morley.

'Except what the bosses plunged it into in the industrial revolution,' said Diana.

'The distinctions drawn between the North and the South are a romantic myth,' said Morley. 'We try to see in the North the kind of strength and simplicity we would like to have.'

'There are some very nice parts of the North,' said his mother. 'Your father and I are very fond of Wensleydale, aren't we George?' (Uproar.)

'We're talking about the real North,' said Diana.

I must join in. I must say something. I mustn't put myself at a distance.

'Anyway this Yorkshire pudding is very good,' said Pegasus.

How old his mother was, he thought. Shrinking. Hardly more than five foot tall these days. Liable to disappear by 1990 at this rate. Beginning to call him Diana by mistake. She had aged at the same rate as him, and so he had never noticed it. She had been there, busy about the house, not sparing herself, a familiar landmark, twenty-five years older than he was. Now overnight she was old. She was a human being. She had been young. He knew nothing about her.

'It'll be warm enough to sit outside,' said his father.

His father looked a little strained, a little haggard, a little baggy. His father too was very pleased about his scientific leanings.

'The temperamental differences between Yorkshire and Lancashire people are considerably more radical than the difference between say Pontefract and Bedford,' said Morley, droning on.

Short work was made of the washing up. It was found to be just possible to sit outside in the deck-chairs, in a sheltered corner of the garden.

They drank their coffee, while all around them the first lawn-mowers of spring whirred, and above them aeroplanes came in towards London Airport bringing carefree foreigners, and over the road Mr Munsford lovingly touched up his repulsive topiary with a very special pair of clippers. Suddenly, in a brief gap between planes, Pegasus took the plunge.

'I'm leaving my job,' he said. 'I'm going to be a chef.'

He was ashamed. The Shah of Persia would never have been so embarrassed about so minor a matter.

'You can't mean it,' said his mother.

'A chef?' said Morley incredulously.

'Good God,' said Diana.

'This is a bit late for April fools,' said his father.

'I've taken a job as vegetable chef in a hotel in Suffolk.'

'It's a bit of a waste of a good second in science, isn't it?' said Morley.

'It's my life.'

'You had a good career at the institute,' said his father. 'Aren't you a bit of a fool to give all that up?'

'Mad,' said Morley.

'Shut up!' said Diana.

'I found it grotesque,' said Pegasus.

He longed to pass overhead in one of those planes.

'But the catering trade,' said his mother, wrinkling the nose of her voice in disgust.

'You make it sound so sordid,' said Pegasus.

'I think food's a jolly good thing to go into,' said Diana.

'You aren't as old as he is,' said their mother.

'And you're a girl,' said their father.

It began to pour, a sharp gusty shower. There was a general rush indoors with rapidly folded deck-chairs. The business section of the *Sunday Times* floated off towards Hillingdon. The rain, which George Baines had not forecast, had saved the situation.

They all disappeared, his father to finish some graphs, his mother to bake a cake, Morley to pack, Diana to go over to Ursula's to do some French. Pegasus recognized this ploy. He was now expected to do the rounds and be lectured by each in turn. If he didn't, they would all come to him.

He followed Diana up to her room.

'Thanks, Di, for backing me up,' he said. 'You know it's rather nice in here.'

'Naturally.'

She was busy with her face.

'You like to be at your loveliest when you do your French, do you?'

'Of course.'

She came up to him with swift movements and kissed him on the lips with her round rather jolly face.

'You're a sweetie,' she said, and then slapped him hard on the bottom and left the room without turning round. He watched her swinging aggressively up the road with her broad hips and slightly muscular white-stockinged Sunday afternoon in Uxbridge legs.

He went out into the corridor.

'Is that you, Pegasus?' called Morley.

He went into the bedroom which he shared with Morley when they were both at home.

'You aren't doing this on the spur of the moment, are you?'

'You're off duty now, Morley. I'm your brother, not a public issue.'

He slammed Morley's door behind him.

'Is that you, Pegasus?' his father called.

His father was at the bedroom window, watching the rain.

'Have you really thought this out, old chap?' he said.

'Of course,' said Pegasus.

'I wouldn't like to feel you were wasting your life.'

'Food isn't wrong, you know, father.'

'Well there you are, you see. Times change. Your mother and I can't quite share your attitude to that. And it's your mother I'm thinking of, Pegasus. This is a difficult time for her.'

'Why?'

'It just is. Take my word for it. Look at this dreadful rain, Pegasus.'

'M'm.'

'Well I'm sorry to be such a bore but that's what parents are like. You'll be one yourself one day.'

Pegasus went out on to the stairs without asking his father how he knew.

'Is that you, Pegasus?' said his mother.

She was busy in the kitchen with her mixture.

'I hope you're doing the right thing, Pegasus,' she said.

'Food isn't wrong, you know, mother.'

'Well there you are, you see. We saw the depression. And your father's very set on your being a scientist.'

'Well, I'm sorry, mother.'

'Your father's a good, sincere man, Pegasus. And good at his job, too. What he doesn't know about warm fronts isn't worth knowing.'

'I'm sure.'

He saw her sniffing, from habit, to see if he was changing his socks often enough. She always did this. Not that he had anti-social feet.

'If your father couldn't forecast this rain, nobody could.'

'I'm sure.'

'I don't want him hurt, that's all,' said his mother. 'We want success for you, Pegasus.'

He looked her straight in the face and what he saw there was love.

After tea he drove Morley to St Pancras. They hardly spoke.

He was longing to see Morley off on to his train. There would just be time to go down to Kensington Gardens before it got dark.

'There's no need to come on to the platform,' said Morley.

22

'I insist,' said Pegasus.

He was irritated with Morley. He was irritated with his parents. He was irritated with Diana for not returning before he left. He was irritated with himself. And the showers had given way now to a soft, remorseless rain.

George Baines watched the rain morosely. They'd be returning now, wet and sad and bedraggled, from Brighton and Worthing and Bognor. George Baines saw their reproachful faces as they stood at the bottom of the garden. 'You were wrong,' they said. 'You, with all your scientific apparatus, you were wrong.'

'Come away from the window, dear,' said his wife Margaret. 'You won't make it stop, you know.'

George Baines came away from the window and sat down opposite his wife.

'Never mind,' he said, and then he added, as if he was speaking about some modern phenomenon that he didn't understand. 'Food's on the up and up, you know.'

'I suppose so.'

George Baines stared at the Constable over the mantelpiece. Looked like a settled spell down there in Flatford.

'Diana's late,' said his wife Margaret.

Diana was kissing Stephen in the back room of number 11, Honiton Drive. Stephen's parents were in Paris, on business. They were often in Paris, on business. When his elder brother Peter had been left at home alone he had invited no less than sixty-three people to a party. Several of them had been drug addicts. Many had stayed all night, getting to know each other better in various parts of the house and garden. A Vlaminck lithograph had been pressed into service as a drinks tray, with deleterious results, and the crocuses had been trampled beyond recognition. Stephen's parents believed that you had a moral obligation to trust your children, especially when cancelling a trip to Paris was the alternative.

Diana kissed Stephen's gorgeous, angelic face. She loved boys with gorgeous, angelic faces.

The rain fell on Tarragon Clump's bonnet as he drove home along the wet, dreary Sunday roads. He had been to see his family, the Clumps of Gloucestershire. He stopped off at Oxford and went to see a film in a huge, half empty cinema. It was a rotten film but it had Pamela Blossom in it, in scanty attire.

The rain fell on Pegasus as he sat on the seat in Kensington Gardens and watched the light beginning to fade from a dismal, featureless sky. In the distance, beyond the Round Pond, there was a woman. It could be Paula. She was coming nearer, a figure from the fieldcraft manual. At 800 yards Paula was a blur. At 700 yards Paula's face was a blob, her legs matchsticks. At 500 yards, Paula's attractive, slightly fleshy legs began to be visible. At 400 yards it was possible to make out Paula's biteable narrow nose. At 300 yards it wasn't Paula at all, but an elderly woman in thick, brown stockings.

He closed his eyes and tried to construct a half-dressed Paula in her suspenders. In vain. He tried to feel the old misery, the betrayal, the silent tears. Nothing.

He looked round the park, his oasis even in the rain. Here he was at dusk, drinking at his waterhole, leaving his Saxone hoofprints in the wet grass. But this scene too aroused no emotion in him any more. He was cured. How sad life was.

He began to walk away, a little ashamed. You wouldn't catch the Nawab of Pataudi hanging around a seat in Kensington Gardens.

He went into a pub and bought himself a pint of bitter. He didn't feel like going back to Hampstead yet, if ever.

His flatlet was full of purple-sprouting broccoli. He had meant to devote the evening to it. He had bought three cookery books and had promised himself three hours' practice a night.

His landlord, Mr Lal, had been furious. 'What are all these good vegetables doing in my dustbins?' he had said. 'Don't you know that in my country there is famine?'

So the next evening Pegasus had taken plate after plate of cooked vegetables to Mr Lal. Later that evening he had seen Mr Lal taking them to the dustbin.

He'd tried throwing them down the lavatory. It had blocked. The water had failed to run out properly after Miss Yarnold's Thursday bath. Mr Waller had used the plunger on it, there had been a loud prolonged gurgle, and several pieces of diced parsnip had floated up into the bath. Miss Yarnold had looked embarrassed, as though she felt responsible for them. The plumber, coming to unblock the lavatory, and seeing all the vegetables, had said in surprise: 'These haven't hardly been digested at all.' Mr Lal had gone steadily berserk.

It had all served to dampen Pegasus's enthusiasm. He was beginning to fall behind. He would persist, but not tonight. He wouldn't do his three hours tonight.

He took a large draught of beer, as if defying the world.

Simon was giving Paula dinner in his flat. He liked to give her dinner in his flat, after evensong.

'I wish you'd let me cook for you,' said Paula.

'Plenty of time for that when we're married,' he said.

Four months. Four months before she was in his fine, manly, hairy arms. Simon knew that she wasn't a virgin. He had forgiven her.

'Lovely pâté, darling.'

'A trifle coarse?'

'I don't think so.'

He didn't like going to her flat and he didn't like going out too often. Only occasionally did she manage to drag him to the pictures. He didn't mind the films but he hated the intermissions. He was a merchant banker. Paula had rarely been to church before, but funnily enough she quite enjoyed it. Dark. Cool. Colour high up. Earl Grey Tea and Simon's dark face bent over a sheet of paper. Small precise writing. Ink, of course.

'Why Ogden Nash?'

'Why not?'

'Well I mean the whole point of Ogden Nash is the funny length of his lines. Isn't all that lost when you put them in hexameters?'

'But that's the challenge. That's the whole fun of it.'

'I'm not criticizing. I'm just trying to get your point of view.'

'Whatever the length of Nash's lines I must turn each one into a hexameter. It's a discipline. I'm not trying to reproduce his humour.'

'No.'

'I couldn't, if I tried.'

'No.'

'Canon Mulgrave was on form tonight, I thought.'

'Yes, very good. I wasn't criticizing, Simon.'

'I wouldn't mind if you were.'

There were watercolours of hunting scenes on the walls. Simon hated hunting but liked watercolours of hunting scenes. A small thing, but irritating.

Pegasus drank on, thinking about the Goat and Thistle. She was an attractive woman. She had given him the job without references of any kind. He believed that this was because they had established an unspoken rapport. It looked a nice hotel. And he liked Suffolk. Though presumably she was married.

5

Pegasus arrived to find that he was staying not in the hotel but at Rose Lodge, a little early Victorian lodge cottage at the back of the village, on the entrance to Lord Noseby's estate. In the car on the way over from the hotel Patsy explained that the staff quarters were full because there was Tonio, the assistant chef, living in and Bellamy the porter and Miss Coward the receptionist and part-time barmaid and also Patsy herself because her aunt had come to stay with them while her uncle was in hospital which looked likely to drag on for some time on account of his liver. Bill Gunter was Lord Noseby's gamekeeper, but his wife Brenda was Patsy's co-waitress, so it wouldn't be like being with strangers.

Brenda Gunter greeted Pegasus warmly. She was a pretty woman with good sharp features, trim legs and a fine figure. She led him up the narrow stairs to his bedroom.

'I hope this is all right,' she said, embarrassed, turning red. 'I was going to remove these books and toys, but I haven't got round to it yet.'

'Oh, that's all right, Mrs Gunter.'

'Brenda, please. The bathroom's straight opposite. You'll have breakfast here and your meals over at the hotel. Come down and have some tea when you're cleaned up.'

'Thank you.'

Left to himself, Pegasus examined his room. It was small, and there was just one window, looking out over a lawn surrounded by masses of roses. There were roses everywhere. The cottage was grasped in innumerable rosy hands, whose colours softened but could not hide its Victorian earnestness.

The ceiling sloped sharply to the right so that there were only about eighteen inches of headroom above the bed on the side nearest the wall. On the other side of the room, where the ceiling was higher, there was a bookcase and three boxes of toys. Pegasus could see a Monopoly set, Snakes and Ladders, stumps and a cricket bat, a lorry, a bus, a few pieces of rail. The bookcase contained *Winnie the Pooh, The House at Pooh Corner,* a large number of very worn Biggles books, and three copies of *Mr Midshipman Easy.*

He went across to the bathroom, apprehensive now. The hot tap was noisy. He had expected to be a part of the hotel, wrapped in its busy ordered life. Now in this cottage he seemed very unimportant, his degree counting for nothing. The late April sky was hostile and windy, with high grey clouds and patches of cold, hard blue. The silence was deafening. When a car went past it was a wound, and a plane was a hysterical gash. He hadn't realized how much he had been looking forward to seeing the landlady, how much he dreaded meeting the husband she was bound to have.

Soap under the armpits never failed to revive him at least a little, and he felt better by the time he went downstairs for his tea, in the small kitchen-cum-dining-room-cum-living-room. Brenda sat by the electric fire with her legs crossed, revealing a large amount of impersonal thigh, apparently unaware of this. Behind her was an ironing board on which stood a large pile of underclothes.

'Bill isn't back yet,' she said. 'I think the pheasants must be proving troublesome.'

'I'm not turning a child out of his room, am I?' said Pegasus, over his bread and jam and tea.

'Oh no, that's all right,' said Brenda, reddening again, unevenly, blotchily. 'No. You see, actually, I'm afraid our little boy was killed.'

'Oh, I'm sorry.'

'Well it was three weeks ago. We're over the worst now.'

'Yes, but still . . . I mean, are you sure . . .'

'That we want to have you? Very much.'

'Well, er . . .'

'If you don't mind.'

'No. No, I don't mind.'

'Have another cup of tea.'

'Thank you.'

'He was knocked down by a car. They didn't stop. He was twelve.'

'But honestly are you absolutely . . .'

'Oh yes. Very much.'

'Well, then, I . . . I'm sure I shall be very comfortable here.'

'I must move all those books and toys.'

After his tea Pegasus sat in his room until it was past opening time. There was nothing else to do, so he glanced at some of the books, imagining the dead boy reading them. He was glad when it was time to go out.

He walked over to the Goat and Thistle, trying not to hurry, wandering round the village in the fading light. A few old houses, one shop, a pub. He hoped she would be alone, and that it wasn't bad form for employees to drink in the bar.

A bat near him, horrible. Nobody about. The main road, relatively main anyway, hardly any traffic. There was the hotel. Nerves. Quite ridiculous. Excitement. Sex. Gables. Porch. Warmth. Light. Voices. Smoke.

A man was serving, presumably her husband. Slightly fat, big face, strong. Hot temper? Unreliable? Receding hair, ha, ha, sandy in colour. An ex motor cycle enthusiast? It was more than possible.

She entered the bar, slight and lovely. He felt as if he was on a big dipper. He must look casual.

'You've arrived,' she said.

'Yes, I've arrived.'

'This is my husband, Tony. Tony, this is the new vegetable chef.'

Greetings. Was he imagining a slight hostility?

He thought of Paula. She seemed so distant now, yet not so distant that he no longer thought of her. He had been to the seat, to say good-bye to it, to put all that behind him.

'I hope you'll be all right with the Gunters,' said Tony.

'Oh, I expect so.'

'Brenda's staff so it won't be like being with strangers.'

'No.'

'They've had a spot of bad luck. Did they tell you?'

'Yes, they did.'

'Hope you'll be comfortable anyway.'

Did Tony suspect? Not that there was anything to suspect.

Pegasus felt secretly attracted to his wife. He had felt secretly attracted to people's wives before. It was part of being alive. He had foolishly dreamt that the wife . . . well, it wasn't the first time he had foolishly dreamt that a wife . . . but she wasn't. They never were. Nevertheless he wondered if Tony suspected anything.

He went home early, not wanting to seem like an alcoholic. Bill was there, short, wiry, grim, quiet, but seemingly benevolent. Like a jockey. He was invited in for cocoa, and felt obliged to go. They switched the telly off, which was a shame. Conversation not too bad, though, despite the dead boy. Facts. Population. Number of pheasants. Brief discussion of rodent life. A short anecdote concerning a badger. Brief character studies of Lord and Lady Noseby. Comparison of country and city life. Not too bad, but what of future conversations when the facts are exhausted? Must go to bed. Rather sleepy. Don't want to be tired on my first day. Good night.

But sleep wouldn't come. Everything was too familiar. The dead child was too real. He dreaded his first day's work. He heard everything, even the sea, two miles away, hissing quietly to itself. At three the wind got up, and bangings and groanings began all over the cottage, magnified by the absence of traffic. The boy sleeping comfortably here in this bed that last of all his nights. At 3.15 a.m. an owl hooted, twice. At 3.17 the rain began, and it was the rain that eventually lulled him into an uneasy sleep.

6

Pegasus felt a sense of helplessness the next morning as he faced up to a great mound of lifeless vegetables. He had to prepare seventy portions of potatoes, forty portions of peas, twenty portions of cabbage, fifteen portions of carrots, ten portions each of parsnips and cauliflower. Vegetables which were not in season had to be unfrozen. There were fearsome slicing and peeling machines such as he had never encountered. Perhaps he ought to have insured his fingers. One day his fingers would be as valuable as Betty Grable's legs.

The pans and stoves seemed very large after his saucepan and gas ring. Everything looked much more mechanical and less artistic than he had expected. This whole venture was absurd.

He was supposed to have previous experience, and the two chefs, Alphonse and his assistant Tonio, assumed that he knew how to begin. He had to be very careful.

'I'm not used to machines of this sort,' he told Alphonse, and Alphonse showed him how to use them. It was easy, really. The vegetables came out just as efficiently for him as they did for Alphonse.

'I'm sorry. We never used carrots,' he told Alphonse, after he had cut up some carrots the wrong way.

'What kind of place have you been working from, with the extreme absence of carrots?' said Alphonse.

'A little place,' said Pegasus. 'The owner had a thing about carrots.'

'Was he having the thing also about other foods?' asked Alphonse.

'One or two,' said Pegasus non-committally, in case there should be other disasters.

He got his timings mixed up. Alphonse was cross.

'I'm not used to these quantities,' said Pegasus.

'This place where you work, she was having no customers?' said Alphonse.

'Not many. The owner had a thing about customers,' said Pegasus.

He needed quite a lot of help, he felt a bit of a fool, but lunch passed off without disaster. And no one sent their vegetables back.

He started early on dinner, and it all went much more smoothly.

31

He began to lose his sense of absurdity. Here he was working alongside these true professionals. Alphonse, with his typical French moustache, and his lean, rather crooked, pimply face with a big nose and stick-out ears. Tonio, hairy and Italian, always either singing or swearing. Pegasus began to feel happy. He was too busy to think about Jane Hassett. Tonight he would sleep soundly. Tomorrow he would work still better. Soon he would be a great chef. And he still had all his fingers. He felt that he was coming to life, that he was starting to live his own natural, destined life. He began to sing, but silently, in case they should think him presumptuous.

7

Jane Hassett changed into an expensive, bottle green costume. She dressed swiftly, her movements charged with nervous energy. Her legs, which were so often heavy and lifeless, felt light, seemed eager to play their full part in the day's activities.

She ran her left hand over her right breast and squeezed the nipple very gently, as if she was reassuring an old friend. The parts of her body often had an independent existence. Often as a child she had been a leg or an arm for several days, without anybody knowing. Never a breast. Not in those days.

Tony was out, gone to Norwich, to see about some new central heating equipment. All lies. Once again there was a woman. She sat down on the bed, lit a cigarette, smoked it urgently, practically devouring it, yet with elegance.

Four months they'd been here, and already it had started up again.

Tony had come into a big legacy last October when his rich

Uncle James had been flambeed to death in brandy during a five course meal at an hotel in Berkshire. Tony went away on a business trip to Suffolk and bought the hotel he was staying in. He had said that the least they could do, in memory of his uncle, was to buy a hotel and never serve meals at the table. She had been presented with a fait accompli, as usual.

She had been nervous. She felt she was too thin to be taken seriously. Landladies were fat, autocratic women, with voluminous chins and loud voices, whose false hoarse laughter shook the mock-Tudor beams and set the antique swords rattling on the walls. Yet she had been a success. She thought she could count herself, to date, a reasonable success. It was Tony who had been the failure. Already he was bored. He'd found a new toy, a doll. The lies had begun again. The accusations and scenes would follow.

And it had all begun with a lie. She had seen his entry in the visitors' book. Mr and Mrs Hassett. So much for his business trip to Suffolk.

She soaked her face-flannel in hot water and applied it to the spot above her lip. She held it there, feeling a sexual excitement in these preparations. Her throat was tickling, the approach of a cold. All his fault. Whenever the lies began she had some minor ailment. It was her system's way of getting rid of the poison.

She took away the flannel and pressed a finger of each hand against the horrid little pimple. It popped and the white poison shot out. She wiped it off with her flannel. It was Tony. It was her husband, in suppurative form, and when it was gone she hated him less.

That was better. Nothing nauseous about a dull, red excrescence. Ready to go now.

She walked over to Rose Lodge, wondering if Tony had sent the poor boy there on purpose. It was sensible enough, on the face of it. There wasn't room at the hotel. It would take their minds off their tragedy. And yet she felt sure that it was done in anger. He was annoyed because she had made the appointment on her own. Only he could do things on his own.

c   33

Brenda showed her up to Pegasus's room.

'He's a nice boy,' she said.

'Oh good.'

'Bill likes him.'

Pegasus opened the door and asked her in. She sat in the armchair and he sat in the hard chair. She had never once been unfaithful to Tony.

'Would you like a cigarette?' she said, offering her packet of tipped.

'No, thanks, I don't. I should offer you some but I haven't any.'

'I just came to see how you were getting on,' said Jane.

'All right, thank you.'

'You heard about their tragedy, I suppose?'

'Yes. They told me.'

'They should have removed all these toys and things. It's embarrassing for you.'

She stood up and went to the window.

'At least you have a nice view,' she said, instantly regretting the 'at least'.

'Yes. Very nice.'

She turned away from the window and smiled at him. He was still seated. She wanted to touch him. She felt a sneeze coming on, turned away politely, sneezed.

'Bless you,' he said.

When she turned round again he looked embarrassed. Why? He seemed tense too, but it wasn't enough to go on. All this was in her imagination. She was in danger of making a fool of herself.

She sat down and took a deliberate puff at her cigarette, keeping herself calm.

'Is the bed comfortable?' she said.

'Very, thank you.'

She crossed her legs, felt this to be a little theatrical, and uncrossed them.

'I must say I wouldn't like having those books and toys there,' she said.

'I would be happier if they were moved,' said Pegasus, 'but I don't like to mention it.'

'No. It's difficult. Well I'm glad to see that apart from that you're very comfortable.'

'Yes. Very. And the view is very nice.'

A hiatus.

'It must seem quiet after London?'

'Yes, it does.'

'Even with all the planes?'

'We get those in London too.'

What a conversation! She must go, and it would be quite wrong anyway to use him as a pawn in her battle with Tony. She had never used anyone in that way. He might even be engaged.

'How did you get on with Alphonse?' she said.

'Very well, I think.'

'We've only had him three weeks. He's very gallic.'

'Yes.'

She decided it was stupid not to cross her legs, just because if done self-consciously it might seem theatrical. So she crossed her legs. Then she sneezed.

'Bless you,' he said, and then he looked embarrassed. Why?

'If you ever have any problems, let me know,' she said.

'Yes, I will.'

She must go. She stood up abruptly and to her surprise found herself not at the door but at the window, looking out over the fields and woods of Lord Noseby's estate. He joined her there and they stood side by side, looking out over Lord Noseby's estate. She could feel his body, touching hers ever so slightly, either by accident or deliberately but made to seem like an accident.

'At least you have a nice view,' she said.

'I'm sure I shall be very comfortable,' he said.

There was a knock at the door. Both of them turned away from the window and returned to their chairs.

'Come in,' she said, forgetting it was not her room.

35

Brenda entered with three cups of coffee and three huge portions of iced chocolate cake.

'I was thinking you might like some coffee,' said Brenda.

'Oh, thank you,' said Pegasus.

'Very thoughtful,' said Jane.

The sun came out. Jane as employer sat in the easy chair. Brenda as landlady sat in the hard chair. Pegasus as Pegasus sat on his bed.

'I hope he likes the room,' said Brenda.

'I'm sure he does,' said Jane.

'I do,' said Pegasus.

'It has a nice view,' said Brenda.

'Yes, it does,' said Jane.

'Little Johnny liked this room,' said Brenda.

'Did he?' said Pegasus.

They took bites of their cake and washed the cake down with draughts of hot coffee.

'We must move all these books and toys,' said Brenda.

8

'Look after yourself,' said Bill.

'Take care,' said Brenda.

They continued waving until he was out of sight. Where do they think I'm going, he thought. Round the world? All I'm doing is going home for the week-end.

He hadn't realized what a relief it would be to get away even for two days, away from the nightly cocoa sessions, the constant plans for a picnic, the 'Wednesday Play' being switched off the moment he came in, as if it was considered quite unsuitable for him.

He'd taken to reading Johnny's books, in order to avoid conversation. Rather childish, on the whole, but there were no others. And Bill seemed to expect it. 'You'll find plenty of books up there,' he said.

It was a lovely Saturday morning. Pegasus felt like singing, would have sung if he'd had the talent.

Forget Rose Lodge. Think how well the work's going. Alphonse likes you. 'Ah, Pegasus, you and you alone do I entrust to my beloved asparagus' he had said. 'You will go on a long road. You are my prodigy. You have the respect for the ingredient.'

On the Ipswich By-Pass Pegasus slowed down as he passed two girls. He opened the window and shouted: 'I'll go on a long road. I have the respect for the ingredient.' The girls giggled.

Nothing had happened with Mrs Hassett. All that had been an illusion. When she came to his room he had been so near to grabbing hold of her, and when she sneezed he had said 'Bless you' more like a lover than an employee, but she hadn't noticed. He had entirely misconstrued her reason for coming to his room.

He was glad, for Paula's sake, that nothing had happened with Mrs Hassett.

'I'm sorry, darling. I just don't feel like going out,' said Simon.

'But it's so nice,' said Paula.

'The sun's shining in the window,' said Simon. 'That's nice, too.'

'It's so nice out,' said Paula.

'You go out, then, if you want to.'

'There's not much point in my coming round to see you if I go out the moment I've arrived.'

'I'm sorry,' said Simon. He was writing, at his desk, in his small neat hand.

'I tell you what I do fancy,' said Paula. 'A bath.'

'Good idea. Have one.'

Simon's bathroom was in a different class from hers. Hers was shared.

'You can have the wireless if you want to,' said Simon.

Paula thanked him. It was a sacrifice. He didn't really like exposing his radio to all that steam.

He came over to her and kissed her in that leisurely way of his. 'We'll make a real night out of it tonight,' he said.

They probably would. He was always true to his promises.

'Do you need the loo before I have my bath?'

'No.'

He never did. A small thing, but irritating.

Pegasus sat on the seat and closed his eyes.

How could you, Paula?

Nothing.

Oh, Paula, Paula, Paula.

Nothing.

He opened his eyes again and looked out towards the bandstand with its pretty curved green roof. Old men were flying kites. One of the kites was a painted eagle, a lectern in the sky. He couldn't see the surface of the Round Pond but he could see the miniature sailing boats sliding across the grass. In the foreground were the sharp cries of children. Behind them, far away, restful from this distance, the hum of traffic, like canned music.

Once more he tried to rebuild Paula, but he couldn't remember her, only his memories of her. Remembrance of Paula past. 'Paula darling' meant 'I remember what a darling you were, Paula, in the days when I used to say to you "Paula darling".'

There is no one else, Paula. If I no longer have you I have no one.

Oh, Paula, Paula. Nothing.

Tarragon walked happily over the duckboards towards his favourite of all the hides, with the best view of the bearded tits and marsh harriers. He was on his own. Occasionally he brought friends to Suffolk, but never to the bird sanctuary.

There was somebody else there, in his favourite of all the hides. A woman, a square woman.

'Plenty of beardies,' said the square woman. 'Gadwall to port, avocet's nest straight ahead, three little stint to starboard.'

Damn the bitch. The pleasure of it was finding the things, spotting them in the far distance, pitting your wits against them, forgetting the banalities. The ability to speak was the curse of mankind, and more especially womankind, and most especially of all, square-jawed authoritative womankind.

'Thank you,' he said.

'Don't mench.'

Damn all square-jawed women. Damn all women. Damn all unsatisfied sexual feelings and all pathetic painful maladjustments. Damn his bloody family, the Clumps of Gloucestershire, and their inhibiting Cotswold seat. Damn all interruptions which spoilt the perfection of the pale filtered sunlight of May by the sea, the magical stillness of a morning without wind, of trees hardly stirring and of mists slowly clearing, and of thin films of white cloud drifting harmlessly overhead.

'Beardies straight ahead. Quick. To the right. Gone.'

'Never mind.'

Focus, Clump. Focus on beautiful creatures marred by cruelty but untouched by malice.

There was a great therapeutic calm in the drawing of his binoculars slowly over the stones and puddles and rank grass.

'Two redshank copulating in line with that upturned rowing boat,' said Tarragon. He looked the square-jawed woman in the face. 'Nice morning for it,' he said.

The square-jawed woman left the hide, and a weight was lifted from him. He had a splendid day, after that. Marsh harriers winging with lazy beats over the marsh, two girls sunbathing on the dunes, swallows and martins swooping and diving, a kestrel hovering, two girls sunbathing, a solitary shoveller flying purposefully towards its mate, two girls sunbathing.

Late in the afternoon, as the wisps of cloud grew thicker and a light wind began to disturb the unnatural stillness, Tarragon set off for the hotel. He began to feel excited. He hurried into a small copse on the edge of the marsh.

Sitting with his back against a tree he had a good view of the hotel. He scanned the upper windows through his binoculars.

I suppose this is voyeurism, he thought, without surprise. A new departure. It was true that he'd often hung around outside underground stations to see the pretty girls returning home from work, and had even followed them, admiring their legs and bottoms, but that was not voyeurism, since it had been his firm intention to speak to them, to invite them to a concert at the Festival Hall, and later to marry them. It wasn't his fault that it hadn't turned out like that.

But this was different, looking at girls from the protection of a bird sanctuary, watching out for Mrs Hassett, squinting through his binoculars, 8 × 35, a good magnification for bird-watching and not too bad for voyeurism. He felt ashamed, yet continued. And was rewarded. At 5.45 he saw her, changing in preparation for the evening's duties. He fancied he could see her breasts—small, neat breasts. He was almost certain that she was applying powder to her armpits. He saw a flash of something pale, her back perhaps, as she twisted into a dress.

'You find Mrs Hassett attractive, no?'

Tarragon jumped and scrambled guiltily to his feet. He blushed.

'I startled you?'

It was Alphonse.

'Yes, you – er – you did. I think there's a swallow's nest under the eaves.'

'Now to me, Mrs Hassett, she has not my sort. She is a little, how you say, not so enough effeminate. A little what I would say Parisian.'

'I thought I saw a hawk of some kind flying past the hotel.'

'Me, I like more the country girl, yes? In my native Provence, there they have the roundness, how you say, swollen. Oh, monsieur, you should see them.'

40

Tarragon had no wish just then to see the swollen girls of Alphonse's native Provence. He set off towards the hotel, with Alphonse at his heels.

'The swallows were rather early this year,' he said.

'You are a coal mine of interesting information, Mr Clump,' said Alphonse. 'I think perhaps my information also to Mrs Hassett and your family will be quite interesting, too.'

'I don't know what you're talking about.'

'I see you by the wood. I think "he is up to some bad". I am very interesting. I watch. I think, this is a man with pictures of the excellent Miss Blossom in his portmanteau.'

'How the devil . . .'

'One of the chambermaids, she is not so discreet. What a shame.'

'All lies. I shall report you.'

Tarragon stalked angrily to his room and opened his suitcase. His pictures of Miss Blossom had gone.

The rain belt drifted in unexpectedly from Northern France and reached Uxbridge during tea.

'George,' said his mother. 'We forgot to show him Edgar's book.'

'Oh yes,' said his father. 'You know your Great Great Uncle Edgar lives in Suffolk.'

'I didn't even know I had a Great Great Uncle Edgar.'

'He's the brother of your father's grandfather, and he lives in Suffolk. And we quite forgot until the other day that we've got a book of his, all about Suffolk.'

'What's it called?'

'*Suffolk.*'

Diana snorted.

'Well anyway,' his mother continued, 'it's got quite a long passage about your hotel in it.'

'Big deal,' said Diana.

'Well it's interesting,' said Pegasus.

'Oh bloody fascinating,' said Diana. 'Far more interesting than

Vietnam or the under-developed countries or non-proliferation or neo-Nazism, which is building up in this country too, you know, or you would if you had eyes to see, or whether organized religion has any relevance to modern life, or the function of the artist in a bourgeois, materialist society. Far more bloody interesting.' And she stormed out, slamming the door.

Try though he did Pegasus thought, thank goodness Tom Graveney isn't here to see all this.

'She's going through a phase,' said his mother.

'I'd like to see that book,' said Pegasus.

His mother fetched it for him. *Suffolk*, by E. Newton Baines.

'The Goat and Thistle came by its name in the following somewhat unusual fashion. It was the custom of the vicar, one Arnold Holyoake, M.A., in an effort to combat the robust heathenism of his flock, to visit the tap rooms of the several alehouses in his parish.

'So easy-going was the nature of the good divine, and so enfeebled his memory, that he invariably forgot the purpose that lay behind his visit. The gentle man of God, therefore, would appear to have learnt more of "Skittle-bowls" and "shove the penny" than his parishioners did of the Almighty.

'One evening, his habitual amnesia heightened by a moderate consumption of strong liquor, he left his coat at the tavern and, wandering home in his shirt sleeves, had the misfortune to trip over an alder sapling and break his leg. He died of pneumonia but two days later.

'When the coat was noticed by Mine Host Will Arnscott, an ancestor of the Big Tom Arnscott whose immense cricket hit was referred to on page 623, a small copy of the Bible fell from the pocket and opened at the Epistle of Paul the Apostle to the Ephesians. The inn became known as the Coat and Epistle, a name which soon became corrupted to Goat and Thistle.'

'Very interesting,' said Pegasus.

'I thought you'd find it interesting,' said his mother.

*   *   *

It was still raining when Tarragon Clump got up on Sunday morning but soon the rain moved out over the sluggish oily sea. Tarragon went down to the river for a sail.

The tide was out, and the river was at its best, secret down there below its rims of mud. Tarragon's spirits rose. He handled the little dinghy well. He got everything he could out of the wind, the wind and he were friends, his face was salty, he would go back and have a drink in the bar, and invite Mrs Hassett up to London for dinner one evening. There would be time to ask her while she was serving him.

He walked up the lane and then across the heath. Tony Hassett served him.

'Nice morning,' he said amiably.

After their Sunday dinner his father suggested a car trip. They went to the National Gallery.

'Rotten luck that chap Turner had with his weather,' said his father.

Tarragon Clump had a puncture less than a mile from the hotel. Damn damn damn.

He drove back aggressively, taking it out on the car, sweating freely, cursing the Sunday drivers with surprisingly violent oaths.

Simon and Paula went to evensong. Canon Mulgrave was on form.

Through Brentford and Shenfield and Chelmsford and Ipswich sped Pegasus towards the beckoning sea, past filling stations and drab dead houses, past grimy cafés and fields full of dead old cars, thinking that this time there was no need to feel excited about seeing Mrs Hassett, from now on he would devote himself solely to the learning of his art, and the last thing you wanted to do was to get tangled up with a married woman.

He looked forward to it all. The steady routine, the heat, the

43

moments of furious activity when the orders came thick and fast, the hearty swearing of his colleagues. Alphonse, convinced that all the English were pigs. Tonio, convinced that all the English were pigs. Pegasus, the Englishman who would prove them wrong and one day outshine them both.

So far he had performed only routine tasks, flexing his taste buds. Soon he would create a great masterpiece – his own. He was so eager to get back to work that he didn't even dread Rose Lodge.

They had some cake for him, and some tinned pears.

'What sort of a time did you have?' said Bill.

'What did you do?' said Brenda.

'Tell us all about it,' said Bill.

There wasn't much to tell, but what there was he told. They listened as if it was the most exciting story they had ever heard.

'I expect you were sorry to leave,' said Brenda.

'Though glad to get back,' said Bill.

'Yes,' said Pegasus.

'We'll have that picnic soon,' said Bill.

9

Even the faint scratching of his nail on her hand or the touch of her lips rubbed across his had been vibrant and thrilling. It had been lovely to live through that thrill. Now these same gestures were already memories, mere expressions of gratitude. And although he knew that this was how it always was, he asked himself whether his desire had all been an illusion.

'Thank you,' he said.

'Thank you.'

44

It was broad daylight in her bedroom. The sun shone in through the window. The afternoon was alive with sunshine and the possibility of unexpected window cleaners.

Tony had gone off for the day, ostensibly to an exhibition of ventilating equipment at Earls Court. He had announced last night, in the bar, that he was going. Mr Thomas, the milkman, had smiled at Mr Block the chandler as if he was a ferret let loose in a warren of innuendo. 'He'll be ventilating his equipment all right, but not at Earls Court,' he had murmured. Pegasus had felt angry.

'Feeling guilty?' said Jane.

'Just reflective,' said Pegasus.

Guilt, you could easily mistake it for guilt. It was a vague sense of absurdity, nothing more. You were in bed, naked together, impelled there by impulses which already belonged to the past. It was impossible to go on without a sense of surprise. And in this case there were added dangers. A married woman. An employer employee relationship.

'I hope all this isn't against union rules,' he said.

'It's a productivity bonus,' said Jane.

'An incentive.'

Jane sighed.

'I'm complicated,' she said.

'How do you mean?'

'Married, for one thing. And I'm complicated in myself, too.'

'Well aren't we all?'

He held her cheek firmly to his, and she shrank away a little, either from his breath or from the patronizing nature of his gesture. This was one of the things Paula had objected to. He had found it delightful and clever that she managed to catch the train, managed to select the right platform, managed to put one foot in front of the other, organized so successfully the circulation of her blood. Paula had resented this.

These things he must not do with Jane. Nor must he think of Paula.

'In what way?' he said.

'I need careful handling.'

'You'll get it from me, darling,' he said.

He fingered her breasts absent-mindedly.

'I'm glad you came in that day,' said Jane.

'I hope you always will be,' said Pegasus.

'What do you mean by that?'

'Nothing.'

'It sounded sinister. Like a premonition.'

'You're imagining things.'

'Well there you are, you see. I need careful handling.'

Pegasus had been having a drink in the bar. They had gazed at each other and then they had realized that the gaze was a declaration of intent. Now here they were in bed.

'What I meant,' said Pegasus, 'if I meant anything, is that so far we've only done the easy bit. To agree what you want out of sex is easier than agreeing what you want out of almost anything else – unless one of you is some kind of a pervert, of course.' He ran his hand slowly up her slim, widening thigh, feeling an echo of his past desire. 'I mean you'd be far more likely to argue over what to have for dinner than about sex.'

'There's more choice.' Her sudden smile was warm, wide and white.

'Sex only becomes a problem between you when you don't want it. Then it suddenly seems unimportant what you have for dinner.'

'You're very talkative.'

'I've never heard of any totally satisfactory way of behaving after making love. Smoking strikes me as repulsive, falling asleep as worse, kissing as an anti-climax. I become talkative.'

He ran his hands over her gently curved, almost boyish, hips.

'Why have you been faithful for so long?' he asked.

'Well I kept hoping things would get better between us. You do. You don't let yourself admit that it could possibly be permanent.'

46

He held her more tightly, as if by hurting her he could convince her of his power to help. Then he let go, sat back and looked at her. She drew her knees up like someone much younger and he held her right knee firmly, enjoying its knobble.

'I'm frightened of running this place,' she said.

'But I think you do it very well.'

'I'm too thin,' she said.

'You're not thin. You're slim.'

She was a little thin. Arms, legs, hips. Not thin, but on the thin side. Nice.

'You're beautiful,' he said.

As he kissed her he felt that she was a little stiff and distant. He wanted to get up, to walk outside, to drink fruit juice. He kissed her arm, and drew gently up his nose her particular range of scents, which reminded him of a tin full of broken biscuits and grass, not that he had ever smelt a tin full of broken biscuits and grass. He pulled the sheet over their heads to make a dark secret place, wanting as he did so to watch cricket, to loll against a gate, to drink fruit juice. Feeling as he wanted that he must seek an explanation of her sudden slight stiffness, of her withdrawal symptoms. And as he sought his explanation still wanting, wanting the sun, laughter, fruit juice.

'What's wrong?'

'Nothing.'

'Yes. Something is. Tell me.'

'It's just me, being me,' said Jane.

'Tell me.'

'No. Quick. Talk about yourself. Tell me all about yourself.'

He was astonished at the urgency of her appeal. But he obeyed. It was nice to be told to talk about oneself.

'Well,' he said, 'I'm a fairly ordinary person.'

'Rub me gently while you talk,' she said.

While he talked he rubbed her gently. His eyes were looking at the soft white clouds. Part of his mind was thinking solely of fruit juice.

He told her about his Uxbridge childhood. School. University. Nostalgic trivia. Selected anecdotes. Humorous self-deprecation. Himself seeing his own life in a wry light. Paula, the only other woman he had ever slept with. A few snatches of self-truth.

'Thank you. That's better,' she said when he had finished.

'Good.'

She explained about her symptoms. Something about seeing herself as something outside herself, therefore being a void looking at herself. Undoubtedly true, yet difficult to believe in. Difficult to comprehend the experience.

'You don't mind?' she asked.

'Of course not.'

There was a knock on the door. They both sat up, alarmed.

'Are you there, Mrs Hassett?' came a comfortingly unconcerned voice.

'Yes. What is it, Patsy?'

'There's been a bit of trouble, Mrs Hassett, over light bulbs. There's two gone and we can't find . . .'

'Just a moment. I'll come and see to it.'

Thank God. It wasn't him.

'Time to get up anyway,' said Jane. 'And you're due back on duty, aren't you? I'm your employer, don't forget.'

'I hope I give every satisfaction, ma'am.'

She jumped out of bed, tip-toed rapidly to her clothes, shy now of her nudity, pale, a few veins showing, her breasts themselves light bulbs, her buttocks superb. She dressed rapidly, kissed him and left the room, locking the door behind her.

Ugh, the necessity for stealth.

This was their bedroom, hers and Tony's. But he didn't feel an intruder, perhaps because it was part of the hotel, or perhaps because there were no photos of smiling innocent children on the dressing table.

He began to dress, keeping well away from the window. Mrs Hassett! He repudiated the Hassett. Did this mean that he was repudiating her past life. 'You won't accept that my whole life before we met has actually happened,' Paula had said. 'You're jealous of my having a past.' Unfair. No, it was just that it was Hassett. Now if it was . . . but he couldn't think of any name that he would have been happy to find her already bearing.

And he must stop thinking of Paula.

Well, Paula dear, we are free of each other and I see now that it is all for the best. Anyway, Paula, I'm sorry that I was such a bore, sending all those awful unfair letters, and visiting the seat in Kensington Gardens like that, though of course you didn't know I was doing that. I only hope that you and Simon will be happy, and that his translations of Ogden Nash are coming along well. Correction – I hope that you and Simon will bust up and that he will find it impossible to continue with his translations of Ogden Nash, but that you will find someone else and be very happy. Thank you for everything, and good-bye.

Duck with honey? Jugged woodcock? You would need either a very large woodcock or a very small jug.

The key scraped in the lock and he had to resist the temptation to hide. The door opened. It was Jane.

'You go downstairs first, looking natural,' she said. 'I'll follow.'

'It's so sordid. Things are going to be a little awkward.'

'I know.'

'I don't really think my place is the answer. We shouldn't broadcast the fact to Brenda,' said Pegasus.

'No.'

'Besides, it wouldn't exactly be the ideal love nest. Not with all those books and toys.'

'Not with Wol and Piglet and Eeyore.'

'Not to mention Major James Bigglesworth, better known to all his friends as Biggles.'

10

Mervyn arrived unexpectedly on the day before the picnic. He came unheralded as always, on the Ipswich bus, just in time to get the last room at the hotel. It was his half-term. He seemed surprised that Pegasus didn't give up all his duties the moment he arrived. Mervyn was the most demanding of all his friends, and the closest. More a mutual need than a friendship.

Tony was present this week-end so Mervyn's presence suited Pegasus and Jane. But it was a pity about the picnic. Mervyn was the last person you wanted on an occasion of that sort.

'Your mind is not over the job,' said Alphonse, noting Pegasus's absent-minded attack on the unfreezing of some fresh spinach.

Pegasus made no reply. He was beginning to think less highly of Alphonse. He was uninspired. No finesse. And lazy. 'Please to open for me a tin of pâté maison. Well, I am not making my own. They are not appreciating it, English pigs.' Pegasus felt that he had drifted into catering simply because he was French, just as, if he was Panamanian, he'd be Sparks on some rusty coaster. He was just doing a job, rather than expressing his essential Alphonseness. But Pegasus remained outwardly respectful, not wanting to get in the man's bad books, and be kept on this routine work for ever.

Steam rising, Tonio swearing, trout sizzling. Enter Jane, busy supervising. Hotel moving towards success. All comments favourable. A special smile from Jane, concealed in an ordinary smile. A rising leap in Pegasus, a salmon leaping, hollandaise sauce spawning. Spurt of water. Tiny pains of hot water alighting on face. Part of great band of men and women creating pleasure and sustenance for others. Romantic brotherhood. Three visits to her room now. Ripening summer, rain and sun. Time for a few pints before closing time. Mervyn in good form, happy in his work. Nostalgia. Sudden access of gloom, feverishly dispelled.

Careful feet on cottage steps, exaggerated care of the drunk. Falling into bed. Soon asleep.

Five hours later he awoke, suffering. He had been dreaming. His dreams had begun again.

The dream had been set at the Ministry of Insemination. The official in Room 511 was Cousin Percy. He was seated at the head of a large round table with twenty-four seats. Pegasus sat at the foot.

'What's your complaint, Baines?' said Cousin Percy.

Pegasus felt instantly servile.

'Well, sir, fifteen years ago I ordered a son.'

'What sort of a son, Baines?'

'A test cricketer, sir.'

Cousin Percy consulted a form. 'Yes,' he said. 'Quite correct. You ordered a test cricketer, who would go in number six, bowl a well-concealed Chinaman, and win the Nobel Prize for left-arm bowling. What is a well-concealed Chinaman?'

'It's the left-arm bowler's off-break, sir.'

'I see. And what went wrong?'

'He isn't what I ordered, sir.'

'You mean he isn't a test cricketer?'

'Yes, sir.'

'How old is he?'

'Fourteen, sir.'

Cousin Percy leant forward, his face stern, his eyes flashing orbs of controlled fury. The room stretched huge and dark in all directions. Pegasus was afraid.

'You're not giving him much time, are you, Baines?' said Cousin Percy.

'He'll never be a test cricketer, sir. He isn't the sort.'

'What sort is he?'

'He's non-co-operative, sir.'

51

Non-co-operative! Nothing could describe the agony of being a parent to such a child.

'In what way?'

'He throws things, sir.'

'What things, Baines?'

'Anything, sir.'

'Anything else?'

'No, sir, just anything.'

'I meant does he do anything else apart from throw things?' Cousin Percy was getting annoyed.

'Yes, sir. He says "sweet and sour pork".'

'I don't see anything so terrible in that,' said Cousin Percy.

Pegasus felt that he wasn't explaining it very well.

'But he says it all the time, sir,' he said.

'Oh.'

'And he's Chinese.'

'What's his cricket like?'

'He refuses to play. He just throws all the stumps at the umpire and says "sweet and sour pork". He's not the sort of thing we had in mind at all, sir.'

'Fetch him in.'

His wife walked listlessly, her spirit broken. Johnny looked so nice in his school uniform, a round jolly contented Chinese face. He sat on Pegasus's right, with his mother beyond him.

'What's your name?' said Cousin Percy, not unkindly.

Pegasus had a wild hope that the boy would tell him.

'Sweet and sour pork,' said Johnny.

'What do you want to be when you grow up?'

'Sweet and sour pork,' said Johnny.

'What's your favourite meal?'

'Sweet and sour pork,' said Johnny.

'You see,' said Cousin Percy. 'He answers sensibly enough in the end, if you just show a bit of patience.'

Johnny jumped up, picked up his chair, and threw it across the table towards Cousin Percy. It didn't reach him.

'Why did you do that?' said Cousin Percy.

'Sweet and sour pork,' said Johnny.

'Take him away,' said Cousin Percy.

The mother led the boy from the room, an innocent smile on his chubby little Chinese face.

'Johnny Chinaman doesn't always take to cricket all that easily. You haven't been forcing it down his throat, have you?' said Cousin Percy to Pegasus.

'No, sir.'

'On balance, Baines, I am inclined to think that this is just a phase he's going through – a phase of being Chinese and throwing things and only saying "sweet and sour pork".'

'But, sir . . .'

'Yes?'

'I wanted an English boy.'

'You aren't a racialist, are you?'

'No, sir, I've got nothing against the Chinese as a race. Only as my son. It seems so inconvenient.'

'Are you suggesting that the Ministry has made a mistake?'

Courage, Pegasus.

'Yes, sir.'

'Well, it's possible. Computers are only machines.'

'I was wondering, sir . . .'

'Yes?'

'I was wondering if the word Chinaman had confused the computer.'

Cousin Percy sat in thoughtful silence for some minutes. His eyes were dark pools, in which his thoughts leapt like trout at dusk. Pegasus could hear a clock ticking high up in the dark, endless room.

'We're always ready to admit our mistakes,' said Cousin Percy at length. 'But we must be sure. I think we ought to wait and see, and if after another twenty years he still isn't a test cricketer, file a PXC 138b/9/7c/X3a/111359R for compensation.'

'But, sir . . .'

'If he stops being Chinese, or shows any sign of going in number six, let us know.'

'But, sir . . .'

'Yes, Baines?'

'Don't you remember me?'

'Remember you? What do you mean?'

'It doesn't matter, sir.'

'The week-end is a very good time for sporting activities and you should consider a business proposition very carefully.'

Pegasus knew that he was dismissed.

He stumbled into the door in his confusion. The shock woke him. He was lying on the floor, unable at first to account for the little room in which he found himself. Then he realized that he was at Rose Lodge, that he had been dreaming, that he had fallen out of bed. 6.25 a.m. A fine morning. Birds singing, none of them with hangovers. He sat in the easy chair, feeling sick. They mustn't begin again, those dreams. There was no need for them, down here.

He began his recovery programme, cold water on the head, liver salts, gradual dressing, one garment at a time, with rests in between, and then some fresh air. With these aids he managed to eat his breakfast without being sick. Bill gave him comics to read, and he felt obliged to glance at them. Bang. Cra-a-ck. Filthy Boche. Stinking Viet Cong. Kids' stuff. Mustn't offend Bill, though, not with the unspoken shadow always inside the house, however much the sun shone in.

'You were late last night,' said Bill.

'A little.'

'Perhaps you'd like to bring your friend with you on the picnic,' said Brenda. She looked like an air hostess and a hangover was an aphrodisiac.

Oh God, the picnic. Why couldn't it rain, today of all days?

Before going on lunch duty Pegasus walked in the sun with Mervyn. Insects were humming insectily, larks were singing larkily, and Pegasus said to Mervyn: 'I've got to go on a picnic

54

with my landlord and landlady this afternoon. I sort of promised.'

'Oh.'

'There's no need for you to come.'

'Oh.'

'It won't be much fun. Don't feel obliged to come if there's anything you'd rather do.'

'I'll come,' said Mervyn.

They took the picnic things out of the boot and went down a path where the cliffs fell away towards the estuary. Pegasus looked across towards the river winding up its broad, empty valley, white sails in the distance. Beyond the river lay the village and the Goat and Thistle and he longed to be back there now, saw a mirage of himself there. Mervyn made no effort to carry anything.

First they bathed. This raised no serious problems. The water was cold, hard, North Sea water. Then they played French cricket. Bill and Brenda ran around with astonishing verve, falling in the sand, laughing at their own wild incompetence, ungainly, unnatural, urging Pegasus and Mervyn to show similar high spirits.

Then they sank into the sand, exhausted. Pegasus gazed at the long, gradual curve of the sea, the sandy cliffs, fishing boats dotted over the sea, two coasters further out. Suddenly a fistful of sand was hurled over him. Bill and Brenda roared with laughter. Then tea began, slowly at first with tomato and egg sandwiches, gathering pace with sticky buns and chocolate cake, finally overflowing in a riot of jelly and bottles of pop.

'O'oh. Jelly and bananas. Pegasus's favourite,' said Mervyn sarcastically.

'Jolly good,' said Bill.

'Jelly good,' said Mervyn, and Bill and Brenda laughed.

Pegasus kicked out at Mervyn when no one was looking.

'Ow,' said Mervyn, looking accusingly at Pegasus.

'That's no way to treat your friend,' said Bill to Pegasus.

Mervyn grinned. Pegasus fumed.

55

'Yum yum,' said Bill, of the jelly.

Pegasus mumbled.

'Don't talk with your mouth full,' said Brenda.

Pegasus looked helplessly at Mervyn, but there was no help from that quarter.

'Are you enjoying yourself, Mervyn?' said Brenda.

'I'm having the time of my life,' said Mervyn.

'Jolly good,' said Bill, measuring his length on the sand and yawning contentedly.

They all measured their lengths on the sand and yawned contentedly. Above them the sky was blue, with white lines where aeroplanes had been. And the great sea teeming with fish. And beyond it the Baltic. And boats rocking gently on the summer breeze in the Baltic, with the rhythmic waters lapping against their hulls, and the long-legged summer girls. Another fistful of sand landed in Pegasus's face.

'Let's go and dam up a stream,' said Bill. 'That's always fun.'

A quick search revealed a complete absence of streams. They played ducks and drakes instead. Neither Pegasus nor Mervyn could equal the flair shown by their host and hostess.

Then they drove home.

'Look,' said Mervyn with mock excitement. 'Cows.'

'Oh yes,' said Bill and Brenda.

'Horses,' said Mervyn.

'Oh yes.'

'Look, a traction engine.'

'Oh yes.'

'Look, an Early English church tower.'

Pegasus felt drained by the nervous tension. Silence was even worse than conversation, because it made him fear what would be said next. But at last they were back. The ordeal was over.

'Thank you very much indeed for a lovely time,' said Pegasus.

'Simply super,' drawled Mervyn, crooking his hand. 'I haven't you know, let myself go so much in years.'

'It was fun, wasn't it?' said Bill.

Brenda rushed over to the hotel to serve dinner. Pegasus, whose evening off it was, went for a drink with Mervyn. They drove away from the village, into the heart of agricultural Suffolk, away from the sea.

At first they didn't mention the picnic. Then Pegasus said: 'I'd say I was sorry I let you in for it, except that you didn't do much to make things any better.'

'Can't you move?' said Mervyn.

Pegasus hesitated. 'I don't like to,' he said.

'You mean you like it there?'

'It's not that. But, you know, I'm all they've got.'

Mervyn bought another round of drinks. The bar was shady and cool. The beer was hoppy, woody, a country beer. Not so many left. The beer at least they could enjoy.

'By the way,' said Mervyn. 'I saw Paula.'

'Good God, where?'

'Kensington Gardens.'

Despite everything Pegasus felt a flicker of excitement.

'With her Simon?'

'She wasn't with anyone.'

'Did she see you?'

'No. I turned away, for some reason.'

'How did she look?'

'I had the impression she was sad. But I'm no judge of women.'

'No.'

'I gather you're having an affair with the landlady,' said Mervyn.

'What makes you think that?' said Pegasus.

'You,' said Mervyn.

'Well yes I am,' said Pegasus. 'In a way.'

'I think I'll hang around till tomorrow afternoon, if that's all right,' said Mervyn.

'That's fine,' said Pegasus. 'In what way did you think she was sad?'

57

Mervyn grinned.

Bill and Brenda were still up when Pegasus got home.

'You're a bit late, aren't you?' said Bill.

'Well?'

'It's becoming a bit of a habit, isn't it?'

'I've got a friend down here, haven't I?'

Bill and Brenda gave each other meaningful looks.

'You think he's a bad example, is that it?' said Pegasus.

Brenda nodded, blushing in her blotchy way.

'I'm not a bloody child, you know,' said Pegasus.

He ran up the stairs and slammed his door behind him. Downstairs he could hear tears. He picked up *Biggles Sweeps The Desert* and flung it into the garden.

11

The next fortnight was glorious. Summer burst into flower ready to welcome its longest day. Mr Thomas sang in Welsh as he delivered the milk and remembered the hills. There were bags under his eyes, from too much drinking too late at night. He sang softly as he delivered three pints at Rose Lodge, that great milk-drinking household. Bill was up, shaving, tetchily, bags under his eyes too, off in a few moments to check on those lazy, stupid pheasants, many of whom he talked to by name.

Soon Jane's mother got up too and complained that it was Wimbledon weather a fortnight too early. Jane's father grunted, and she went downstairs to prepare breakfast for Jane's father. It had really been rather unfair of Jane to dislike tennis, thought Jane's mother. Jane's father read the *Daily Telegraph*, while Jane's mother opened Jane's letter and commented: 'Reading between the lines, Jane's marriage is on the rocks.' Jane had made a bad marriage. If only she had persisted with her analysis. Angela Curvis had persisted with her analysis, and she had married a barrister. Jane's mother sighed, and Jane's father, hearing the sigh, grunted.

Each day the sun rose higher, and twice Mr Thomas had punctures. Each time he found sharp nails in his tyres. The Baineses breakfasted at 8.30 in their Cotswold Guest House, and planned which villages they would visit. Alone in Uxbridge Diana luxuriated in a series of ludicrously eccentric breakfasts. Cousin Percy and his friend Boris ate honey with their rolls on the terrace of their Bavarian hotel. Tarragon Clump rolled back his sleeves and began to operate. He was the master here.

Morley Baines sat in the hot dusty newspaper office with the typewriters clacking and wrestled with his feature. Are dogs intelligent? Morley Baines conducts an enquiry into the canine mind. Stacks of letters from readers.

'The moment the TV comes on our West Highland Terrier goes to sleep and doesn't wake up until the end of the epilogue. If that isn't intelligence I don't know what is.'

Hot. Pity he hadn't a car. Holidays soon, to Norway with Tim. Pity he couldn't go down to see Pegasus this week-end. Pain that Pegasus had not written, nor invited him. Much love in this relationship, well hidden.

Day after glorious day Pegasus helped prepare lunch and dreamt about his future masterpieces. He had a feeling that he would invent the first masterpiece any day now.

Every morning Mr and Mrs Baines drove through the pleasant Cotswold lanes. One morning they passed a particularly pleasant old house and Margaret Baines exclaimed: 'Oh look, a wedding' and it reminded them of their own wedding and they didn't know whether to be sad or happy.

And Tarragon Clump, dressing for the wedding of his sister Parsley, took out the letter in his bedroom in the particularly pleasant old house and read it once again. It was made up of printed letters taken from various newspapers and periodicals in the traditional manner.

'Dear Mr Clump,' it read. 'If I am not receiving £100 before 10 days of this day I am sending then my next letter to Mrs Hassett, your family also. Please to leave monies to that extent withinside the old woodpecker's nest in the blited oak tree in Blounce Copse beyond the gate with five planks holding to N of copse'.

Tarragon put the letter back in his pocket, thinking that it was all too idiotic to be true. And then in the church he looked at his father, encrusted in eccentric style and benevolent prejudice, a vintage port to whose friendship only those who could identify the year were ever admitted; at his mother, busily idle, proud, domineering, living for the social life that she had entwined around herself in this her corner of England; at his sister Parsley, a long, tall cumbersome girl of thirty-four, all elbows and knees and good intentions, radiant and unembarrassed at the altar with the dull but wealthy Martin Smith-Peters; at his brother Basil, forty, solid, a farmer, with five radiantly dangerous children who indulged in an inordinate amount of outdoor activity and always had at least two broken legs between them. When Basil was two his parents had found a delightfully novel egg cup for him, marked with his own name, Basil. It came in a set of six. The other five were marked Tarragon, Parsley, Mace, Thyme and Sage. But they only had three children.

Tarragon looked at them all in the quiet church and he thought, ridiculous it may be, but I can't risk their knowing. It would be incomprehensible, absurd, worse than a thumping great traditional scandal. He knew then that he would endure the humiliation, next week-end when he visited Suffolk with his friend Henry Purnell, of depositing £100 in the old woodpecker's nest in the blighted oak tree in Blounce Copse beyond the gate with five planks holding to N of copse. Of course if there were further demands after that, that would be a different matter.

60

In the afternoons the sun was really hot and a pall of dirty heat hovered over the city.

'Our Alsatian always carries my purse when I go shopping. Recently I have suspected our Pakistani shopkeeper of giving me "short change", but I said nothing as I didn't want to cause "trouble". Then last month the dog fell ill and the vet found £14 7s. 9½d. in his stomach. My dog has opened my eyes to the dangers of racialism. Count me among the keenest supporters of our friends from the sub-continent from now on.'

Perhaps it was his fault there had been bad feeling between himself and Pegasus last time. Perhaps he ought to write.

And Pegasus, preparing vegetable after vegetable as the evenings wore on, thought sometimes of Morley and the keen edge of their past affection, and thought, perhaps I ought to write to him, though he hasn't written to me.

Tarragon Clump excused himself shortly before dinner, left his friend Henry Purnell, the up-and-coming society dentist, walked the half mile to Blounce Copse, found the five-barred gate and the blighted oak, made sure no one was watching, and slipped the money into the old woodpecker's nest. There was no sign of the Hassett husband that week-end but he couldn't talk to Mrs Hassett because of his friend. Next time, when he came alone, he would take action.

The evening drew on. Mr and Mrs Baines drove slowly towards London in a congealing mass of traffic. Diana tidied up and looked forward to their return. Stephen and his angelic face tended to pall when there was nobody around to think that he was Ursula.

The sun sank slowly in the West, unaware that it was a cliché. It looked like being a good start to Wimbledon, thought Jane's mother. Jane, quite suddenly, in the bar, decided to institute proceedings for divorce. Tony, ostensibly visiting friends in Yorkshire, would not return for some time.

Tarragon and Henry Purnell had a last drink before setting off for London. They chatted amiably about the breeding habits of avocets, while Tony Hassett was taking precautions so that he wouldn't breed in a windmill just off the Norwich Road.

Alphonse counted the notes hungrily. The garrulous starlings arrived at their roosting places. Bill and Brenda waited for Pegasus. Morley went up on deck on his Fred Olsen line steamer and stared fascinated at the wake for half an hour. Cousin Percy drove sadly back along the M.2, sadly humming Viennese hums. Mr and Mrs Baines arrived home and Diana kissed them both and made them a pot of tea and said: 'Enjoyed your greedy fortnight while the world slides nearer to starvation?' The sun dotted its cliché with a thousand glorious tints.

Simon struggled with his Ogden Nash. They had been to Blackheath, followed by evensong. Now they were home. Paula sat in his room, writing a letter slowly, with several drafts.

Not long to go now till the wedding.

'Who are you writing to, darling?'

'No one special.'

'Oh. Who?'

'Carol.'

'Ah. How is Carol?'

'Recovering.'

There was no such person as Carol. Paula began again.

'Dear Pegasus, I expect you'll be surprised to hear from me after all this time but, as you have said so often in your letters, when two people have been "close" to each other they obviously want to know how the other one is getting on. Real warmth between people in this world is so rare that . . .'

No good at all. On the way home she would deposit it in a distant litter bin with all the other false starts.

'I thought Canon Mulgrave was a bit diffuse tonight, didn't you, darling?'

'Possibly a bit diffuse,' said Paula.

'No one can avoid being diffuse all the time,' said Simon. 'Not even Canon Mulgrave.'

He saw her to her bus and as he kissed her good night he said: 'I'm glad Carol is recovering.'

The sun disappeared. The last boats drifted on the tide up the slow East Anglian rivers. Gulls finished their last greedy morsels, cows stood deserted in the dewy fields, Mrs Thomas went to bed early and left a note on the bedside table saying 'Not today, thank you' and fell asleep with her mouth open. The light faded and a warm darkness enveloped the once lovely land of Britain. The glorious fortnight was over.

I 2

Paula was on the telephone arranging some air tickets to Madrid when Cousin Percy walked into the office and smiled at her. It was Wednesday morning and raining hard. The tickets to Madrid were not for her, they never were, and so she was pleased to see Cousin Percy.

'It's Cousin Percy,' she said.

'I'm not your cousin,' he said.

She thought of him as Cousin Percy because he was only an appendage to Pegasus. They had gone out with him from time to time. On one of their Italian holidays they had met him, quite by chance, in Venice. She gave him another smile as she calculated whether the 15.00 hours plane would give Mr Bartram time to get to the airport from his lunch appointment. Cousin Percy's long face was healthily tanned. He was tall. Was it because of this or because he was an appendage to Pegasus or simply because it was raining that she was so delighted to see him? Yes, the 18.00 hours would probably be better.

'What brings you to Punic Films?' she asked.

'You,' said Cousin Percy.

'How do you mean?'

'I was sheltering from the rain, waiting for a taxi, and suddenly I saw Punic Films on the door, and I thought, hullo, Perce lad, that's where old Paula used to hang out. I wonder if she's still there.'

'Oh, I'm still here.'

'So I thought I'd come up and see how you were. How are you?'

'Fine.'

'What's the link with Carthage?'

'What?'

'Why Punic Films? Or did they want to call it Pubic and then get cold feet?'

'You're in spritely vein today.'

'Oh, I can sprite, when the mood takes me. Anyway, what about lunch?'

'Lovely. Marvellous.'

They went to the nearest place, because of the rain. It was a salady sort of place, very health-giving.

'Well, it's nice to see you again,' said Cousin Percy.

Paula wondered, was that story true – or are you spying on behalf of Pegasus, or are you trying to get your own oar in?

'You're not looking radiant,' said Cousin Percy.

'It's the rain,' said Paula, 'and the routine.'

'Not married yet?'

'Not quite. It's due quite soon.'

'Ah.'

She asked him about his own affairs and he told her about his musical holiday and about all his work, including his horoscope column.

'Would you like me to tell you yours?' he said.

Paula gave him all the details of her birth.

'A change will bring you new personal interests,' said Cousin Percy. 'A good time for initiative in private matters, with Tuesdays particularly favourable for romance. Have some more cucumber.'

'A bit vague,' said Paula. 'Except for the cucumber.'

'Well it's got to be true for quite a lot of people as well as yourself,' said Cousin Percy.

'I suppose so.'

'This man you're marrying, is it . . .'

'Simon. Yes, it is,' said Paula.

They ate in silence for a few moments.

'Have you seen anything of Pegasus recently?' said Paula.

'Not for a while. He left his job, you know.'

'No, I didn't.'

'He's working as vegetable chef in some pub in Suffolk.'

'Good lord. Is he happy?'

'As far as I know.'

'Good.'

'You'll make a good mother, Paula,' said Cousin Percy. 'I see you running a rambling, idle, lazy, civilized hospitable kind of home.' Paula laughed, delighted.

Soon the meal was over. Cousin Percy didn't fancy coffee.

'I don't like this place,' he said. 'There's a man in a dark suit over there eating a salad full of raw grated carrot and drinking a glass of milk. I can't stand that sort of thing.'

'You don't like health.'

'It's one of the most morbid things I know.'

'You're just reacting against your parsonical past,' said Paula, before they hurried along the pavement to her doorway.

'It was nice,' said Cousin Percy.

'Yes, it was. Thank you,' said Paula.

During the long afternoon Paula found it hard to keep her mind on the job. She wasn't due to see Simon that evening. It was his evening for uninterrupted Ogden Nash. He was having trouble with 'The song of canaries – Never varies . . .'

When she left work at five-thirty Paula realized that it would be well over an hour before Simon got home. She decided to go to the cinema, so she bought an *Evening Standard*. It boiled down to a choice between a Godard she had seen twice and a Losey she had seen once. In the end she plumped for the Losey on mathematical grounds.

She enjoyed the Losey. It wasn't the master at his best but it had his stamp upon it. Art was a great sedative.

After the film she had a spaghetti, despite her figure. Then she set off towards Simon's.

She half hoped there would be a sudden bus strike and an enormous traffic jam through all the streets. But the bus soon came.

She thought, I wonder if all along I was just using him. I wonder if I'm a bitch. I never thought I was one of those. No, I'm sure I'm not. Well, pretty sure.

She shivered. She closed her eyes and thought of Venice, the Fenice Theatre, the Accademia Bridge, the vaporettos buzzing past the Ca' D'Oro even now. But Simon interposed himself, standing on the Rialto Bridge, dark, serious, measured, shaving twice a day, with the hirsuteness of the righteous, vulnerable.

From the bus stop towards his house her feet dragged. On the stairs to his flat she met the man from the flat below, who smiled as if this was just another casual visit.

She rang. He would be annoyed at the disturbance.

He was surprised to see her.

'Well,' he said. 'This is a surprise.'

Not delighted. Not frightened. Not annoyed.

'I'm leaving you, Simon,' she said.

'Perhaps it's all for the best,' he said.

13

He had to escape from Rose Lodge. He couldn't stand it any longer. Night after night, sipping cocoa and ploughing through all those books. Already he'd read *Winnie the Pooh*, *The House At Pooh Corner*, all three copies of *Mr Midshipman Easy*, and almost half the Biggles books.

He smiled at the Gunters. They smiled back. They approved of his reading.

He read on, half his mind in the kitchen. He'd taken to the work well. He'd learnt all he'd ever learn from being vegetable chef under Alphonse. One of these days someone else would be doing the boring chores, and he would be the master to whose restaurant people flocked to sample his Suffolk oyster patties. 'What a character' observed Algy shrewdly as the pock-marked mulatto limped . . . hake. Something with hake.

He had to escape.

'I'm going for a walk,' he said.

'But it's bed time.'

And so as Paula walked away for the last time from Simon's flat Pegasus was walking up the lane past the Magnet and Cowslip, past the modern bungalows where quantity surveyors from the town were discussing the charms of rural life. Behind a hedge an electricity sub-station hummed venomously, and a bat flickered erratically past his head. His sexual desire rose sharply. Damn Tony for not being away. He hurried on. The hedge was overgrown with wild rhubarb. That might be it. Hake with rhubarb.

A double row of pylons led towards the sea, towards the nuclear power station whose bulk could just be made out against the night sky. Bold, impressive, but contemptuous of the gentle contours of the land. Hubris.

Pegasus could hear humming in the wires, perhaps imaginary. He remembered a recurring childhood dream, himself sliding along the telegraph wires, coming to a spot where the wires ended, falling, falling into a pit of writhing snakes. He felt that there were things in the hedge, emanations of evil. He set off for home, feeling that the humming was a formless evil that would overtake him. He wanted to run but forced himself not to, forced himself to resist all this absurdity. Nevertheless he was glad when he got back among the houses.

He climbed wearily up the narrow, squeaking stairs to his room. He hardly had the strength to undress, and the moment his head touched the pillow he was asleep.

He was woken by Bowen, the foreman.

'Time to get up, sir,' said Bowen.

'Oh, thank you, Bowen.'

He leapt out of bed and dressed hastily, then went out into the main processing area, where Bowen was waiting.

On all sides were pipes and machines. Bowen explained how the largest pipe, from whose joists water was steadily dripping, was connected to the main steam reconservation boiler, where the pre-sluiced water from the cooling plant was washed off the purification rollers before being pressured back through the smaller pipes to be neutralized in the reduction chamber.

'I don't want to be told about all this,' said Pegasus.

'Then I shouldn't have told you about it, sir,' said Bowen, ducking neatly to avoid a de-icification flange.

'No. Kindly see that it doesn't happen again.'

'When, sir?'

'All the time.'

'Then when will I do my other work, sir?'

'What other work, Bowen?'

'Well, sir, my duties.'

68

As they crossed the floor towards the bulbous steel boilers Pegasus gave Bowen an almost pitying look.

'I don't give a fig for your duties, Bowen. Can't you understand that?' he said.

'No, sir.'

'Why the devil not?'

'I see human nature through rose-tinted spectacles.'

'Carry on, Bowen,' said Pegasus, opening a small door in the huge wall and stepping out into the bright sunshine.

He was surprised to find that there was no bright sunshine, that it was raining steadily, and that he was in the garden of Rose Lodge in the first light of dawn.

On his way upstairs he met Bill.

'You woke me. What on earth are you doing?' he said.

'I couldn't sleep,' said Pegasus.

'You're wet.'

'I didn't realize it was raining.'

He went back to bed, but couldn't sleep. I'll have to leave this place, he thought, it's getting on my nerves. He thought of Jane, only a few hundred yards away, and of Paula, very distant now, almost forgotten.

He got up early, and read the paper till breakfast was ready. Bill came in for his breakfast round about eight o'clock. Brenda was in her dressing gown. Pegasus didn't like to see people around the house in their dressing gowns. It made him think of early morning breath.

'You're up early on your day off,' said Bill.

'I couldn't sleep.'

Brenda asked him what he was intending to do.

'Go out,' he said.

'That's right,' said Bill. 'Get some fresh air.'

'Well you can't go out looking like that. You're a sight,' said Brenda.

'What do you mean?'

'Just look at you.'

She led him into the bathroom. Bill stood by the door, watching. She was washing behind his ears before he could decide what to do. He hated the bathroom with its stained bath and cracked blue toothmugs, but he couldn't hurt their feelings, not with things the way they were, not even mentioning the death of their son to himself except in euphemisms now.

'There. That's better,' said Brenda.

Pegasus got his coat from his room and hurried down the stairs. Bill was standing by the door.

'Brush your hair,' he said.

Pegasus opened his mouth to protest, but no sound came. So he thought, well, there's not much point in opening my mouth if no sound is going to come, and perhaps it's all for the best. So he went back into the kitchen-cum-living-room and after a few moments he ran his comb through his hair, hoping that it looked as if he would have done it sooner or later in any case.

Bill came back into the room.

'Shan't be back to dinner,' he said.

Brenda gave Pegasus a white pill and a spoonful of cod-liver oil.

'You haven't been today,' she said.

How the hell does she know?

He washed down the pill with the cod-liver oil, thinking that he might as well go through with it now he'd got this far, feeling embarrassed for Brenda and Bill as much as for himself, thinking, I'm glad King Feisal isn't here to see this.

'You won't what?' said Brenda.

'Be back to dinner,' said Bill. 'Not with the stoats the way they are.'

'Well you might have told me.'

'How was I to know the stoats were going to be the way they are?'

'Well I'll expect you anyway, Pegasus, at one,' said Brenda.

'But I don't eat here,' said Pegasus.

'Then it's about time you did,' said Bill.

Pegasus set off angrily for the hotel, intending to demand a move. But he couldn't find Jane, only Tony.

He met Tarragon in the lobby.

'Hullo. Off to work?' said Tarragon.

'No. It's my day off,' said Pegasus.

'Come down the marsh with me,' said Tarragon.

'All right.'

'I thought I saw a black-tailed godwit yesterday.'

Tarragon walked fast. Pegasus, whose desire to see black-tailed godwits wasn't so strong, found it difficult to keep up.

'Funny chap, your boss,' said Tarragon. 'Armande, isn't it?'

'Alphonse.'

'Oh yes. French, anyway.'

'In what way, funny?'

'Don't know, really. Had a chat with him. He struck me as funny.'

'I don't think he's all that brilliant as a cook,' said Pegasus.

'No.'

Tarragon began to scan the marsh and the dunes with his binoculars.

'Got him. Just to the right of that little hut. Biggish fellow. Handsome chap. Have a look.'

'Thanks.'

To his surprise Pegasus found he could see through the binoculars.

'Oh yes. He's feeding.'

'Where else has he been a chef, do you know?'

'I'm afraid I don't. There are two of them.'

'What's she like?'

'She looks much the same as him.'

'Good Lord. I'd heard she was rather attractive.'

'I'm talking about the godwits.'

'Oh.'

'Why do you want to know?'

'Oh, no particular reason.'

71

Suddenly Jane walked into Pegasus's field of vision along the path that ran round the bottom of the dunes.

'Good Lord. There's Jane. Mrs Hassett.'

He had given himself away with that Jane but Tarragon didn't seem to have noticed. She was walking quite slowly, looking not exactly sad but rather as if she was thinking about sadness. She was wearing black trousers, tight over her neat legs and precise buttocks.

'Which way is she going?'

'Towards the godwits.'

'She'll disturb them. Let me have a look.'

Regretfully Pegasus handed over the binoculars. He watched Tarragon with surprise and annoyance. The binoculars were moving almost imperceptibly to the right, and Tarragon let out a small sigh as he watched Jane. Then he must have sensed Pegasus's eyes upon him because he moved the binoculars over to the hut where the godwits had been.

'I was thinking we might move on and go back via the sea,' said Tarragon.

'Yes,' said Pegasus.

This meant that they met Jane. She seemed pleased to see them.

'I'm showing your staff the birds,' said Tarragon.

They climbed over the dunes, their feet sinking into the sand. The sea was grey, flecked with white, and the power station dominated the southern horizon.

'Little terns,' said Tarragon, pointing at the two fragile sea birds which were slowly working their way up the tideline into the wind.

'Rather lovely,' said Jane.

'I have a slight problem,' said Pegasus. 'Things are getting worse over my accommodation.'

'Pegasus lodges with the Gunters, one of our waitresses, Mr Clump,' said Jane.

'I know her. Brenda.'

'Their son was killed in a car crash. They seem to see him as

72

something of a substitute.' She turned to Pegasus. 'Why don't you come and discuss it with me tomorrow afternoon, Pegasus?'

'Thank you.'

'It's so important to keep one's staff happy these days, Mr Clump,' said Jane.

Suddenly Pegasus had to rush back, impelled by the evident efficacy of his pill. He hated going to the lavatory in the cottage. He was inhibited about making a noise.

Oh well, he thought, I may as well eat now that I'm here.

It was steak and kidney pie. Brenda gave him an enormous helping. He almost mouthed the words, 'You need it while you're growing' but she didn't say them.

She was nervous. The blood was running up her neck underneath her sharp chin.

'It's not often we both have the day off,' she said.

Pegasus plied her with questions as assiduously as she plied him with food. She talked about her father, a Nottingham businessman, told him how she had worked in the same firm as Bill, how they had moved to the country and the new life Bill had always dreamt about, how much she missed the city life now.

Afterwards they had apple pie. Then Brenda made coffee. It was warm in that small room in that small cottage. They sat over their coffee in the two high-backed wooden chairs with soft brown cushions. These chairs stood beside the range, which was rarely used. On the ironing board there was an untidy pile of underclothes. It looked as if Bill was rather hard on pants.

'Pegasus?' said Brenda.

'Yes?'

'It's awfully nice of you pretending to be our son and everything.'

'What?'

'But I see through it.'

'Well – er . . .'

'Reading all those Biggles books every day. Always looking so guilty if you did anything wrong. You did it well, but, you know, it never quite rang true.'

'Well – er . . . I . . .'

'It was very kind of you, but it couldn't work.'

'I – I suppose not.'

'You're too old.'

'Yes.'

'I think we should drop the pretence now.'

'Yes, well, you know, fine. I mean, that's all right with me.'

Her blushing became intense.

'If you really want to help me,' she said, staring into the empty range. 'I mean, if you want to – you know – I . . .'

'Well – you know, I – I mean . . .'

'I mean . . . you see . . . I hope you . . .'

'No. Not at all. But . . .'

'Bill won't be back.'

'Well – er – you know, it . . . I mean, it's so sudden. I mean under the circumstances it might seem . . . well, a bit, you know, Oedipal.'

'Oh, Pegasus, it's all so awful. Bill's getting so strange. You've no idea.'

Pegasus put his hand in hers and squeezed it encouragingly.

'I'd like to help, but, you know . . .' he said.

'I understand.'

'It's my aunt's birthday tomorrow, and actually I ought to go and write.'

'Oh.'

'And my uncle's actually, too.'

'Oh.'

'I mean we could have some tea or something a bit later if you, you know, wanted to.'

'I hope you didn't mind my . . .'

'No. No.'

'We must remove those books and toys.'

'Yes.'

74

14

Paula's mother lived in a semi-detached on the outskirts of Lough-borough. Behind the house rose the broken outline of Charnwood Forest, those attractive volcanic foothills to a mountain range that due to the British love of understatement does not exist. There had been a manor house and its spacious grounds where now there were regular suburban streets. In the manor house had been born Sir Bernard Colthard, the famous dermatologist, author of *Pustules can be fun* and many similar works. It was in his honour that all the streets had been named after skin diseases. The spacious cul-de-sac where the larger houses were set in their leafy gardens was known as The Shingles, but Paula's mother lived with her widowed sister in a more modest house – 32, Impetigo Close. On her long walk from the station Paula would find those street names depressing, but when she entered the house she was always charmed. Its anonymous exterior hid a sanctuary of femininity. Two widows, one with one unmarried daughter, and the other with two unmarried daughters. The mothers had gone the whole hog and had made a virtue out of necessity. Being women, they loved gossip and family news. Being women who knew all about the sadness of life, they made no easy moral judgements.

Paula arrived home late on the Friday night and told them all about it, and they made no criticisms but merely provided an extra slice of cake all round to fortify them during the long dis-cussion which would follow. They paid Paula the compliment of assuming that if she had anything to feel guilty about she would already be feeling guilty without prompting from them.

'I suppose I wanted Simon because I was bewildered and he

was so steady,' said Paula. 'And then when I wasn't bewildered any more I didn't want him because he was so steady.'

'His steadiness was a protective shell,' said her mother, 'and you can't marry someone whom you've never seen in an unprotected moment.'

Paula told them all about her lunch with Cousin Percy. They were a little shocked that she had left Simon purely because of a horoscope, but she assured them that she had been building up to it for some time.

A bottle of wine was brought out, to steady Paula's nerves.

'I had a letter from Cousin Percy this morning,' she told them.

'What did he say?'

'Dear Paula, how lovely it was to see you again yesterday. For once I felt grateful to our British rain. Unfortunately it was all too brief and the atmosphere in the restaurant was not very congenial. Why not allow me to take you out to dinner one evening, far from the madding cry of raw grated carrot, and then we could go on to a play or concert. At the moment I am extremely busy, and so many of my evenings are taken up. However, I am usually free on Tuesdays. Drop me a line and name your first available Tuesday. Looking forward to it immensely. Love, Percy. P.S. Less of all that "cousin",' said Paula.

'What are you going to do?'

'I don't know.'

'Well I must say he's got a nerve,' said Paula's mother. 'Telling you Tuesday is a good day for romance and then only being available on Tuesdays.'

'The question is,' said Paula's aunt, 'is he really only available on Tuesdays, and is the horoscope a lie, or is the horoscope true and his availability only on Tuesdays a lie? Either way he intends to be romantic, and he's a liar. You'd be rather silly not to go.'

'Go this Tuesday,' said her mother. 'I'm having my hair done on Wednesday morning, but you could ring me after two and tell me all about it.'

'I'll be in all day,' said her aunt.

'I'm her mother. I ought to hear about it first,' said her mother.

'The only reason why I hesitate is that it's Pegasus I really want to see,' said Paula.

'Good lord. Why?'

'I love him.'

'Paula! And you never told us.'

'I wanted to be sure.'

'And now you are?'

'I think so.'

'I must say it would be rather exciting if all that started up again,' said her aunt.

'Provided that you marry him this time,' said her mother. 'To have an affair with someone once is permissible. To do so twice is debauchery.'

'I don't think I ought to give up without trying,' said Paula. 'And I mean we're quite a lot older. It should work this time.'

'People seem to take much longer to grow up these days,' said her aunt.

'It's because they mature much more quickly,' said her mother.

'The girls will be sorry they missed this,' said her aunt.

And so at about 11.30 on Saturday morning Paula walked down Impetigo Close, into Eczema Crescent, down Eczema Crescent to the junction with Psoriasis Grove, and there she dropped an envelope into a fat red letter box.

Later a postman would collect the letter and it would be sorted and delivered. And the postman would never know that the letter said:

'Dear Pegasus, I heard of your doings from Cousin Percy whom I "ran into" the other day, and I thought how nice it would be if we could meet and jaw over old times. It seems such a shame to lose contact altogether after everything we've "been through" together.

'I'm still working at the same dump, Punic Films, and I'm sharing a flat with Sue just now. If you write, write to the flat, but for telephoning the office would be better. Easily the best day

77

for us to meet from my point of view would be a Tuesday as we are working late every other evening on a "rush-job". I wonder how you are fixed as regards Tuesdays. Perhaps your days off are a little irregular. If you cannot come to London I could of course come down to see you but as I have no car it would be better if you could come to see me, though of course I don't mind coming down if it's difficult for you to come up.

'Sorry this letter is so scrappy, but if we are going to meet it's best to leave news till it can be given "in the flesh", which is always so much more satisfactory than letter writing. If you can't make it on a Tuesday, I could possibly manage another day, but Tuesday would be best. I do hope you can come. Love, Paula.'

As she walked down Psoriasis Grove, into Acne Avenue and back into Impetigo Close Paula was regretting that the letter fell so far short of being the literary masterpiece that she had desired. What in particular had possessed her to use the phrase 'jaw over old times'? It sounded like old men with false teeth nodding off over the port. Or false men with old teeth.

When she got back home Paula wrote another letter.

'Dear Percy, Yes, it was nice to see you again, and I would simply love to go out for the evening as you suggest. Unfortunately however something has "cropped up" at Punic Films which will involve my working late on Tuesdays for the next two or three weeks. But most other days will be free . . .'

15

Pegasus's eye caught Alphonse's, and there was a flicker of hostility. Alphonse didn't like Pegasus so much now, because Pegasus didn't like Alphonse so much.

'Three peas.'

Pegasus hadn't liked Alphonse so much since he had found out that Alphonse was not so good a cook as Alphonse himself thought he was.

But Alphonse still appeared to have a high opinion of Pegasus's powers. Pegasus believed that Alphonse knew that in time Pegasus would be a much better chef than he could ever be.

'Two sauté, two new, one mashed.'

Alphonse had said 'You will go on a long road' and 'You have the respect for the ingredient.' Despite his shortcomings, he could recognize an artist when he saw one. Pegasus's famous hake with rhubarb was only one of the great dishes he would concoct. There would be something rather startling with fresh apples. Alcohol would be involved, tia maria perhaps. In all probability something really rather amusing would be done with cream.

'Two new, one mashed, one sauté, two broccoli, one peas, one spinach.'

A busy night. But then every night was going to be a busy night one of these days.

No self-respecting gourmet would ever fail to visit the Plough if he found himself within motoring distance of Wignall Andershoot, for under the ownership of Pegasus Baines and his delightful spouse Jane this modest hotel has blossomed into the finest restaurant in England.

Not that Mr Baines, who is himself chef and supervises all the cooking even on his nominal day off, would ever accept that word 'gourmet'. His customers are just people like anyone else, reasons this Uxbridge-born and almost entirely self-taught genius of gastronomy.

In fact Mr Baines abhors the prima-donna approach which he believes has marred the work of so many of his predecessors in the glittering history of gormandizing. Anyone is welcome at the Plough, provided they can get in! 'I reckon I'm here to serve the public, not they to serve me,' shrewdly opines this wizard of the casserole.

79

It is ironic then that this modest restaurateur is likely to be known to posterity not for his many ingenious and unpretentious country dishes, such as the now legendary hake with rhubarb and the no less famed dill-flavoured oyster patties, but for that aristocrat of sweets, that veritable Château Mouton Rothschild of the dessert table, Apple Rosanella.

'Two sauté, one new, three peas.'

For this was the one dish which Mr Baines was ever persuaded to create for a particular individual, the lovely Italian actress Rosanella Bolognionioni. The great actress, famed for her Pirandello, was appearing with Jean-Louis Henriques, Heinz Schnitzler, and Anna-Maria Von Schwitzendorf in the British prize-winning film Z, directed by Lev Zziblorwsky, several scenes of which were to be shot in the vicinity of Wignall Andershoot. Baines insisted that in order not to disrupt the life of his 'regulars' only four of the film's personnel could stay at the Plough. Among them was the sultry Pisan red-head with the fruity chuckle and the enigmatic Giaconda face.

Captivated by her unforced Tuscan charm and vitality, and thrilled by her assertion that she had never eaten better even in the eternal city itself, Mr Baines lovingly created his superb leaning tower of – apples-and-er – and – and – and –

'Come on. Stop dreaming of the day.' The Gallic voice cut in on his dream with harsh insensitivity.

'Sorry.'

At last the dull routine was over. He washed the worst of the smells off himself and went into the bar for a pint. Mr Thomas the milkman was indulging in flights of dull rhetoric, as if he were depressed by the responsibility of representing Wales in this taciturn outpost. Mr Plumb, the fisherman, was telling Mr Block, the chandler, what a bad year it was for shrimps, and Mr Block, the chandler, was telling Mr Plumb, the fisherman, what a bad year it was for chandling. Six quantity surveyors from the bungalows were lamenting the changing face of the countryside. Jock 'Merganser' Bardswell, the warden of the bird sanctuary, was discussing the decline of English beer with an eater-out from the *Good Food Guide*, several of the hotel's male guests were talking noisily, two Danish tourists were asking questions about everything with characteristic Scandinavian curiosity, and Mr Flitch the seed merchant was making caustic comments about the merchandising of seed to anyone who was prepared to listen. It was, in short, a characteristic evening in the bar of an English country hotel in summer. Serving behind the bar were Jane and Miss Coward. Both were hard pressed. There was no sign of Tony.

Miss Coward served Pegasus with his first pint, but Jane served him with his second.

'Tony's away. He won't be back,' she said.

'I could stay on a bit,' said Pegasus.

He was in talkative mood. He wandered round the crowded bar, chatting to everyone.

'This is a bad year for shrimps,' Mr Plumb told him.

'The countryside isn't what it was,' the quantity surveyors told him.

'The government has it in for us chandlers,' Mr Block told him.

'The merchandising of seed is harder than it used to be,' Mr Flitch told him.

And to all of them Pegasus replied, and chatted briefly, and passed on.

'Aalborg,' he told the Danish tourists, a Mr and Mrs Larsen from Aalborg, 'is one of the four largest cities in Denmark. The others are Copenhagen, Aarhus and Odense.'

'My word, you are very well-known in Denmark,' said Mr Larsen.

'Yorkshire is the largest county in England, but it is divided into three ridings,' said Mrs Larsen.

Closing time came, but a few of the residents decided to carry on drinking. This meant that Jane had to stay up to serve them. She couldn't really burden Miss Coward.

'I couldn't really burden Miss Coward,' she told Pegasus.

'Of course not.'

'It's all right about the room.'

This was marvellous news, which successfully called for another drink. Miss Coward was leaving and they had already decided that if she could be replaced by somebody local, Pegasus could have her room. And this had happened.

The group of residents had settled down in a corner of the bar, and were testing each other with sporting questions out of a diary. Pegasus sat on a bar stool and felt his desire slowly ripening. He ran the nail of his index finger very slowly across Jane's left hand as they talked.

'I love you,' he said. He found it difficult to say except when the mood was on him, and then it was all too easy.

'Darling,' said Jane.

'Who was the leading trainer in 1963? Three to one.'

'I've made up my mind,' said Jane. 'I'm going to divorce Tony.'

'Paddy Prendergast.'

Pegasus found himself thinking of small wiry men leading strings of horses on to misty downs in the first light. Jane had said 'I'm going to divorce Tony' and some kind of reply was eagerly awaited. The reply was not expected to feature small wiry men and strings of horses. He took hold of her hand firmly and squeezed it hard and long, forcing a simulated passion into the gesture, but it was only an interim measure, to bridge the gap between the announcement of her momentous news and the arrival of his first reaction to it.

'Aston Villa have won the cup seven times. Which two teams have won it six times? Two to one each, six to one the pair.'

Still no reaction came. He began to feel something close to panic, akin perhaps to what Jane would feel if he didn't reply. Voices in the bar were dim but curiously resonant, he had an impression they were all walking across a cobbled void. 'Newcastle,' said someone, centuries away in time. 'Yes.' Disembodied voices.

'I love you,' he said, and he pressed her hand harder. 'I love,

love, love, love, love you.' Yet this too was an interim measure.

'You're hurting,' said Jane.

'Sorry.'

He let go and began to stroke her hand absent-mindedly, with his little finger this time. He withdrew it as one of the men came up to the bar, announcing that this was the last round they would have. Now the sense of distance had gone. The men were close at hand, across the dimly-lit bar. One of them was saying 'West Bromwich'.

'No. Blackburn.'

'Oh yes. Damn!'

And Pegasus thought, do I love her? Surely I'm glad?

'I'm glad,' he said.

'Are you?'

'Of course.'

'That's all right, then.'

Was her tone a little mocking? Had she sensed the inadequacy of his response?

'Who won the World Amateur Road Cycling Championships in 1964? Ten to one.'

Pegasus wanted the moments of deception to end, he wanted to be able to put his arm round her openly and run his hand over the gentle curve of her hips as they passed the church, should he so desire. But did he want his commitment to be total? Did he really want to marry her and live with her and turn her into Mrs Baines as the result of a few embarrassing moments in a registry office?

'I give up.'

'Merck (Belgium).'

'Oh yes.'

What about Paula? She flashed briefly across his mind, distant but still there. And had he ever really wanted to marry her?

'Let's have another drink, to celebrate,' he said.

Jane got the drinks.

83

'The women's doubles world table tennis champions 1964-65. Fifty to one.'

'This is getting ridiculous.'

Jane handed him the drink.

'It can't go on. You can't go on patching up a failed marriage,' she said.

'No.'

'I don't want him to find out about us until it's all under way,' she said.

'It's understandable. Where's he supposed to be now?'

'In London at a furniture exhibition.'

'Does he ever buy anything on these trips?'

'He has once or twice.'

'Lin Hui-Ching and Cheng Min-Chin (China).'

'I'd never have got it.'

Pegasus saw her sitting on a sofa with her dress worked up just over the top of her stockings and her thighs looking pale and jellified under her suspenders. These moments would be his regularly soon. Of course it was what he wanted. He would be a husband in whom manly virility and sensitive delicacy were judiciously admixed. He would be a kindly father, if they decided that despite the population explosion one or two children were permissible.

'We're going to be so happy,' he said.

As if she had read his mind Jane said: 'I didn't want children. I suppose that was my fault.'

'Ever?'

'No. It was just that I kept wanting to put it off. I didn't feel ready to be a mother.'

'It's not something that would worry me all that much,' said Pegasus.

'Who won the 1962 Open? I'll give you five to two. An easy one.'

Pegasus whispered: 'There's only one place I want to be just now.'

'Where's that?'

'Inside you.'

Suddenly the group were on their feet, there was a tidal wave of good nights, they were alone.

When they were upstairs they undressed each other slowly. Pegasus kissed Jane's back with its smooth off-white skin and the tiny blood blemishes. He kissed the mottled awkwardness of her elbows, which looked as if they had just been pressed against rough soil.

'I wish I wasn't so thin,' said Jane.

'You're lovely.'

'I want to make a success of this place. I've got to put on weight.'

'Nonsense.'

He hopped into bed. The sheets were cold. She had to clamber over him, her small breasts close to his face. He put his hands gently round her hips and pressed her buttocks inwards. It was galling that he would never be able to experience the physical sensation of her buttocks rubbing against each other.

He held her tight. 'Avoirdupois isn't everything,' he whispered.

'It counts for a lot.'

He eased his tongue into her mouth.

'Perhaps if I got a mackaw,' she said, as distinctly as one can with a man's tongue in one's mouth. Then they kissed hypnotically and rhythmically.

Someone tried the door. They both stiffened.

There was a soft knock. A voice said: 'Hullo. It's me.' It was Tony.

Pegasus looked under the bed but it was full of suitcases. Jane signalled to him to get into the wardrobe. He nodded.

'Hullo. Are you awake?'

Jane made a reasonably realistic moan.

'What?' she said sleepily.

'It's me. Let me in.'

They crept carefully out of bed.

'What? Who is it?' said Jane sleepily.

'It's me, Tony. Let me in.'

'Just a minute.'

They gathered up all Pegasus's clothes. He moved over to the wardrobe. Jane put on her pyjamas.

'Just coming,' she said.

'What the hell's going on in there?'

'I can't find the key.'

'It's in the door.'

'Oh yes. Just coming.'

Pegasus lowered himself on to the floor of the wardrobe and carefully shut the door.

'Come on. I'm cold out here.'

He heard Jane open the door.

'What a palaver,' said Tony irritably.

'I was fast asleep. I wasn't expecting you.'

'I decided I didn't want to go to this exhibition.'

Had he got all his clothes? Perhaps the bed would look suspicious. Perhaps there would be a smell of man in the room. Wouldn't Tony open the wardrobe to put his clothes away?

Apparently not. Presumably Jane knew his habits well enough.

Pegasus settled down for a long vigil. He was squatting on the floor, holding all his clothes in a pile on his stomach. The floor was soft and furry, almost alive. His bottom was resting on a pile of dirty clothes, most of them socks, to judge from the smell. People get the feet they deserve, he thought. He wondered whether Don Juan's feet had smelt. Above him was a rack of coats and trousers on coathangers. They tickled his bare back. He was cold and cramped, and he wanted to pee. It would be impossible not to move and make a noise.

He heard Jane say: 'Good night. I'm sleepy.'

Tony said: 'What a welcome.'

Jane said: 'Well, I was asleep.'

Tony said: 'It really makes you feel wanted.'

Jane said: 'Good night.'

Tony said: 'Good bloody night.'

He heard the bed creak. Perhaps she was turning to give him a kiss after all, or was it he making advances? Surely they wouldn't make love? Or was the villainous husband exerting his fatal charm and causing the resolve of the hapless heroine to weaken?

No, it was just routine movements, as they tried to get comfortable.

Movement! Comfortable!

Tony would be touching her at some point, no doubt. But only through two pairs of pyjamas, so to think about it was just bearable.

Pegasus tried to pass the time by remembering the capitals of all the countries in the world. He tried to think of new dishes to cook. He began to compose a crossword but after doing seven clues he forgot the lay out.

He almost slept and dropped one of his shoes. It fell on to the pile of clothes and made only a dull noise. The bed creaked but nothing was said. After a few minutes he cautiously moved one of his arms and picked up the shoe.

A rhythmic complacent male snore began. Pegasus let it continue for about five minutes. Then he leant forward and pushed the door very carefully. It swung open with a low whine that seemed immensely loud to Pegasus. The snoring dipped, stuttered, and then regained its even monotonous tone.

He had his arms out in front of him now and his chest was pushed out so that the clothes couldn't fall between his arms and his body. Carefully he put all his clothes down on the carpet just in front of the wardrobe. With his hands pressed against the floor he managed to slide himself out of the wardrobe along the floor. The clothes stirred and the coathangers jangled lightly. The snoring dipped again, but continued. Pegasus moved the clothes out of the way of the wardrobe door, and then shut the door. Jane, he knew, was wide awake only a few yards away, listening.

He carefully put as many of the clothes as he could over an arm, then scooped the remainder up between his hands and hobbled cautiously to the door. He was extremely stiff even though he had been less than an hour in the wardrobe. He hoped that if he had left any clothes behind Jane would make sure that she found them before Tony was up.

He put his clothes down again by the door and opened the door slightly. A narrow shaft of light poured into the room but not in the direction of the bed, and the snoring continued. He picked up the clothes, went out through the door, shut it carefully.

He began to check through his clothes to see if they were all there. He was frozen. He heard footsteps. A man came round the corner, looking for the lavatory. He stared at Pegasus in astonishment. Pegasus recognized him as one of the men who had been drinking in the bar. He looked altogether greener now.

Pegasus gave him an embarrassed smile.

'Arnold Palmer,' said Pegasus.

16

As he drove up to London Pegasus felt his nervous excitement growing steadily. By the time he reached Witham his senses were already exceptionally alert. The trauma of Chelmsford was even more acute than usual. And then the vast dead oyster of London closed round him like a trap.

Paula's letter had been both a complete surprise and no surprise at all. It had not been too hard to get the following Tuesday off, and after that he had let the question of Paula lie fallow while he dealt with the more immediate problem of the Gunters, their begging him to stay and their resigned acceptance of his departure, and the ordeal of the cocoa sessions, which he hadn't the heart to bring to an end, although he was careful to be very adult, to avoid all comics and eschew Biggles entirely. Now he was amazed to find how much he was looking forward to seeing Paula again.

It was exciting to be alive on this cloudy, humid July morning, when the trees hung so limply on their trunks and the lorries and vans droned so monotonously along the A.12.

London nineteen. First love. First meetings. Plays and films and modest Italian dinners. Visits to Paula's flat when Annette was out. Visits of Paula to Cambridge, while his room-mate Fogden roamed the streets moodily.

London seventeen. Why was he coming up like this at her command, not even altering the day lest she have second thoughts? Why the excitement? Why was he so worried about being late? The traffic was growing heavier all the time, and he had been delayed by a puncture just after leaving the hotel. He feared she'd be gone before he got there.

Paula fifteen. Was it wise to be meeting at the same old seat? Wasn't this an unwarranted concession to nostalgia?

Paula fourteen. No, because he wasn't involved. His visit was purely experimental, to find out what it was like to see Paula again after all this time, and so as many of the incidental details as possible must be kept the same.

Paula thirteen. Jane was going to get a divorce. She was seeing her lawyer tomorrow and soon she would tell Tony. It was hardly the time to start seeing an old flame, even experimentally. He must turn back.

Paula twelve. This was the grey country of grimy allotments where even to have aspirations towards being a carrot was to enter into a bitter fight against one's environment. It was the land of works sports grounds and forgotten tidal creeks. It was the peeling back door of a civilization. The wet warmth of the day was closing in over the bleak housing estates and over Pegasus. The clock on Lexton Aerated Waters showed 10.27.

Paula eleven. Violent death opposite a row of shops built in thirties mock-Tudor. A scream of brakes and tyres, a splattering of blood and glass. Pain and shock. A gaggle of hesitant by-standers. Help from a chemist's assistant. Clerks peering from the windows of the Westminster Bank. Life suspended to stare at death. Mr McGregor summoning the clerks back to work, behind their plaques, Miss E. A. Hayward, Mr F. Knowles. The blaring of police cars and an ambulance, a noise to finish off the shocked and injured. Cars filing slowly past and faces peering eagerly out at the wreckage. Hard to believe that it hadn't happened, that it was only hanging there in the atmosphere waiting to happen. Hard to believe you were still alive and safe.

Paula ten. Not only safe, but eager. Increasingly eager. The nervous excitement very much an echo of the old excitements of their meetings long ago. He weaved his way adroitly through the traffic, making better time now, driving well.

Paula nine. A day for sweating. He didn't want to be smelling stale for her. Difficult. 10.35 by the clock on Pogson's Jellies. Why had she written? Did it mean she had finished with Simon? Was she just taking him at his word about having future meetings to keep in touch, or did she want to begin their relationship all over again? He couldn't do that, of course, because of Jane. He felt rather guilty about deceiving Jane, and rather guilty about not feeling more than rather guilty about it.

Paula eight. There was no reason to feel guilty because he couldn't feel more than rather guilty. He was only deceiving her in order not to cause her totally unnecessary worry. The reason for his visit was simply what he had always said to Paula in his letters. They had been close to each other, and therefore they should always be interested in what happened to each other.

Paula seven. What he was feeling primarily was drama. He was in transit from one woman to another. He was therefore a person of importance, a person to whom things happened. Hardly head-line news – London. Baines sees old flame. Peking. More anti-British riots – but it was sufficient to give him pleasure. What he dreaded was becoming dangerously involved in things that were happening to someone else, of walking along a promenade on the periphery of life, of having to jump in and risk his life to save someone else's, and then when all the fuss had died down having to continue his walk along the promenade, as peripheral as ever.

He rarely felt completely inside an event, but he felt that now. That was why as he waited at a set of lights alongside a van he looked across at the driver and thought, you fancy yourself with the birds, mate, but let me tell you, they go for me as well. Some of them, anyway. Two, actually. And they're all the world to me, all I want.

Paula six. He tried to recreate her as she would appear before him. The outline was there, but the features he had forgotten. Colour of eyes? What a blind insensitive fool he had been.

He would be there first. She would appear from the right, smiling. He would rise from the seat, smile warmly, kiss her with a touch of becoming formality, and find out whether or not his senses still responded to her in any way.

'You're as lovely as ever, Paula,' he would say.

Unless she wasn't.

Paula five. If he didn't still want her, why the excitement? Why was he becoming more and more nervous?

It wasn't a question of the future. They had no future together. Nor of the present. He had no need to see Paula. He had lived without her twice, once before they ever met and once afterwards, and he could do it again

So it must be because of the past, perhaps because the memory was so precious. In his memory it had all been so wonderful, so moving, so real, and he was afraid of discovering that it had not really been like that at all.

Paula four. It had all been a great mistake. It would be a fiasco. He had been wrong to come. He would turn back the moment he found a suitable turning point. It was unfair to Jane, to Paula and to himself.

Passing through the City now. A complete fiction, it had always seemed to Pegasus. A defect in him, no doubt, but there it was, he just couldn't believe that teas were really firm, tins yielding, rubbers ambiguous. Amsterdam and Frankfurt weren't really sluggish and irregular, the creamy trams groaning under the weight of the constipated burghers.

Not there. Too much traffic. And not there. No right turn.

Paula three. There? No. Too difficult.

You know, Pegasus, it really would be better if you turned. And you could have done it there, if you'd really wanted to.

But I don't. Until I turn round I can go on or turn round. Once I've turned round I can't go on. It's silly to limit my freedom of action unnecessarily early. The Prime Minister said it himself only last week – and the week before – and the week before that. We must keep all the options open.

Paula two. Or perhaps he would rise to the occasion and say something witty, make some amusing crack. An epigram to remind her how many amusing moments she had foregone.

'Hullo, Paula. The present is a double agent between the past and the future. Never trust it.'

'Hullo, Paula. Reality is the romantic's only form of escapism.'

'Hullo, Paula. People have the courage to persevere only because they are afraid of giving up.'

'Hullo, Paula. There cannot be a military mind. It is a contradiction in terms.'

It wasn't a very good morning for epigrams. Too sultry. Not enough wind.

Paula one. She would be walking slowly along the path. He would see her before she saw him, and he would smile at the laziness of her walk. Then she would see him.

'Hullo,' he would say simply, as he kissed her in an impersonal but masterful manner.

'Hullo,' she would reply, with a no less affecting simplicity.

Assuming, of course, that he didn't turn back.

Quick. A parking place.

He'd made good progress over the last few miles, and he wasn't going to be late after all.

Paula Hour Minus Two. He walked slowly towards the seat. This was the very last moment in which it would be possible to draw back. He could turn away now, and return to Jane, whom he loved.

There was indeed a hesitancy in his step, a possibility of turning.

Paula Hour Minus One. To turn would have been cowardly. It would have meant that he was not sure of his love for Jane.

Paula Hour. She was not there. An elderly man sat on the seat, fast asleep. He had white hair. It was symbolic of the fact that old people have white hair and fall asleep in public parks.

Paula Hour Plus Five. Pegasus had walked round the Round Pond, and now he was back where he had started.

It was annoying of that man with white hair to have chosen their seat. In the mythical past the seat seemed always to have been free.

Oh, the nervous ache now. Come on, Paula. Where are you?

Pegasus Hour Plus Six. Paula had decided to be exactly seven minutes late, so as not to seem too eager. After all, she had made herself eager enough by writing the letter.

God, she was eager. She walked slowly, trying to remember exactly what he would be like. She loved him, of that she was terrifyingly sure. She had given up the struggle far too soon, due to inexperience and a naïve belief that love was absolutely wonderful.

If only her great mountainous breasts wouldn't heave.

When she said love she meant commitment. She was prepared to commit herself to Pegasus, for better or for worse, in Antonioni or in Losey, until Jean-Luc Godard did them part.

They would go to a film. People said she was obsessed with the cinema. Not at all. She loved it, but she loved life as well. Of course she had once been secretly addicted to *Picturegoer*. Who hadn't? She had identified with Joan Rice and had loved Humphrey Bogart, which was better than her friend Jennifer, who had identified with Humphrey Bogart and loved Joan Rice.

She prayed that he was still available. She had been glad when he'd finished sending brooding letters but she hoped it had just been the healing balm of time and not another woman.

There was the seat. Her heart seemed to . . . to do nothing. That wasn't Pegasus at all. It was an old man with white hair, asleep. Life was rather like Antonioni, beautiful, sad, and a little over-deliberate.

Where was he? Where was Pegasus?

They came face to face about twenty yards from the seat and somehow they found themselves walking towards the Albert Memorial without having kissed or really said anything.

Pegasus's first impression was that she was both shorter and bigger than he remembered. And fairer.

Paula's first impression was that he was both taller and thinner than she had remembered. And darker.

'Well,' said Pegasus. 'Here we are again.'

'Yes,' said Paula.

'The question is, what are we going to do?'

Paula smiled.

'I seem to have heard that before,' she said.

Pegasus took her hand. It was a little sticky. Was this nerves, or was it ever so?

'Hullo my sweet,' he said, uncharacteristically.

'Hullo.'

'It was nice to get your letter,' he said.

'I'm glad you came,' said Paula.

'I think the first thing we should do is go and have a little drink,' said Pegasus.

'While we decide what to do,' said Paula.

When they were seated with their little drinks Pegasus looked her straight in the face and said: 'Well, and how are you?'

'I'm all right,' she said.

She was wearing a blue summer dress. He compared the gentle fleshiness of her arms with Jane's. Her figure was full and good. The face was rather broad, with a slight but attractive bagginess. It was all so familiar and yet so unremembered.

'And how's things?' he said.

'They're not too bad.'

'Work all right?'

'Much as usual.'

He smiled. She smiled back. Her nose wasn't really narrow at all. It was hard for him to ask about Simon without seeming to be sexually interested. She came to his aid.

'I'm sorry I couldn't see you earlier when you wanted me to, but it would have upset Simon,' she said.

'Won't it still upset him?'

'I'm not seeing him any more.'

'Oh.'

It was no real surprise. He had assumed it, from her letter. But it came with a shock of pleasure none the less.

'I'm sorry,' he said. 'I mean, that you've been unhappy.'

'Not all that unhappy,' said Paula. 'Except about Simon. I feel rather guilty. I can't help thinking I used him as an excuse to get away from you.'

'Was I so awful?'

'Of course not. I only meant . . .'

'I know.'

'It could never really have worked out. He translates Ogden Nash into Latin.'

'You told me.'

'You can't marry men who do things like that.'

'I imagine not.'

There was a pause. Paula had established her position. Soon he would have to establish his. He dreaded that.

'Well I always wanted you to leave Simon,' he said.

'I imagined that from your letters.'

'I'm sorry about those letters. They must have been awful.'

She shrugged.

They had lunch in that commonplace pub.

'I heard about your work from Cousin Percy,' said Paula.

'It's going pretty well,' said Pegasus.

95

'And you're happy in your . . . your personal life?'

'Well, you know . . . I . . . I'm having a sort of affair with the landlady of the hotel.'

'Oh. Why sort of?'

'I don't know.'

'Do you love her?'

'I don't really know. Certainly I came up here today.'

'You did, yes.'

She gave him an amused look and spoke the words a little mockingly. Her feelings were revealed in the movement of her breasts in the low-cut dress and he felt a flicker of sexual warmth.

Desire was a delicate plant whose growth depended on so many different elements. Nostalgia, social success, love of nature, aesthetic admiration, sexual energy, secretiveness, self-esteem, humour, the competitive spirit, greed, narcissism, rebellion, warm-heartedness, a love of self-dramatization, the need for exercise and liberal humanism were elements that he himself had at one time or another recognized – and no doubt there were many others of which he was unaware. The first thrusting now of this delicate plant was a most delicious moment. He let his hand touch hers loosely for a moment, and propped his right leg against her left.

He had another woman, but there was still desire in him for her. Paula decided that, difficult though it might be, she would reveal her love only if and when he asked her for it.

She closed her eyes and saw the main square in Siena. This was disconcerting, and she opened her eyes again hastily. It would be pretty awful if her love of Italian architecture turned out to have been phallic all the time.

'I think we should have a nice, easy, relaxed day. A film, a leisurely dinner, and a talk.'

'That would be lovely.'

They chose a double bill which paired a Jean-Luc Godard with a minor Swedish film, full of subtitles of the 'I say, chaps, guess what? I've just seen the two daughters of the horse-knacker in the baptismal pond together, going further than they ought to with each other' variety. They held hands and Pegasus placed Paula's hand in his lap and ran his right hand up the warm barrel of her left leg. The cinema was a huge cave with little pricks of light in the roof. Pegasus leant across to whisper something to her and smelt her Paula smell, groundsheets drying in the sun after a shower.

'Wow,' he whispered and she lightly kissed his ear.

Pegasus drank cinzano bianco after that and Paula drank amontillado, and then they went to one of the Italian restaurants that they had known. Little had changed. The mats showed Portofino where in the past they had shown Assisi. The young waiter had left, the old waiter remained and recognized them delightedly, so that their coffee and petit fours were free, the prices were higher and the carafes smaller, and it was nice to be back.

'Did we really quarrel in here?'

'We quarrelled everywhere.'

'Why?'

'Oh, it's too long ago. Who can tell?'

The recall of these quarrels was a big shock to Pegasus. It didn't tie in with his idea of a golden past, too beautiful to endure.

'You used to accuse me of being possessive,' said Paula.

'I suppose I thought you were.'

He remembered insisting on retaining his privacy and independence. Tuesday evening had been Hugh evening. Friday night was Mervyn night. On Saturdays he went to football matches. He had forgotten all this.

'You were possessive too, in your way,' said Paula. 'You didn't want to share your friends with me, because they belonged to you. You clung to your way of life.'

'I suppose so.'

'I wanted to share everything.'

After dinner they drove up to Hampstead Heath. It was growing dark. The hills of the heath had a quality, especially against the evening sky, of looking wild and impressive far beyond their size.

The mauling began. Pegasus kissed her long and slowly with his tongue as with his hands he pulled off her stockings and explored her legs. He put his hands on her breasts and reached under the bra to fondle the nipples. Her tongue was surprisingly small but her breasts and curves were large and comfortable. He warmed to her womanishness, her dreamy receptive sexuality.

The mammoth kiss ended and Pegasus kissed her quickly several times on her wet lips, and then suddenly it was two wet faces against each other, absurd in a family saloon, and he felt no more desire. You wouldn't find Peter Ustinov messing around in a car on the edge of Hampstead Heath. He looked down at her face and it was a strange face, years away, and he was ashamed of himself.

'Is this altogether wise?' he said.

'Now you say it.'

'Well, you know . . .'

'No, I don't. I don't know.'

'I'm sorry.'

'If you think it's not wise, don't do it.'

He drove her home. They drove in silence most of the way.

'I'm sorry,' he said.

'Don't keep apologizing.'

'Sorry.'

He kissed her good-bye in the car.

'I've enjoyed it very much, Paula,' he said. 'I don't want to, you know, go too fast, that's all. I'm cautious.'

'I've enjoyed it too,' said Paula.

He reached Shenfield before he remembered that he had forgotten to look at the colour of her eyes.

He drove more rapidly than usual. There was little on the roads. Shortly after Woodbridge an owl flew across in front of the car. Pegasus thought of the marsh, and felt no pleasure. He thought of tomorrow's work and felt no pleasure. He thought of everything that might give him pleasure. He even thought of hake with rhubarb. Ugh!

He thought, we all have moods like this sometimes. But he didn't. Depression to Pegasus was something that was caused by your circumstances, and whenever he thought of the prospect of doing something pleasant, then however great his depression he felt a prospect of pleasure, Not so now.

It began to rain, hard vicious summer rain.

He turned off the A.12. Nearly back now.

He thought of Jane and felt nothing.

He thought of the things one tries not to think of – starving black children with swollen bellies and rich women with four minks.

He could have dismissed this comparison with all sorts of rationalizations, but they were not the defence against it. The defence was the sum of all his particular pleasures, of all the diversions that filled his life and made it his and not all lives. Now there was no defence.

He almost lost control on the wet road, but managed to pull up safely. Another puncture!

He had changed the wheel after the morning's puncture so there was nothing for it but to leave the car and walk. There was a very slight slope and he managed to push the car off on to the verge. His bad luck with punctures reassured him. He was going through an unlucky phase, and he would feel more cheerful when the luck turned. That was all it was.

He walked back through the warm, heavy rain. The country-side was very still. Trees became people, owls were ghosts, there were footsteps behind him. He broke into a run and the footsteps also began to run. He forced himself not to run. He walked for two miles or so through the vertical rain, and all the time the footsteps followed. They only ceased when he shut the door of Rose Lodge carefully behind him.

He squelched quietly up the stairs, his shoes and feet sodden.

He opened the door of his room and the heat struck him in the face.

'You can't come to work in that state. You're soaking wet,' said Bowen.

'I'm sorry,' said Pegasus.

'Take off your clothes, sir, and I'll dry them for you,' said Bowen.

'Won't the men object to seeing me in the nude?' said Pegasus.

'They're used to it, sir. They don't shirk the seamy side.'

Pegasus took his clothes off and helped Bowen to arrange them on the hot pipes, where they began to steam profusely.

'How's it going, Bowen?' he asked.

'Quite well, sir. Pressure's high. And Mr Prentice's new purification technique is working wonders with the pre-sluiced water.'

'Excellent, Bowen. Excellent.'

Bowen coughed discreetly.

'What is it, Bowen?'

'With respect, sir, you look splendid in the nude. Not meaning to be personal. Just trying to reassure you, sir,' said Bowen.

'Thank you, Bowen, I understand. You – er – you really think I look all right, do you?'

'A great example to the men, sir.'

Bowen turned on a switch, and the heat ratio dial rose to 177·3.

'177·3, sir,' said Bowen.

'Is that good?'

'Excellent, sir.'

'Good. Well done. Oh, I feel tired, Bowen.'

'I can look after things. Why don't you turn in?'

'I think I will.'

Pegasus opened the door of one of the huge bulbous boilers. Then a thought struck him.

'Bowen?'

'Yes, sir.'

'As head of this project, Bowen, I feel I have a right to know what's going on here.'

'Yes, sir. Absolutely, sir.'

'All this stuff we're making, this – er – thingummy. . .

'Nuclear energy, sir.'

'That's it. It is for peaceful purposes, isn't it, Bowen?'

'I wouldn't know, sir. Ask no questions, get no answers, that's my motto.'

Pegasus went into the boiler. It was even hotter in there. He lay down on the floor, and the heat pulled the lids gently over his eyes.

When he awoke the boiler seemed to have become bitterly cold. He was frozen. He couldn't move. He couldn't open his eyes. He tried to shiver but couldn't. A body, suspended in ice, frozen in mid-shiver. Perhaps this was Hades, and he was undergoing his eternal punishment. But for what?

He wanted to sweat, but the sweat would have frozen. He managed at last to move his legs and arms. The cold seemed more intense still, as if a million icy pins were scratching his insides.

And then he could open his eyes. He was sitting in a marble bath, his body encased in a block of melting ice.

He managed to stand. The pain began to grow less intense. He scraped the remaining ice off his body. He was thawing out, drying off.

A man came in and gave him a denim suit. He put it on. He could feel the last of the cold passing out of his body. He felt warm, drowsily, sexily warm.

'Follow me,' said the man.

The man walked straight towards the wall and disappeared through it. Pegasus stopped.

'Come on,' said the man. 'It can't bite you.'

Pegasus felt for the wall with his hand. The hand went straight through and he felt nothing.

'There's no wall there,' said the man. 'It's all done with beams.'

Pegasus walked through the wall, flinching but feeling nothing. The man led him down a long corridor and through another wall into a drab hot office.

He sat at the desk, facing Cousin Percy.

'You are Pegasus Baines?' said Cousin Percy.

'You know I am.'

'You have been kept in cold storage, Baines, since 1988.'

'I don't understand.'

'It's 2363 now. You've been asleep for 375 years.'

'What is all this?'

'You were stored away under the Important Persons Refrigeration Act of 1986. What the papers called the "sage freeze". Do you recall none of this?'

'No, sir.'

'The Government had powers to make refrigeration orders on people whom it felt would be needed more in the future than they were at the time.' Cousin Percy's manner was impersonal but not hostile. 'In 1983 a method of reviving frozen people was discovered. It was tested on rats with 2·3 per cent success. By 1986 it was clear that eventually total success would be achieved. The bill was passed by 287 votes to 253. The liberals abstained.'

'I'm a liberal.'

'Shut up. In 2026 100 per cent success was achieved. Since then all our frozen people have been able to be unfrozen in times of emergency.'

'Why was I frozen, sir?'

'Because you are the world's greatest chef. You turned the Plough at Wignall Andershoot into a veritable oasis in the gastronomic desert that was Gloucestershire. Don't you remember?'

'It's beginning to come back to me.'

'And then the famine came.'

He did vaguely remember the famine. It was disturbing even to think of it.

'The world's population was completely out of control. Haute cuisine was declared illegal. The introduction of chemical foods was speeded up. The concept of a chef became an anachronism. You were obsolete, but you were a genius. You were an obvious candidate for refrigeration. So, a Refrigeration Order was duly issued, you appealed against it, there was a public enquiry, you lost, the Minister upheld the decision, and here you are.'

The memory was coming back.

'Yes, you took it pretty hard. We gave you seven days' notice, told you to take a holiday.'

'I remember it, sir.'

'Did you tell your wife?'

'No. I thought it best not to.'

Cousin Percy leant forward and spoke in a manner that was almost friendly.

'How are you feeling now? Better?' he said.

'Yes thank you, sir, but very randy.'

'Really? You had your oats, I presume, the night before you were frozen?'

Pegasus thought back, trying to live again those awful last moments.

'No, sir,' he said.

'Didn't you read the pamphlet? You're supposed to have your oats the last night.'

'It was the wrong time of the month, sir.'

'Damned bureaucratic incompetence. You must have them tonight. What would you like, blonde or brunette? Plump, slender, or average?'

What did it matter now? And yet he would like it.

'Well, sir, I – average would be safest, I suppose. And, er, I think brunette.'

Cousin Percy spoke into the intercom on his desk. 'Lay on average brunette oats for Baines, will you, 238^4?'

He switched off the intercom. 'Bloody incompetence that. I'd give the man responsible a damned good bollocking if he hadn't been dead for 350 years.'

350 years. He thought back over the last days, the attempt at a holiday, the forced cheerfulness, the parting which his wife didn't know was a parting, the injection. And then he thought of all the time that had elapsed since then, and he lying in a block of ice, and the world changing.

'We saved you up for a rainy day. Well, that rainy day has come,' said Cousin Percy. 'The file, 238^4,' he barked into the intercom.

238^4 entered the room with the file. Pegasus recognized her. It was Miss Besant. She smiled at him and he desired her pink plumpness, her fleshy legs, her shapely plumpkins.

She handed Cousin Percy the file and left through the wall. Cousin Percy glanced at the file.

'It won't be easy, but it may give you a chance to get even with an old friend of yours, your arch enemy, Erich Von Stalhein. Now Algy and Ginger . . .' Cousin Percy shouted into the intercom: 'Baines, not Bigglesworth.'

238^4 hurried in, blushing profusely, with another folder.

'Terribly sorry, ninety-one,' she said.

'All right, but don't let it happen again or you'll be relegated to the power of five.'

238^4 left through the wall and Cousin Percy looked briefly at the new file.

'A crisis is occurring, Baines,' he said. 'People are bored. They are losing their interest in life. Now One has decided, though no doubt Three is behind it as usual, that the monotonous diet is one of the major factors. Your job will be to create a varied diet out of the existing ingredients of modern food. We need different recipes for each new city, Francetown, Englandtown, Chinatown and so on, based on their old traditional foods. Steak and kidney, sweet and sour pork, chicken chasseur, the lot. Supposing we give you, say, three years. Then we'll refreeze you and keep you for another rainy day.'

Pegasus was afraid, bewildered, but above all full of self-doubt.

'I may have lost my powers, sir,' he said.

'Nonsense. You're at the height of them. Now, you'll have a flat, a laboratory, thirty assistants, your oats whenever you want them and a salary of £64,000,000 a week.'

Cousin Percy summoned 238^4, gave her £38,000 and asked her to get a copy of the *Evening Standard*.

'Any questions?' he asked Pegasus.

'Yes, sir. Is my – my wife, sir – I suppose she wasn't frozen?'

'I'm afraid not. She died in 2012.'

'Oh.'

'Natural causes. In her sleep. Quite painless.'

He felt that he was going to cry. Cousin Percy gave him a drink. It was fiery but tasteless. It made him feel better.

'Why couldn't she have been saved too, sir? She was a lovely woman.'

'Our examiner found she rated very highly for certain qualities – heart of gold registered 86 per cent. But she just wasn't essential. Lovely, Baines, but not essential.'

'It would have made my task much easier, sir.'

'I know. They brought in a private member's bill about it in 2033 – the Spouse or Other Essential Emotional Partner (Except in Cases of Lesbianism and Homosexuality) Refrigeration Accompaniment Bill. In 2174 homosexuals were admitted as well, and Lesbians were admitted in 2303. We stumble towards humanity, Baines. Ah, here's 238^4.'

Pegasus took the paper from her. The main headline read 'Piccadilly to get Holford Piazza soon'. It all meant so little. He was lost, without bearings. It was clear that even Cousin Percy was no longer, in any meaningful sense, Cousin Percy.

'You're a very important person,' said Cousin Percy.

Pegasus shivered.

'Yes, sir.'

'You will be known as 680^1. It's pretty good to get a power of one straight off. You will do well to persevere at work, and you will be much in demand at social gatherings. The week-end . . . what's wrong? You're shivering.'

'I'm very cold, sir.'

'You shouldn't be.'

Cousin Percy was alarmed. He came across to Pegasus's chair and felt his forehead.

'My God, you are cold. Fetch 3,619[1] and 227[2] immediately,' he shouted into the intercom.

Pegasus felt the heat draining away, the cold gnawing once again at his insides.

'I'm losing heat fast, sir.'

'Hang on. They'll soon be here.'

His brain was slowing down. The icy chill passed through his veins. His eyes became glazed.

He woke up. He was lying on his bed but he was naked and he had no bedclothes on. The bedclothes were strewn all over the room and his clothes were draped across the top and bottom of his bed.

17

Tony seemed genuinely surprised.

'But why? Nothing's changed,' he said.

'That's why.'

'Everything would be all right if we'd had children,' he said.

It had been wrong of her to be frightened of having children. She was ready now. She wanted them now. But not his. A tiny infant helpless in a pram, brought into this world to cement a failing marriage. Pathetic.

'It's too late now, Tony.'

'Are you really surprised if I go off with other women?' he said.

'What do you mean by that?'

Knowing what he meant. Standing stiffly, unable to look at him, like a bad actress, her body expressing the gauche banality of the arguments.

'Well I don't get much of it at home, do I?' he said.

'It was all right before you went off with other women.'

'I can't help it. I'm made that way,' he said.

'You're not made to be a husband then.'

The situation was too strong for her. She couldn't feel herself, be herself. She could only be wifehood caught up in impending divorce.

'Don't let's quarrel,' he said.

How like a man. It takes two to quarrel but it only takes one man to say 'Don't let's quarrel', placing all the burden on the woman. If you said: 'Must you set fire to the house like that?' he would say 'There you go. Nag nag nag.'

'Do you think I want to quarrel?' she said, continuing the quarrel, as angry with herself as with him, her body heavy and lifeless, the bedroom suspended in air.

'Please, darling, do try,' he said. As if she hadn't. As if it was all her fault. 'I still love you.' And perhaps did too, by his own lights. And she could still remember loving him. Here came a kiss. 'Please.' No response. She mustn't allow herself to respond. They had been through this before, and she had responded, and nothing had changed. 'This time it'll be all right.' He meant it. And perhaps, who knew, it might. This time, or the next, or the next. If she could stand the risk of further lies, further nights waiting, further quarrels.

'You've said that before,' she said.

'I know. But it really will be different this time.'

Don't let him.

'That's what you said in Manchester, 1965.'

'Oh for God's sake,' he said.

She was sorry. Nasty to throw that at him. But nastiness was what was required of her. She herself was of no account.

'So you're trying to turn me out, is that it?' he said.

'I'm afraid so, Tony.'

Nothing else to say.

'You cold little bitch,' he said.

Violence coming. Cushions, first. Then a vase, narrowly missing her. God, if he hits me. I'm terrified. He's mad. A chair.

107

Escalation. The chair hurled at the window, falling bathetically short. Wanting to laugh, nervously. Mustn't. Fatal to laugh. Might be clawed to death.

Standing over her, no longer her, no longer him, just something big threatening something smaller with a table mirror.

He hurled the mirror to the floor. His strong hands thrust her back on to the bed.

'You bloody stupid little coward. You're scared stiff, aren't you?' he said.

Its skirt was up around its waist. Pain of nails in its thighs, scratching hard. A stinging slap across the cheek, and then he had left the room, not even forgetting to slam the door.

It inspected the pain in its legs. Red blotches. Deep nail marks. Blood.

It tried to think, he's mad. The words meant nothing. It tried to think, look what a justification his behaviour is. But that was horrible, to think of justification. A vague shame, that was all it could feel, scaling down into nothingness. Into being a nothing, something that was but was nothing. No use saying: 'It thinks, therefore it is' or 'It believes itself to be nothing, therefore it is.' Equally true to say: 'It considers itself, therefore it is something other than itself.' All sadly useless statements, when the chips were down. One of the girls at school saying once: 'Oh don't worry about Jane. Leave her alone and she'll soon disprove herself.'

She tried to feel. To feel something, anything, was the solution. She took their wedding photo out of its drawer and gazed at it, two meaningless grins taking each other in perpetual smile-lock. She felt nothing. She took one of his unwashed shirts out of the wardrobe and smelt it – the back, the armpits. Nothing. She looked out over the marsh towards the sea, grey under the disturbed sky. Nothing.

She got a piece of paper and a pencil from her handbag, and sat down at the dressing table to write. She had tried this before and it had seemed to work.

The idea had come from Dr Patterson, her psychiatrist. This

was before Tony. Angela Curvis swore by Dr Patterson and Jane had reluctantly allowed herself to see him. Dr Patterson had made her write down certain things about herself and bring them to him. Once, annoyed, she had written: 'I am not a banana or a chair' and he had seemed pleased with this and had said: 'Do you feel you are as much not a banana as you are not a chair?' as if you could find out your point of truth by doing a map reference on everything you weren't. She had said: 'For God's sake, I didn't mean it seriously' and he had said: 'You think you didn't. You chose the words at random. So much the better. Why for instance didn't you say: "I am not a corn exchange"?' and she had said: 'Because it's self-evident. I haven't the frontage for it,' and this too had interested him, and she had asked him why he had chosen at random to ask her why she wasn't a corn exchange. Why hadn't he asked her why she hadn't said she wasn't a lighthouse? Did he shrink from the phallic? And he had said that at last they were getting somewhere. And she had realized that you were forced to take it all seriously, that was what was so unfair.

Of course she had no idea whether Dr Patterson was a good psychiatrist or not. Perhaps he didn't either. Certainly Angela Curvis got on all right with him.

One day Jane had told Dr Patterson that her problem was that of excessive self-involvement. Surely therefore she would be helped not by considering herself but by considering someone else. Why didn't they analyse Frank Sinatra together? But Dr Patterson had explained that if one suffered from a tendency to excessive self-examination one must examine oneself to find out why.

He had said: 'You could fall in love with someone and marry them, and cease to examine yourself because of your love. But it would be dangerous. The cause of your previous self-examination would not have been eradicated.'

She had said: 'Unless lack of love was the cause.'

He had said: 'Look, Jane, you could feel cured. You could lead an entirely happy life. You could become a warm, generous, loving person, happy in marriage, doing rewarding and useful work, never giving a thought to your problems until the day you died. But all that would be a cheat. You can't win the Grand National by going round the side of the fences.'

She had said: 'I don't want to win the Grand National.'

He had said: 'A lot of the saints became saints because of their personality defects.'

She had said: 'I suppose you would rather they'd all been having analysis.'

He had said: 'They might well have rathered it.'

She had said: 'Thank you for doing your best for me, Dr Patterson, but I don't think I'll come any more.'

He had said: 'That's interesting. Why not?'

She had said: 'Well frankly I think that in my case it's simply pouring money down the drain.'

He had said: 'What makes you use the word drain?'

And Angela Curvis had married a barrister and she had married Tony. And Angela Curvis had what her mother described as 'three bouncing babies', and she had none. So leaving Dr Patterson hadn't been much of a success either.

Jane had decided after leaving Dr Patterson that the answer might lie in writing down observations not about herself but about the outside world.

So now she sat at her dressing table and resolutely set her mind to consider the rest of the world. She wrote busily. She wrote: 'Rock Hudson is not an intellectual.' '1961 was a good year for Burgundies.' 'Waterspouts are not common in the Irish Sea.' 'Community Singing is a ritual act of shared emotion.' 'The Portuguese oyster is a bisexual bivalve.' 'A belch is a mark of respect in some countries but not in others.' 'A rusty lawnmower is a doubtful asset' and many other remarks of a similar nature, until both sides of the page were covered. Then she hurried downstairs and threw herself busily into her work. So the ruse seemed once again not to have been a total failure.

* * *

The marsh to himself, even in July. The crowds all in strips along the roads and coast.

Birds in the distance, feeding, guarding, rearing, fighting, nothing to worry about except survival. The marsh occupied to its maximum density without the aid of statutes. Pegasus felt cut off from this world, only too conscious that if he advanced on it he would disturb the whole bang shoot.

It would be easier if he had binoculars. He decided to buy some binoculars.

'It's the ideal site for it, sir,' said Bowen.

Pegasus jumped.

'You startled me,' he said.

'Sorry, sir.'

'The ideal site for what?'

'The number three power station, sir.'

'Oh yes. Of course. I'd thought perhaps a little more to the left, Bowen.'

'No sir.'

'I expect you're right. Bowen?'

'Yes, sir.'

'I wonder if you'd mind leaving me alone for a few minutes. I've a rather thorny problem to work out.'

'Not at all, sir.'

The thorny problem was, did Bowen exist? Pegasus stared at the marsh for a minute or two, at the birds whose lives were over-flowing with necessity. Then he turned and scanned the horizon. There in the distance was the great mass of the power station. Far away by the edge of the heath a man was walking. Bowen couldn't have got that far in the time, and there was no one else in sight.

He hurried back to the kitchen. Bowen hadn't been there. There was no such person as Bowen. He was cracking up. He would have to take himself in hand. No one else would.

He closed his eyes, knowing that if they were opened he would see a carrot. He imagined the carrot in his mind's eye. He opened his eyes and there it was, red and tapering, exactly as he had expected.

'Stop staring into the space and give me kindly my parsnips, is it?' said Alphonse.

'Sorry,' said Pegasus.

There was no getting away from it. Bowen did not exist. And yet . . .

'What you do now? You are smothering that plate with the colossal extent of a parsnip,' said Alphonse.

'Sorry.'

'Put your mind to the job. The cooking, she is ninety-nine per cent of the perspiring, and one per cent of the inspiring,' said Alphonse.

On the Saturday Tony came back and intimated that he had decided to agree to the divorce.

'Adultery, I presume,' he said.

'Yes,' said Jane.

'Fair enough,' said Tony.

Jane offered him a drink. They were in the bar. It was four o'clock.

'You offer me a drink as if it was yours to give. I still own this place, you know,' said Tony.

It was true. She had forgotten – or chosen to put it out of her mind.

'Have a drink,' said Tony.

'Thank you. I'd like a gin and tonic,' said Jane.

'I'm sorry I was so brutal,' said Tony. 'Do the marks still show?'

'A little.'

He lifted up her skirt and kissed her legs where the marks were.

'Let's hope that makes them better,' he said.

Jane wanted to say, I'm still very fond of you despite everything.

'What do we do about the hotel, then?' she said. They were both behind the bar, landlord and landlady, serving no one.

'I don't want to come back here. It's too quiet a life for me,' said Tony.

'So?'

'And I've got rather a good plan for making some money.'

'I can't afford to buy it,' said Jane.

'Would you like it?'

'Yes, I would. I love this place.'

'I dare say we can sort something out. We'll have to see. There's no rush, is there?'

'No. None at all.'

'I'd better go off and start committing adultery, anyway.'

'I don't think I'm supposed to condone your adultery, am I?' said Jane.

'You don't condone it. You only suspect it,' said Tony.

'You'll let me know when and where to suspect it, will you?'

'O.K. I imagine it'll be with a girl called Wanda.'

'Wanda?'

'Yes.'

'Well I suppose the least sordid way is for you and Wanda to go to a nice hotel somewhere, behave in a thoroughly conspicuous way, and then I'll send my detective round afterwards. Apparently that usually works all right provided everyone's agreeable.'

'If you say so. And don't forget, Jane. I didn't want this divorce. It was you.'

'Where can I find you?'

'169, Bulstrode Street, Norwich.'

A vision of a crumpled bed in a terrace house.

Soon he left. She saw him to his car.

'Cheerio then, Jane.'

'Cheerio, Tony. Sorry it had to end like this.'

He shrugged.

'Don't worry about the hotel, anyway,' he said.

'I won't.'

'Good-bye.'

'Good-bye.'

H

18

Tarragon and his mother sat on the terrace munching buttered toast and drinking China tea. It was one of the rare sunny afternoons of that wet July. Somewhere in the house his father was asleep. It was peaceful on the terrace but Tarragon felt gloomy. In London he was a successful man. Here he was an infant.

Two days ago he had received a demand for a hundred and twenty-five pounds, to be placed in a box in the boot of an old Morris Eight which lay rusting in a ditch at the side of a cart track just outside the little hamlet of South Green. Clearly Alphonse was going to step up the demands slowly, to find out how much he could get away with.

All day Tarragon had been wondering what to do. He had finally decided that he would tell his mother, when they were alone together. It would only be a matter of a few moments, and he needn't look at her while he was speaking. He would wait until some interesting bird came along, and he would look at that while he told her.

A beautiful cock chaffinch, hunting for seed on the stone path. Now.

'Mother?'

'Yes, dear.'

'Er – nothing.'

Damn! But perhaps it was all for the best.

He had thought first about telling the police. It would come out in court. He would bring disgrace on them all, on all this, the elegant stone gables of this glorious Cotswold house, the clipped hedges of sober well-bred yew, the close-cropped terraced

114

lawns. A show place. The garden open twice a year. His mother a pillar of local society.

A wren. Now. Seize your courage in both hands, Clump.

'Mother?'

'Yes, dear.'

'Er – nothing.'

On his week's holiday he hadn't spoken to Jane. He had meant to, but somehow as always he hadn't. It would be harder even to tell her than to tell his mother but once he had told his mother he thought he might find the courage.

The alternative was to go on paying out to that swine.

A great tit. Try again, Clump.

'Mother?'

'Yes, dear.'

'Er – nothing.'

'Are you all right, dear?'

'Quite all right, thank you, mother.'

'Have some more tea, dear.'

'Thank you, mother.'

'You're getting enough sleep, are you, dear?'

'Yes, mother.'

'You're not haunting the nightspots, are you, with all those vulgar businessmen and dirty-minded hairdressers?'

'No, mother.'

Impelled by the need to find an excuse for inactivity he suddenly felt sure that his suspicions of Alphonse were right.

Tarragon sipped his tea miserably. Suspicions or no, he was determined to make one more effort.

A starling. Hardly what he had hoped for, but it would do. Beggars can't be choosers.

He took his sinking stomach in both hands and prepared to say: 'Mother'. But at that moment his mother spoke.

'I'm giving up all this social work,' she said. 'I'm getting too old for it. And if their own families cared for them properly none of it would be necessary. People have no family feeling these days.

There were only eight entries for the home-made jam competition this year.'

I wanted to be brave and tell the truth. That would have meant utter disgrace. Mother would never understand, but she would think she understood, which would be worse. No, I must pay up this time, and in the meantime I must find out a little more about our so-called Alphonse.

He eyed the starling with more generosity now.

'It's very nice, sitting here together, just the two of us, mother,' he said. 'Alone in the garden, just us and the odd bird. Odd's the operative word.'

The starling flew away as Basil's car screeched to a halt in the drive and his five children yelped cheerfully round the corner, their noses bleeding and their legs encased in plaster.

19

After Pegasus had gone Paula had felt quite desperate. She hadn't slept a wink and had got up at five o'clock to have a bath, after which she had roamed the streets, wearing herself out and getting strange looks, until it was time to go to the doctor's for some sleeping pills.

When he hadn't written or telephoned she had itched to ring him up and hear his voice. Twice she had dialled the hotel only to ring off when it wasn't he who answered. She had a lot of baths, walked as much as she could, went out with Sue every night and arrived at Punic Films each morning with a head thick from sleeping pills.

Sue was a brick. She threw herself into the business of cheering her up with tremendous enthusiasm. Sue was a neat, slight, attractive, dark girl with cool eyes who only liked to kiss men if they didn't put their tongues in her mouth. She had several boy friends, of whom her favourites were Cornelius, an American painter who fascinated her because he was growing tired of her, and Don, a freelance zoo critic. She was being determinedly chased by Philip, a talented trombonist with feminine hands, and faithful old Mike, fat and self-denigrating, who took her out once a month and made her regret that she couldn't love him, he was so kind and such fun. Sue liked the social side of sex, but she couldn't find it in her to entertain the same enthusiasm for the physical side. None of the men understood this except Mike, who nevertheless hoped constantly for a transformation.

'In a sense I envy you,' said Sue. 'You at least have had something very precious. I'm still looking.'

Paula smiled wanly.

They went out with Cornelius, who rang Paula up the next day and asked her out. She refused to steal a man from Sue, and neither of them ever saw Cornelius again.

They went out with Philip, who was extremely annoyed and treated Paula with contempt. Nevertheless they arranged to go out with him again.

They went out with Mike, who accepted with resignation that he would have to take out two women, and then thoroughly enjoyed the evening. Since attempts at sex were doomed to failure, as he told Paula when Sue was in the loo, it was more fun when you had no opportunity to make them.

They had Don to dinner and in return he took them round the zoo.

Once Cousin Percy took Paula out. They went to the opera, he was courteous and kept his hands off her, saw her home in a taxi, came in and had a cocoa, was studiously charming to Sue, seemed bored, said what tremendous fun it had been, arranged to take her out again the following week and left without kissing her. She told him nothing about Pegasus.

Gradually she grew calmer. To have started the affair again

after it had failed once would have been madness. She reduced her baths to two every three days. And then a fortnight after their day out he rang her at the office and they arranged to meet at six.

She rang Sue to cancel their evening out.

'I hope you don't mind,' she said.

'It can't be helped,' said Sue. 'I only wish it wasn't Philip night, that's all. I can't stand it when he touches me with those strange fingers of his.'

'Perhaps he won't touch you.'

'He will. These jazz musicians have hot blood.'

Let's hope Pegasus does too tonight, thought Paula.

Pegasus was feeling very disturbed. He had not meant to see Paula again, and he was appalled to find how much he was looking forward to it. The humid, thundery weather had given him a headache. He had slept badly. He was tired. He was still worried about seeing Bowen on the marsh. All these things contributed to his state of mind.

He entered the store to buy his binoculars. It was even hotter in there.

In the lift it was stifling.

He stepped out of the lift. On the third floor it was hotter than ever. Steam was rising from all the pipes and from one of the huge bulbous boilers.

'I think you ought to inspect the suppuration tanks, sir,' said Bowen.

'Right.' They walked over towards the suppuration tanks. Pegasus could hear the furious swishing of the water before they reached them.

'We're getting a bit of excess suppuration, sir,' said Bowen.

'Is that bad?'

'Yes, sir.'

'Oh dear.'

Bowen stopped at the third tank and turned on a switch. 87.9 per cent density.

'Very dense,' said Bowen.

'Oh dear.'

Pegasus sensed that such density was bad.

There was a strange smell, a smell of putrefaction.

'Can you smell putrefaction, Bowen?'

'No, sir.'

'I can.'

'With respect, sir, you're too sensitive.'

'Do you think so?'

'Yes, sir. Everyone does. There was a resolution passed at last week's union meeting to the effect that you ought to be altogether more thick-skinned.'

There was a violent blast which knocked Pegasus to the ground. As he fell he saw a mushroom cloud of yellow gas rising from one of the suppuration tanks.

When he came to he found himself surrounded by women, fanning him with bras.

'Where am I?' he asked.

'Lingerie,' said one of the women.

'You passed out,' explained a second.

Pegasus looked round the lingerie department. A few moments ago he had mistaken it for a nuclear power station. The error seemed barely conceivable now. The absence of any machinery would give the game away even if the neat rows of bras and underclothes didn't. But perhaps he had only had the illusion as he fainted, in a kind of dream, a split second as he fell.

He looked round for the lifts. They were about twenty yards away.

'I'm all right now,' he said. 'I've been overdoing things recently.'

'What you need is a change,' said a third woman.

'A change is as good as a rest,' said a fourth.

'Too many late nights,' said a fifth.

'This modern generation's too keen on pleasure by half,' opined a sixth.

'There's always a day of reckoning,' said a seventh.

'This modern generation's too keen on pleasure by half,' re-opined the sixth.

'I'm all right now,' said Pegasus.

Willing hands helped him to his feet.

'Where's the binocular department?' said Pegasus.

'They'd be with cameras, wouldn't they?' said the first woman.

'Straight through menswear,' said the second.

Half-way through menswear Pegasus felt that he couldn't stay in the shop a moment longer. He hurried down the stairs out into the street and took a deep gulp of fresh carbon monoxide.

He arrived at the seat three quarters of an hour early and spent the time experimenting with Bowen. He closed his eyes and willed him to appear. He blinded his eyes with the sun and looked for him in the resultant glare. He focused on distant men and tried to turn them into Bowen. But Bowen did not reappear.

The moment he saw Paula he desired her. She melted into his arms. That was something Jane didn't do. Paula melted and she also nuzzled up to you. Jane wasn't one of nature's nuzzlers. Jane was quicker, like the lick of a snake. Harder, fiercer.

He must stop these odious comparisons.

They walked in the park.

Sex was only a very small part of it. He must stop thinking in physical terms.

'You're beautiful,' he said, putting his arm gently round her. They were looking out into the Serpentine. She smelt slightly of sweat. No doubt he did too. It was immensely humid.

'I'm getting fat,' said Paula.

'Nonsense.'

They sat on a seat and watched a swan and several boats of laughing young people, many of them tourists, of every race, creed and colour.

'Why didn't you write?' she asked, and she bit her mental lip in annoyance. She mustn't reveal that it had upset her.

'I'm a bad correspondent,' said Pegasus.

Their hands mingled, convoluted, gently sweaty. The heat hung on, a freak one-day heatwave, soon to burst. The water was limp, artificial. The sun was half hidden by a film of haze.

'You really are as beautiful as ever,' said Pegasus.

'You never used to say things like that,' said Paula.

'I'm older and wiser.'

Brown. Her eyes were brown.

'Did you tell your hotel manageress about me?' asked Paula.

'No.'

'Why not?'

'I don't know.'

'Will you?'

'I suppose so.'

He let his hand rest on her knee, tapping it nervously.

'It's all very awkward,' said Pegasus.

He told Paula about Jane's divorce.

'I just don't know what to do,' he said.

'So it seems.'

'I'm being honest with you, Paula.'

'But not with her.'

'No. I wonder what that means.'

'Yes.'

'I'm not trying to put any burden on you, Paula, but you've rather thrown things into the melting pot by coming back like this. Can you be patient with me?'

'I don't know. I hope so.'

He clasped her knee more firmly.

'You ought to be honest with her as well, you know,' she said.

Later they went to another Italian restaurant of their acquaintance. It smelt of garlic and human sweat.

They only mentioned Jane once, when Paula said: 'Where does she think you are?'

'At home.'

'You should be.'

'Yes.'

The rest of the time Paula filled him in on all the films he hadn't seen, and he realized how much he missed them. He told her about his work and the great dishes that he would one day cook, though he was too coy to mention hake with rhubarb or the hare which was just beginning to take shape.

As they walked back to the car he said: 'That wasn't bad, but one day I shall cook you a meal five times as good as that.'

On the way home down the cursed A.12 Pegasus thought about Paula and Jane. The part of him that had loved Paula still existed, but a new part of him had been born, and this part loved Jane. And polygamy just wasn't on. If he was Polynesian he could have sixty-four wives, but he didn't really want that either. A lot of the depth would go from the relationships. He could hardly imagine taking sixty-four wives to see *Monsieur Hulot's Holiday* on successive nights, or having sixty-four honeymoons in Venice, or being anxious whether his parents would like all sixty-four of them.

It was as if each of the two women had her own administrative area. At first he was in a Paula mood, sorry to leave London and its noisy backcloth to his Paula life. This gradually weakened as he drew near to the borders of Paulashire. Somewhere along the route he must have passed a sign announcing: 'Janeshire welcomes careful lovers'. London was monstrous, the countryside warm and rich, he looked forward to seeing Jane again.

He began to feel guilty. Jane had only to have rung his home and found that he wasn't there, and the fat would be . . .

At this moment he had yet another puncture. The car skidded, there was a moment of horror, the hedge was flying towards him, he was in the ditch.

When he had recovered from the shock and had found that he was unharmed except for some slight bruises, he set off on the six mile walk to the hotel. He wondered if the punctures were an omen, and if so, of what?

After he had walked about half a mile he got a lift from Mr Flitch, the seed merchant.

'That your car in the ditch?' said Mr Flitch.

'Yes. I had a puncture and lost control.'

'There's something funny going on around here,' said Mr Flitch. 'I've had three punctures in the last month, and before that I hadn't had a puncture for six years. And each time I've had a puncture it's been a nail.'

'I had two punctures on the same day a fortnight ago,' said Pegasus. 'And each time it was a nail.'

'Do you know what I think? I think someone is putting nails on the road,' said Mr Flitch.

'It's beginning to look that way.'

'You can say that again.'

But before Pegasus had a chance to say that again Mr Flitch had a puncture. Pegasus stood around while Mr Flitch changed the wheel. Then they drove on.

'Someone ought to tell the police,' said Mr Flitch, and after that they dropped the subject. Mr Flitch had some caustic comments to make about the merchandising of seed, and very soon they were back at the hotel.

Pegasus went quietly up to his room. Beside the bed he found a plate of salad and a note which read: 'In case you're hungry. Love. Jane.'

The salad made him feel ashamed, but also pleased. He smiled as he admired the hand-writing. There was a knock at the door. A voice said: 'Can I come in?'

'Do.'

Jane entered the room, wearing yellow pyjamas.

'Hullo, darling,' she said. 'I couldn't sleep.'

'Thanks for the salad.'

'You're late,' she said.

Did this imply mistrust or not? He felt acutely guilty and was terrified it would show.

'I had two punctures.'

'Again!'

'Well one of them was Mr Flitch's.'

'You seem nervous.'

'I am a little. It's shock. I got thrown into the ditch.'

'Oh my darling.'

He was hungry. They sat on his bed and shared the salad, eating through a hard-boiled egg until their lips met. He told her about the possible maniac. She asked after his parents. He dissimulated. She said how much she had missed him. He replied, ditto.

He toyed with the idea of telling her about Paula, but somehow he didn't get round to it.

They finished the salad.

'One of these days I shall cook you a meal fifty times as good as that,' he said.

20

On the following Saturday morning Pegasus took Paula's letter out on to the heath and sat among the gorse bushes reading it.

'My darling Pegasus, Thank you for your note on Thursday. I'm glad you enjoyed our evening out, but I was sorry to hear about the puncture. Of course if the car is damaged you'll have to have it repaired before you next come up. And of course I realize that it's a bit awkward for me to come and see you "in situ".

'In any case I am fairy busy just now as we are just setting up our new production, "You can say that again". Also, don't laugh, but two nights a week I am going to go and train with the South Rickmansworth Harriers. I know a vision mixer who puts the shot for them, and I thought I'd go along and see if I could get my weight down, because whatever you say, darling, I am a "bit on the broad side". So next time you see me I hope to be "in good shape".

'You remember I was going to have dinner again with Cousin Percy? Well, I did, and afterwards we went to see the new Antonioni. I'm looking forward to seeing it again with you. Cousin P. gave me a message for you. Work is all important and you should beware of distractions, especially at week-ends. He wants me to go to a party he's giving on Saturday but I may put him off.

'I miss you quite . . .'

'Hullo.'

Pegasus put the letter away guiltily. It was Tarragon.

'Oh hullo.'

'Got a minute?'

'O.K.'

They walked slowly over the heath towards the derelict cottages. They passed underneath the lines of pylons leading to the power station on their left.

'I've got myself into a very stupid mess,' said Tarragon.

They walked on in silence. Tarragon was obviously very embarrassed, and Pegasus thought that if they stopped walking it might make things easier, so he climbed a gate beside the Forestry Commission plantation. He sat on top of the gate with his legs straddled over it and composed his face into what he hoped was a look of encouragingly impersonal sympathy.

'I shan't sit myself,' said Tarragon. 'Farmer Giles.'

Pegasus looked hurriedly round. There was no one in sight.

'Farmer Giles?'

'Piles.'

'Oh. Would you rather walk, then?'

'I would, if you don't mind.'

They walked on in silence beside the Forestry Commission land, back away from the sea towards the old quarries. Pheasants were honking on all sides.

'Painful,' said Pegasus.

'Yes.'

There was another period of silence. Three planes screamed overhead. Pegasus was uncertain how to help.

'I'm thirty-seven,' said Tarragon.

Pegasus waited. He assumed that there was more to come.

'I haven't been able to tell this to anyone else,' said Tarragon. 'But somehow I know it won't be quite so hard with you.'

They had come to a knoll from which the heath descended towards a lane.

'I don't want to be within sight of the road,' said Tarragon. 'Do you mind if we turn back?'

'Not at all.'

Tarragon smiled apologetically at Pegasus.

'Where was I?' he asked.

'You were thirty-seven,' said Pegasus.

'Oh yes. Actually I've got myself into a very stupid mess. Very undignified. Yes, I'm thirty-seven, and I suppose I'm a reasonably successful man. Tarragon Clump, the renal surgeon. But I've got myself in a very stupid mess. If we go right here towards the sea . . .'

'All right.'

'I can't thank you enough for this. You're making it so easy for me. I thought I'd never be able to tell anyone, and here I am talking to you about it as if we were just taking a casual country stroll.'

'You haven't actually told me anything yet.'

'No, I suppose I haven't. Do you mind if we sit down?'

'Not at all.'

They sat on the dry grass, cropped short by rabbits, covered in little balls of dung, hot under the summer sun. The sweat was glistening on Tarragon's broad chunky brow.

'The truth of the matter is that I've got myself in a very stupid mess,' said Tarragon. 'I'm thirty-seven, and I'm very shy. You might not think it, but I am. Especially with women.'

'Well, you know, lots of people are.'

126

'As a doctor I naturally meet quite a lot. Under the anaesthetic, though, most of them, and of course that does make a difference. But I do meet women doctors and so on, and I can make small talk all right, chat to them about kidneys and abortions and things till the cows come home, but I just can't talk about personal things. I can't make the first move. I can't ask them out to dinner.'

'A lot of people don't find it all that easy.'

'Bittern booming. Listen.'

They listened.

'It's all right if I don't find them attractive. But if I find them attractive I can do nothing. And it seems to be getting worse the older I get. Red-backed shrike, look. On that branch over there.'

'Which branch?'

'Gone now. Normally I'd be fascinated by it but just now I couldn't give a damn. Where was I?'

'Getting worse the older you got.'

'Oh yes. I've followed women. There was one used to get the tube at Bond Street at 6.10 every evening. Lovely legs. Worked up Wigmore Street and lived at Ongar. Once or twice I followed her all the way home. I suppose I fully believed that one day I would talk to her. I suppose I'm an odd fish really. Odd's the operative word.'

'I don't quite see where I come in,' said Pegasus.

They sat looking out towards the sea, the leisurely sea riding complacently at its own anchor. The sun went in behind a black cloud and a cool wind sprang up. There were a few large spots of exploratory rain.

'Mind if we walk?' said Tarragon.

'Not at all.'

They walked towards the sea. The power station loomed larger. Pegasus felt its malevolent pull, felt he ought to go in and give some instructions to Bowen, told himself that Bowen did not exist.

'The fact is, I'm being blackmailed,' said Tarragon.

'Oh, I – I'm sorry.'

'You know the landlady?' said Tarragon.

'Mrs Hassett? Of course.'

'She's an attractive woman, isn't she?' said Tarragon.

'Well, I've never really . . . Yes, I suppose she is, in her way.'

'Well, anyway, this is where I come to the difficult part.'

Pegasus looked at his watch.

'I'm on duty in half an hour,' he said. 'In fact I think we ought to turn back.'

'O.K.'

They turned back.

'I don't know why I worry. What is it to you what I am?' said Tarragon. Pegasus made a non-committal sound. 'I'm not what's known as a voyeur. But one day . . .' Tarragon sighed. 'One day I was coming back through the marsh. There's a little copse behind the hotel, nuthatches nesting there, and I thought, perhaps I would see Mrs Hassett.' Tarragon paused.

'So you had a look?'

'Exactly. Through the binoculars.'

'Did you . . . see anything?'

'I caught a glimpse. Nothing more.'

'Just a glimpse?'

'Yes. Her bedroom looks out that way.'

'Oh. Does it?'

'I wouldn't have done it if she'd been happily married, but she isn't. She's getting a divorce, you know.'

'I had heard a rumour, but I dismissed it as typical below stairs gossip.'

'Well it isn't. It's true. Her husband is an absolute bastard. Ex R.A.F.'

'And somebody saw you, did they?' said Pegasus.

'Your boss. Alphonse.'

Pegasus whistled. More and more interesting.

'He also took some photos I have. Stole them, from my room.'

'Of Jane?'

Once again Pegasus gave himself away. Once again Tarragon was too wrought up to notice.

'No. Of Pamela Blossom, the actress.'

'She was at Cousin Percy's prediction party, wasn't she?'

'That was the main reason why I went, that and loyalty to Percy. Oh, by the way, it looks as if I will be operating on a royal personage soon. A third cousin of Ex-King Zog of Albania.'

'I suppose that just about qualifies.'

'Of course it does. Anyway he has twice got money off me – a hundred pounds and a hundred and twenty-five pounds. I have to leave it in all sorts of stupid melodramatic places. It's all so sordid.'

'Why don't you tell the police?'

'I don't want my family or Jane – Mrs Hassett – to know. I couldn't bear that. You don't know my family, do you?'

'No.'

'And I still have hopes, you know, that one day I may bring myself to – to ask Mrs Hassett to dinner or something.'

Pegasus felt sorry for Tarragon. It was probably his public school's fault, not his. The man was physically awkward. He seemed to have got his body off the peg – it was expensive, but one size too large. He and piles seemed to have been brought together like a perfect love match, and Pegasus instinctively marked him down for athlete's foot as well – wrongly, as it chanced.

'I see. So what exactly do you want me to do?' said Pegasus.

'I want you to help me to clip Alphonse's wings.'

'I must admit I'm not over-enamoured of the man. He isn't French culture at its best,' said Pegasus.

'Do you think he is French?' said Tarragon.

'What do you mean?'

'I suspected him from the first, without knowing what I suspected him of. Then it suddenly came to me. That pidgin English of his is quite absurd. Would any Frenchman ever really speak like that?'

'I've always thought he ladles it on a bit,' said Pegasus.

'Would you ever believe he was French if he wasn't in a kitchen? Would he look French without that moustache?'

'I wouldn't be at all surprised if you weren't right.'

'I am right. I know it. Well, will you help me?'

'What exactly can I do?'

'Just keep your eyes open and let me know if you find anything out. Does he ever go home?'

'He hasn't while I've been here, but it's been high summer.'

'Does he have a car?'

'Yes. An old green thing.'

'I'm certain he's English. Probably got a completely false set of French credentials. So if he ever goes off home, all I have to do is follow him.'

'He'd see you. Or you'd lose him.'

'I can try. Will you help me?'

'Well, yes, all right – if I can.'

'I feel so much better now I've told someone,' said Tarragon.

Back in the kitchens Pegasus looked across at Alphonse, and he thought, we'll get you, you phoney. It was an offence against the whole profession, the noble art.

It would mean promotion for him. Tonio would take Alphonse's place and he would take Tonio's. More chance of displaying his genius then. Before long this would be his kitchen.

Soon the Goat and Thistle would be a centre of pilgrimage. Its hake with rhubarb would be legendary. And a second equally luscious concoction was forming itself in his head. Hare braised in honey and grated chocolate, stuffed with oysters wrapped in seaweed, and served on a bed of banana and pimento. Yum yum.

21

'Have you told her about me yet?' said Paula in the pub after the Antonioni.

'Not yet,' said Pegasus.

'It's obvious you never will.'

'Not at all.'

'Your affair is going on just as before.'

'I've told you, Paula, this is a difficult situation for me.'

'She thinks she's the only one. I know I'm not. So I feel insecure and she doesn't. So she's pretty well bound to win, isn't she?'

'It isn't a match.'

'If you're at all serious about seeing me again, you ought to tell her.'

'It's not easy.'

'Give me up altogether then. That's easiest.'

'Exactly. So if I wanted to give you up I would. And I haven't, so obviously I don't want to. Don't be stupid, Paula.'

A pause. A moment of silence. A sudden impulse.

'Why don't we go to a hotel, Paula?'

'You mean now?'

'Yes.'

'You'd stay the night?'

'Well, no, I couldn't really do that. But we'd have two or three hours.'

'I'm worth two or three hours in a sordid Bayswater hotel, am I?'

'It's not that.'

'What is it then?'

'It's just that I wanted . . .'

'You wanted me to be your little bit of spare, is that it?'

'Don't be so stupid.'

'I'm stupid, am I? Get what you can out of your stupid Paula and then buzz off back to your cold comfort farm or whatever it is. Well you've picked the wrong person.'

Paula hurried from the bar, and was gone before Pegasus could collect his wits. Life seemed to hold on the door for a few long seconds, then to pan round the unconcerned faces in the pub, before returning to Pegasus and his search for his wits. He found them, and hurried out after her, just in time to see her stepping into a taxi.

Another taxi was coming down the street. Pegasus hailed it.

'Follow that taxi,' he said.

After they had crossed Westminster Bridge Paula began to play games. Her taxi started to travel at a reckless speed.

'Wait till I tell the missus about this,' said the driver as he swung his taxi violently to the left. 'We're only just married, you see.'

Pegasus didn't see, but there was no time for questions. Paula's driver had doubled back on his tracks in an effort to shake them off.

Pegasus closed his eyes in fear as his driver mounted the pavement in Tulse Hill and squeezed between the shop fronts and a letter box. If he was to die, please let it be by drowning in an Italian bay and not in a taxi in Tulse Hill.

This girl has been seeing too many films, thought Pegasus, as they swung to the right in front of a bus.

It would end in certain death but he couldn't humiliate himself by giving up. He must prove to her that he cared. At the end of the journey they would fall into each other's arms, never to leave them.

Paula's taxi pulled up outside a typical 1920s villa in a quiet, residential street in South Norwood.

Pegasus gave the taxi driver thirty shillings.

'Keep the change,' he said.

As he hurried towards the spot where the other taxi had been

Pegasus gradually became aware that it was not Paula who was standing on the pavement, but the most enormous man he had ever seen. He was seven and a half feet tall, and had a girth to match. His left eye and most of his right ear were missing, and a huge scar ran across his right cheek. He was totally bald, his remaining eyelid was curiously hooded, and his mouth seemed to be permanently twisted in a vicious parody of a grin. His hands were covered in tattoo marks but even if Pegasus had had more time to examine them he would not have recognized the tiny crescent moon which indicated to the underworld that the man was a member of the inner circle of the infamous Pung Chow Brethren, who masqueraded as an innocent non-gambling Mah Jongg school in their Shanghai waterfront den.

He did not have more time.

'Where's Paula?' he asked.

'Keep your nose out of our affairs,' said the enormous man in a grotesque, high-pitched effeminate voice.

When Pegasus came to, the street was empty except for his taxi driver, who was bending over him solicitously.

'Where am I?' he moaned feebly.

'Acacia Avenue, South Norwood.'

'What happened?'

'He hit you. You've got a real shiner coming.'

Then Pegasus remembered.

'What happened to Paula?' he asked.

'I never saw a bird at all.'

Pegasus tried standing up. It was not a conspicuous success.

'Lean on me,' said the taxi driver.

'Oh. Thanks.'

'Nobody treats a fare of mine like that.'

The taxi driver helped him back to his cab.

'Did you see who got out of the taxi?' Pegasus asked.

'Yeah. Just that dirty great brute.'

'No woman?'

'No woman.'

133

'Oh.'

They must have been following the wrong taxi. And now here he was stuck in South Norwood with his right eye closing and the whole right side of his face on fire.

'What do we do now?' the taxi driver asked.

'Just what I was wondering. Go back to town, I suppose.'

He seemed disappointed. He had done well. And he was just married. Pegasus didn't like to see him so dejected.

'I've got to make him think he's frightened me off,' he said.

'That makes sense,' said the taxi driver, brightening up. 'Where to?'

'Oh. Yes. Leicester Square, I suppose.'

When Paula had gone off after an argument in the old days they had usually met up later at one of their restaurants. Better try the Vicenza, the Siena, the Assisi and the Rapallo first.

'Anything to do with the Ruskies, is it?' asked the taxi driver.

'I'm not really supposed to tell,' said Pegasus.

'No. I suppose not.'

After tantalizing the driver with a brief silence Pegasus said: 'The Russians aren't the real enemy any more.'

Another brief silence.

'The Chinks, is it?'

'They aren't the real enemy any more either.'

Another silence.

'Oh well, I'm sure it'll go no further.'

'What do you think I am?'

'The Americans. They're the real enemy.'

The taxi driver whistled. Then after a moment's thought he said: 'I can't say that really surprises me.'

'It's the usual story. Germ warfare.'

'There's a lot of it about,' said the driver.

'Between you and me, and this is in strict confidence, they're poisoning our milk supply.'

The driver let out a stream of asterisks.

'They're filling it with a substance that makes anyone who

drinks it impotent. It's colourless, odourless, damned difficult for our boys to detect.'

'Too bloody true.'

'So far it's only the gold tops. But it'll spread. My boss, F, thinks it'll be in the yoghourt by Christmas. The boffins are helpless.'

'Just wait till my wife . . . doesn't hear about this.'

They drove on in silence for a while. Pegasus was thinking that if he met up with Paula that night he would forgive her. Otherwise he would be very cross indeed. Five or six times in the old days she had walked out like that, over nothing.

'Who was that bloke at Norwood, then?'

'A thug. One of their villainous henchmen. One of the twelve most ruthless killers in the orient. A member of the inner circle of the infamous Tang Pu Brethren, who masquerade as an innocent non-gambling Fan-Tan school in their Hong Kong waterfront den.'

After that Pegasus felt in too much pain to make up any more. So when the taxi driver asked another question he said: 'I really think I've told you too much already.'

It had been tiring leaning forward to talk through the little window in the panel, but the driver had deserved it.

It was half past eight when they arrived at Leicester Square.

'Thank you,' said Pegasus.

'Thank *you*, sir. Best fare I ever had.'

'Oh. Thank you.'

'17s 6d.'

Two very frail elderly Americans got into the taxi. The driver set off with a huge jerk which must have sent them flying across the cab.

Paula wasn't at the Vicenza or the Siena, but he found her dejectedly leaving the Assisi, on her second time round.

'Good God, what have you done to your face?' she said.

They went into the Assisi and over a cinzano bianco he told her about his evening's adventures.

135

'I left my taxi almost immediately and went back to the pub, but you'd gone,' said Paula.

'If this sort of thing is going to happen again we'd better always arrange a reserve meeting place,' said Pegasus.

'Oh, I'm sorry. But it's better than just going on quarrelling.'

'So you've said before. Oh, zuppa pavese and steak pizzaiola.'

'Lasagne and escalope valdostana.'

'Why did you go? That's what I want to know. Oh. Well, a carafe of — is red all right with you?'

'I'll change to steak and then we can both have red.'

'I could change to the veal.'

'No. I feel guilty. It's for me to change.'

'The food doesn't have anything to do . . . sorry, waiter. Make it two steak pizzaiola and we'll have a bottle of the valpolicella.'

'You know why I went.'

'I don't.'

'Well you should.'

'Well I don't.'

'I told you. I left because you seemed to think that the way to prove your affection for me was by taking me off to a sordid Bayswater hotel for two hours.'

'Who mentioned Bayswater?'

'Don't introduce irrelevancies.'

'Well I can't see the harm. We've made love hundreds of times.'

'Barely more than eighty.'

'There's no need to let the whole restaurant know.'

'They aren't interested.'

'They are. Look at them.'

'I mean have you ever seen Jeanne Moreau going to a hotel like that without her regretting it afterwards?'

'We're old and good friends, so it wouldn't be sordid.'

'And as we're old and good friends there's no need to do so.'

'Well, anyway — yes, thank you, very good — we aren't going.'

'That's what I came back to say. If you want to, I don't mind.'

'Then why are we arguing about it?'

'We aren't. We're arguing about why I left the pub. If you really want to go . . .'

'I don't, now.'

'Are you sure?'

'Quite sure. You're right. It would be sordid.'

'O.K. This lasagne's good. Is your soup all right?'

'Very good. This isn't your qualms again, is it, Paula?'

'There's a world of difference between qualms and two hours in a Bayswater hotel.'

'I'd just like it to go on record, Paula, for posterity's sake, that it wouldn't have been Bayswater. It would have been East Ham. Oh dear, what a sad smile.'

'Well here we are already, botching up our evenings again.'

'It's understandable. As you say, you must be feeling insecure. Oh, thank you.'

'Thank you.'

'I've been thinking, Paula, and you're right. I must tell Jane.'

'They've given me the larger one. Shall we swop?'

'Well are you sure?'

'Yes. It's too big for me. It doesn't fit in with my slimming plans.'

'Nor does lasagne.'

'I forgot.'

'I will tell her. I promise.'

'Oh dear. The moment I'm offered what I want I don't want it. I'd hate you to tell her just because I've made you.'

'You won't have made me. I make my own decisions.'

'Well that's all right then.'

'You are lovely, Paula.'

'Please, Pegasus. Not here.'

'Did you have a good evening?' said Sue.

'Marvellous.'

'Percy rang,'

'What did he say?'

'Be cautious in matters of the heart. Concentrate on financial and business affairs, where a recent contact could prove beneficial. A good time for athletic activity, and he has two tickets for *Othello* next Tuesday.'

22

He told Jane on the sea shore, where the wind would blow away some of his guilt.

'I saw Paula yesterday,' he said.

'Oh.'

'I got a letter from her and I thought, you know, it would be silly not to see her.'

'And how did it all go?'

'All right.'

Jane bent down and picked up a handful of stones.

'How's her affair going?'

'It all seems to be off.'

'Oh.'

She tossed one of the stones into the sea, then another, and watched them hopping over the wavelets as if nothing else in the world interested her.

'We had quite a nice time, I suppose,' he said.

'Good.'

'Oh, Jane, you don't mind, do you? I mean there's nothing wrong in seeing an old friend like that, is there?'

'Well you might have told me.'

'I thought you'd be, you know, worried if you knew beforehand.'

'Why should I be worried?'

'I don't know.'

A kicking of shoes against stones. A hurling of a stone into the sea. A falling of that stone, to the total disinterest of a large variety of marine creatures.

'Paula and I meant a lot to each other once, Jane. It's natural that we should still like each other and care what happened to each other, isn't it?'

'It isn't natural, no. Possibly it does you credit, I don't know, but it isn't natural.'

'O.K., then, it does us credit. If I didn't go and see Paula it would suggest that I was frightened that if I did see her I might get involved again.'

'I suppose so, in theory,' said Jane.

'So if I have confidence in our love, and I do, then I'm pretty well obliged to go and see her, aren't I?'

Jane laughed.

'Why are you laughing?' he said.

'You're so funny.'

'What's funny about me?'

'The way you find arguments to justify yourself.'

They kissed warmly in the open air. Pegasus licked the salt off her cheeks. Gulls watched them, wondering if they were missing something out of life. A porpoise broke the surface, a buoy came lazily to life, and went under again, seeming to decide that it was missing nothing. Pegasus thought, she is so lovely to me, I mustn't let her down, and I won't. With his tongue he said I won't, I won't, won't, won't, won't.

'I don't think I can stand any more insecurity,' she said.

They were happy that August. Without throwing discretion to the winds, they were no longer offensively secretive. Once, at high tide, they put a message in a bottle, declaring their love for each other and giving in English, French, Dutch and German a list of wedding presents for the finder to choose from. Then they bathed, joyously, despite the cold unfriendly waters of the North Sea, the artisan ocean.

Pegasus's happiness with Jane was marred by guilt. Jane knew that he hadn't gone to see Paula again and she was obviously pleased by this, but she didn't know that this was because Paula had gone to Ibiza with Sue and four other girls on a long-arranged holiday.

Pegasus's dreams got no better, but they got no worse either. Twice more he met Bowen, and the day after the second meeting he went down to the power station. At the guard room he asked to see Mr Bowen and said he was a relative. He expected to be told that there was no Mr Bowen there, and was discomfited when the guard said: 'I'll see.'

The guard spoke briefly on the phone and then told Pegasus: 'He's just coming.'

Pegasus felt apprehensive and excited. After a few minutes a total stranger appeared.

'I'm sorry,' said Pegasus. 'I meant Mr Bowen the foreman.'

'There's no foreman called Bowen here,' said the mystified Mr Bowen.

'I must have made a mistake,' said Pegasus.

He was glad King Hussein hadn't been there.

Sometimes Pegasus saw Brenda and she said: 'When are you coming to see us?' and he said: 'Soon.' Once he tried his appalling schoolboy French on Alphonse.

Alphonse said: 'Please, Pegasus, I am no speaking French in England. I try to learn the English more better. She is terrible, my English, no?'

Tarragon didn't dare go away on holiday in case the opportunity to spy on Alphonse should occur. He made a week-end visit to the Goat and Thistle, was again too shy to make any advances to Jane, and deposited a hundred and fifty pounds in a box in a rotting upturned rowing boat on the marsh.

It was the busiest month of the year in the kitchen.

Alphonse had no time to go away and Pegasus had no time for

thinking about the dishes he was going to create. The only real progress he made was in deciding that the hare with oysters would be served with curried pumpkin.

Mervyn came down for a week-end with another friend, Hugh, but nothing happened that hadn't happened before.

One day Pegasus had a day off and as it happened to be his father's day off as well he decided to go home.

Diana was away in Italy, enjoying High S, which was centred thirty miles south of Diana and moving towards her. On their own his parents seemed lonely. Morley had been home the previous week-end, with his slides of the Hardangervidda, but they didn't see him often.

Over lunch Pegasus thought, I'm glad Escoffier isn't here to see this. And then he was annoyed with himself, for thinking that.

As the afternoon wore on he talked to his mother.

'I'm rather worried about your father,' said his mother.

'Why?'

'I think he's a little bit worried about you.'

'What about, mother?'

'All this concentration on food. He thinks you may be wasting your life. We're old-fashioned, I suppose.'

'It's my life, mother.'

'I know, dear.'

Pegasus kissed his mother, much to her astonishment. That sort of thing was usually reserved for arrivals and departures.

'He dreams, you know,' said his mother. 'He dreams about the holidaymakers rebuking him for his wrong forecasts. At first it was just the day trippers. Now it's the fortnights coach tours as well.'

Perhaps I've inherited dreaming, thought Pegasus.

They went to the window and looked out over the garden where his father was working.

'He did so want you to be a scientist and win a Nobel prize,' said his mother.

141

'I know. I'm sorry.'

'I tell him it's not his fault. Modern science isn't omnipotent. You can't be right every time.'

'He's a perfectionist.'

'He comes from a long line of perfectionists.'

His father saw them and smiled affectionately – quite cheerily, it seemed to Pegasus.

'Look at him. He's a soul in torment,' said his mother.

'I don't really like discussing him behind his back,' said Pegasus.

'Go and have a word with him,' said his mother.

Pegasus went out into the garden to talk to his father in front of his back.

'Been talking to your mother?' said his father, still digging.

'Yes.'

'Well?'

'Well what?'

'How do you think she is?'

'She seems all right.'

'I'm worried about her,' said his father. He stuck the spade firmly into the ground and unbent. They stared at the vegetable patch desultorily.

'Your beans look good,' said Pegasus, who knew nothing about gardens. Beans were things which arrived in the kitchen out of nowhere.

'They are good. Yes, I'm a bit worried about your mother.'

'What's wrong?'

'She's a little worried about you, old chap,' said his father.

'In what way?'

'I think she feels cooking isn't quite the thing.'

'She'll feel different when I'm famous.'

'She saw you winning the Nobel Prize, and all the aunts proud of you. She's fond of you.'

'I know, but . . .'

'But it's a burden. Do you think life would be worthwhile without burdens, Pegasus?'

'Yes.'

Tony and Wanda booked into the Red Lion at Norton Snoddering under the name of Mr and Mrs Hassett. Wanda was quite blasé about it. After all, it was her third citation.

'What's she like?' Wanda asked as the waiter served them.

'My wife, you mean?' said Tony.

'Yes, your wife,' said Wanda.

'As wives go I suppose she's not a bad wife,' said Tony. 'But she turned out to be cold. Always jealous. It's a thing I just can't stand, jealousy. And I mean I was never jealous of her.'

'It's not always easy not to be jealous,' said Wanda.

'Well you're never jealous of me,' said Tony.

'Yes, but we aren't married.'

'Too right we aren't.'

Tony leant across the table and kissed her on the lips.

'Your tie's gone in your avocado pear,' she said.

'Damn. No, I've learnt my lesson.'

'Me too,' said Wanda.

'But you've never been married,' said Tony.

'No, but you don't get cited in three divorces without knowing what hell it is.'

'Did you enjoy your others?'

'Yes. I told them both I'd be available if they ever needed the same thing again.'

'I hope you'll enjoy this one too,' said Tony.

Afterwards they drank vodka leaning against the bar.

'Where does your wife think you are?' said Wanda in a loud voice.

'S'sh,' yelled Tony.

In the morning when the early morning tea came they asked for an extra bath towel. When it came they dropped it in the tea pot and rang for another one.

After breakfast Tony paid the bill. He left an enormous tip consisting entirely of threepenny bits.

'They should remember us all right,' he said, as he drove away.

But when the detective turned up everyone made a point of being very discreet and denied all knowledge of any 'goings-on'. They weren't the sort of people to let a handsome tipper down.

As soon as the police began investigating the East Suffolk Puncture Mystery, the punctures stopped. And so they got no further with that. Not that they tried very hard. Nobody was trying very hard. After all, it was August, it was summer time, it was the silly season.

23

September. The godwits had bred successfully, and the avocets had enjoyed a record season. Summer returned, Indian summer. Bookings in the hotels were slacker, and Tony set about providing the evidence in earnest.

At the White Horse at Potter Sneighthinghampton and the Green Man at Nether Wadsbridgeworth no one could remember them. As the landlord of the Green Man told the detective: 'Look, old boy, if we get a couple who *are* man and wife, that's when I sit up and take notice. This is the modern world, you know. It isn't 1960.'

But at the Bull at Cludd they finally got their evidence.

'Well, that's that,' said Tony.

'I'm sorry it's all over, really,' said Wanda.

'It was fun, wasn't it?'

'The best of the three.'

'Honestly?'

'Without question.'

'Easily the best?'

'Easily.'

'Wanda?'

'Yes, Tony?'

'Will you marry me?'

'Darling, I thought you were never going to ask.'

Paula was back, and Pegasus went up to London to see her. She was brown, smoothly richly brown all over her strong legs and arms. She was destined to be the envy of the South Rickmansworth Harriers. She had the smell of the heat still upon her, and she was wearing a kind of deck chair cover which went well with the sunburn. Sue was out, and Paula took him back to the flat. She had pale strips where she wasn't sunburnt. Nudists didn't know what they were missing. Nor did Simon.

Back at the Goat and Thistle Jane was pallid, and he thought, she's had no chance to get sunburnt, she's been working hard, everyone ought to be entitled to their fair share of sunburn, on the national health. Not that Jane's skin would ever sunburn like that. It had all been a dreadful mistake.

'I gather it all went well with Paula,' Jane said.

'How do you mean?'

'It did, didn't it?'

He shrugged. Jane just looked at him, emptily.

'I can't cry. I've lost the knack,' she said.

She had either been asleep or pretending to be asleep when he got back. She called on him early in the morning, tense.

He had to make some kind of admission. It was called for.

'I don't deny I was attracted to her,' he said. 'After all, I'd already been attracted to her before, hadn't I?'

'You didn't know me then.'

'Well you know how it is. You know, it was just one of those things. She was all sunburnt and . . .'

'My God, trust a man to fall for the superficial.'

'Exactly. It was just superficial. Nothing to worry about.'

'You didn't have sex, did you?'

'Why do you ask?'

'Did you?'

'Of course not.'

'You did, didn't you?'

'No, I tell you — we did actually.'

'I knew it. Oh God.'

He said: 'I'm sorry, Jane,' and she must have seen how true it was at that second in time because she allowed him to hold her firmly in his arms.

After that Jane was tense and nervous, distant, cool, almost uninhabited, frightened presumably of getting so close that she would suffer the moment of growing more distant again. He felt that anything would be preferable, even violent anger.

Pegasus felt increasingly sorry for Jane and guilty about his behaviour. He even promised that on his next visit to see Paula he would break things off.

He meant to, undoubtedly. Otherwise he would not have been in such a nervous state as he walked towards the seat.

Her sunburn was fading, subtler now, infinitely lovely. She wanted him to go back to her place again but he refused.

'Why? Is it your turn to have qualms now?' she said.

'Of course not.'

'I know. You felt guilty with her.'

'Yes, I did. She was so unhappy. She found out we'd slept together.'

'You mean you told her?'

'No. She sort of knew.'

There were kites in the sky. And children's voices. And white sails on the Round Pond. A clean scene. One of the cleanest.

'This situation is intolerable,' said Paula.

'I agree.'

Suddenly on this seat he felt a desire for anything but sex. It wasn't a qualm, exactly, just a desire for something more original, less clogging, freer and gayer.

'I'm going for a fortnight's holiday,' he said. 'I know this sounds awful and arrogant, Paula, but I'm going to have to sort things out. This is making everyone miserable. By the time I get back from my holiday I shall have decided.'

'Whether to give up me or Jane?'

'Well, you know, I suppose so, yes.'

'That's awful and arrogant.'

'I said it was.'

'That doesn't excuse it. We're just supposed to sit here and wait for your decision, are we? We aren't seeking permission to build a greenhouse in our back garden, you know.'

'You both have a perfect right to reject me. I realize that. But so far you haven't.'

'That's true.'

Paula smiled, faintly, but it was a smile.

'I hope everything'll be all right for us, Paula, that's all.'

'You'll tell her that as well.'

'No I won't. Honestly.'

'Oho!'

'I'll get in touch when I get back, and I'll, you know, let you know.'

'Don't ring us, we'll ring you.'

'I'm sorry. And now let's go and see a nice sad film and enjoy ourselves.'

When he got back Jane was waiting for him and he thought, I can't stand much more of this.

'Well? Have you broken it off?' she asked.

'Not exactly.'

She smiled, a smile which had love and sadness in it.

'You see, I'm helpless in your hands,' she said.

'We didn't make love anyway,' he said.

'I'm grateful for small mercies,' said Jane.

Pegasus outlined the projected holiday programme.

'Do you accept?' he asked.

'Yes. I'll sign on the dotted line. I have no choice.'

'I only hope everything'll be all right, darling,' he said.

'I expect you told her that, too.'

'No, I didn't. Honestly.'

'Your problem is that you can't break off with any part of your past,' said Jane.

From then until his holidays in nine days time Pegasus was busy in the kitchens. And in the background were his dreams, insistent, despite his growing weariness.

And all the time the cooking continued, and he dreamt of his masterpieces. Oh heedless youth, not to take warning from the gulf between your ambitions and your achievements. A man who forgets his trousers is rarely complimented for his taste in ties. (Old Suffolk Proverb.) A horse fly may ride on the back of the Grand National winner, but it won't receive a prize. (Old Suffolk Proverb.)

He decided to go motoring in Europe. He would start in Amsterdam, because he liked it, and then he would move on to France. He would stay in quiet places, where he could solve his problems in peace. He would eat three meals a day conscientiously, because your true professional is never idle. It would be a voyage of personal and culinary discovery, and like so many other discoverers he would keep a journal.

On the week-end before he left for his holiday, Pegasus suffered a disappointment. Alphonse took a long week-end off, in order to visit Provence, where his elderly mother had been taken ill. Tonio took over his duties and naturally Pegasus assumed that this would give him the chance of doing some of Tonio's work. Not a bit of it, however. A floating chef, one Angelo Fabbricione, was recruited to tide them over.

Pegasus remonstrated with Jane – but in vain.

'We just can't have any suggestions of favouritism,' she said.

'But there wouldn't be. I'm the ideal person for the job.'

'I know you are, darling, but can't you see what would happen? Not everyone is as noble-natured as you. There'd be envy, jealousy, ill-feeling. You know what these Latin races are.'

'But you think I'm the best man, don't you?'

'Of course, but I mustn't let my better judgement affect my love.' She was so pleased with this as to be seriously discomfited. So she left the room without saying any more.

She had been playing a part, making fun of him. Oh well, he couldn't blame her. He deserved it.

Later on he said: 'I do think you were mean,' and she said: 'I know how you feel, darling, but I must put the Goat and Thistle first.'

Pegasus telephoned Tarragon to tell him that Alphonse's duties would end at 8.45 p.m. on the Friday, and that he was going off for three days to visit his ailing mother in Provence.

24

Alphonse's duties did not in fact end, due to an unforeseen contretemps with a pork chop, until 8.51. Tarragon, sitting in his car in the main road, saw him leave the hotel by the yard entrance and set off down the road. He saw him turn left into the lane which led to the heath. He did not see him walk up the lane and enter the house where he lived with his attractive wife Lucienne.

A few minutes later Tarragon drove into the lane and parked some fifty yards short of Alphonse's house.

When Alphonse did not re-emerge Tarragon realized that he was not going to leave until morning. This was a blow but it was by no means unexpected.

At 9.40 the bedroom light in Alphonse's house went on and at 10.03 it went off. Tarragon waited a few minutes longer and then drove on up the lane, past the foundations where six new desirable residences had just been begun. He parked in a small copse of widely spaced trees which stood between the houses and the heath.

He lay across the seat and tried to sleep, and did indeed manage a few spells, one of them lasting almost an hour. At three o'clock his alarm went. It was possible that they would make an early start, and he didn't dare sleep on any longer.

He drove back into the lane, and pulled up by the foundations of the new houses. He ate his smoked salmon sandwiches and drank his thermos of strong, hot coffee. And waited. Trying not to nod off. Gradually the dark grew less intense and he thought of the sea, dawn coming up, the whole tossing expanse of the sea on all sides, and considerable prospects of porridge. He was a good man at sea, Tarragon, not so much of an ugly duckling. He wished he was at sea now and not in this ludicrous mess.

The foundations of the building site grew clearer, till every brick was visible. Soon there would be twee little houses there, nostalgically named after remembered beauty spots now made hideous by houses just like these.

Just after half past six Alphonse's car slid out into the lane. Tarragon ducked out of sight, peeping up again in time to see which way the car turned into the main road. It turned right. He gave it a minute and then followed.

When he caught up with the car it was doing only about thirty-four miles per hour on the deserted road, and he realized with dismay that this was its maximum speed. It was therefore impossible for him not to overtake without becoming conspicuous. So he overtook, and drove on out of sight.

When he came to the junction of the A.12 and the A.145 Tarragon turned south down the A.12, then turned round and waited, as far away from the junction as he could get without losing sight of it. He felt very conspicuous, told himself that Alphonse, with no possible suspicion that he was being followed, would hardly question the sight of a car standing at the roadside, but still felt very conspicuous.

He soon saw the bright pale green car at the junction, turning up the A.145.

Tarragon waited a few minutes and then set off in pursuit. The next likely divergence of the ways was in Beccles, so he overtook the car, parked in the town, and kept watch. As he expected, Alphonse took the Norwich road.

Tarragon bought himself a bottle of milk off a cart, and drank the clean cool liquid with gusto. Then he drove on. He overtook Alphonse at Loddon and drove on to Norwich where things became rather more difficult. He soon picked up the bright pale green car but lost it when he was held up by traffic lights.

A glance at the map confirmed what he had thought. By far the likeliest route for Alphonse to take was the A.47 to King's Lynn. Roads to the north of this would lead only to the Wash and the North Norfolk coast, and he felt certain, in view of the early start, that Alphonse's journey would be longer than that. Roads to the south all led to places which could have been reached without ever going as far north as Norwich. So, King's Lynn it must be.

And was. Tarragon felt gratified when he saw the bright pale green car proceeding sedately along the road some two hundred yards in front of him. He overtook, sped rapidly to King's Lynn, parked, and had time for a hurried breakfast in a self-service café before, as he expected, the car struggled past on its way to join the A.17, bearing inside it the man whose alias was Alphonse, and his attractive wife Lucienne.

He followed his prey as far as Newark without straining his powers of deduction or motoring, but here things grew more complicated. He lost him in heavy traffic and failed to see whether he took the A.1 for the north or the A.616 towards Sheffield.

After driving a few miles up the A.1 Tarragon realized that he had made the wrong choice. So it must be the A.616, with the possibility, as the reader has no doubt already observed, that Alphonse would either continue along the A.616 or would take the A.617 towards Mansfield and Chesterfield. Tarragon plumped for the A.616, a choice he would never have cause to regret. At

Tuxford, therefore, he turned left off the A.1 on to the A.611, a road so engineered as to cross the A.616 at Ollerton, thus affording him, by means of a simple right turn, the opportunity of rejoining the A.616, an opportunity which he did not spurn.

From Ollerton he bustled up the A.616 and just beyond Clowne, oh joy of joys, there was the bright pale green car struggling valiantly on its slow painful noisy way.

With every mile that it travelled the likelihood of its ending up in Provence became more and more remote. Tarragon was a hunter who has the prey in his sights. He was a cunning stalker who had got down wind of his adversary. He was gripping the wheel tightly, so that his knuckles stood out white. He tucked himself in behind a large lorry. Here he could safely remain, without rousing the suspicions of his quarry.

Past Renishaw they went, past Eckington, into the suburbs of Sheffield, city of the short knives, over the switchback of high hills on which the bleak treeless suburbs are built. And the bright pale green car nipped across a junction just as the lights were changing, but the lorry ground squeakily to a halt. And when they moved off the car was nowhere to be seen. Tarragon drove on, as fast as he could, down into the smoky pit of the city, but no bright pale green car did he see.

He was tired, but he wasn't giving up now. After a quick meal and a wash and brush up he drove back to the spot where he had last seen the car. He was reasonably certain that it would not have turned off at that point unless its destination was somewhere within the city boundaries of Sheffield.

He explored the streets to the left until it was dinner time. Then he booked into a hotel, ate an indifferent dinner, and returned to examine the streets on the right. On into the cold sodium night, long after the last cream buses had passed through the inhospitable unlovely streets, he searched. It was 1.30 a.m. before his exhausted body sank into a comfortable bed, and at 8 o'clock he was at breakfast, ready to continue his search. All day he searched, but he didn't find what he was looking for.

It was 2 a.m. on Monday when he arrived home, stiff and exhausted, and 8.15 that morning saw him perusing his mail over a plate of kidneys.

He only had one letter. It ran:

'Dear Mr Clump, Please to leave £175 in the sailing sloop Godwit, that you are finding in Woodbridge Harbour in the first section of the new marina nearest beyond from the old mill. The door from one of the lockers is not holding its size so good due from the warpings (bad British workmanship!) Please to be sliding envelope in locker before October 1. Then I buy a new car.'

25

Amsterdam, Sept 25

Heated terraces, canals, fat women at windows, rijstafels in the Indonesian restaurants, trams, hurdie-gurdies and trees. Heated trams. Fat women at rijstafels. Stop it, Pegasus.

Had a rijstafel tonight. Excellent, but too exotic to be much use to me personally. There was so much food, and it was so oriental, that I got to thinking about poverty. If I hadn't eaten the meal and had sent my fourteen guilders to India, India would have been fourteen guilders richer and the restaurant would have been fourteen guilders poorer. Fourteen guilders makes much more difference to a small restaurant than to India, so I enjoyed my meal. But afterwards I sent fourteen guilders to Oxfam.

Amsterdam, Sept 26

Had my usual dream last night. Bloody nuisance. I'd hoped they'd stop while I was on holiday.

Went to Aalsmeer to see the flower auctions today. We were divided into six language groups and a multi-lingual girl showed us round. The only thing she knew in the six languages was the names of the flowers and they were always the same. Chrysanthemum, chrysanthe, Chrysanthemadre, Chrysanthomos, Krisanthemitz, Chroesanthemoos. When she took us upstairs I looked up her long, elegant, multi-lingual legs and desired her. I'd have asked her out if there hadn't been 128 other people there, divided into six language groups.

I thought perhaps if I was unfaithful to both Jane and Paula I might find out who I loved the best by finding out who I felt more guilty about. But I'm glad now I didn't. It would only have made matters worse.

I wish they were here. Now all I've got to do is decide which of them I wish was here the most.

But I don't want to break it off with either of them.

Question: Is this feeling selfish (I am greedy) or unselfish (I don't want to disappoint them)?

Answer: I must decide this during my holiday.

Question: Even if my main desire is not to disappoint them, isn't this also partly selfish, because it suggests that I think highly of myself as an eligible bachelor?

Answer: So do they.

Question: Am I an eligible bachelor?

Answer: I'm certainly a bachelor.

Amsterdam, Sept 27

Bought two postcards, one for Jane and one for Paula. One of a canal and church, the other of a canal and flower market. I can't decide which is the more attractive card, and I can't decide who to send the more attractive card to when I have decided. So it shouldn't matter two hoots which card I send to which girl, but I can't help thinking that my whole future may depend on my decision.

Amsterdam, Sept 28

Saw the Rembrandts today. Marvellous. Tried imagining Jane

154

and Paula as Rembrandt would have painted them. Marvellous.

Played billiards with a student called Jan Pumpernickel. Lost 4-3. But played him secretly, without his knowing it, at using adjectives, and beat him 112-73.

I must leave Amsterdam tomorrow. It's lovely, but no use to me gastronomically.

Can't seem to think of much to say today. Have to do better than this or my journal won't be worth keeping.

Namur, Sept 29

Food much richer here. Took great care to eat sparingly because it would be so humiliating to get diahorrhea (spelling?). Must run my stomach in gradually.

Sent cards to Paula and Jane. The same card to each this time. The same message, too.

Must try and get further with analysing my motives.

What sort of person am I?

The sort of person who makes notes about what sort of person he is.

The restaurants are good. They have a sense of style. I don't seem to mind being on my own. If Prince Rainier and Princess Grace came in and saw me I wouldn't bat an eyelid.

Dijon, Sept 30

France at last. Two excellent meals. This seems a nice city. No great inspiration with my masterpieces yet, or with my thoughts, which is a worry, but that will come and at least I'm on the right road now. This question of knowing where you're going in life, doing what it's natural for you to do, is it anything to do with religion? Does God exist? I don't know. Except that some sort of standard exists whereby it's right for me to do what I'm doing. Is that God?

Do my talents in any sense make me better than other men of less talent? Is Progress the way to achieve progress? Is increasing scientific knowledge consistent with a richer human life? Is stan-

155

dardization a bad thing? Can there ever be a revolution which respects the right of the individual? If not, can a revolution ever do good? Has society the right to ban experiments with drugs? Why do I support Fulham but hate Chelsea, and do so become convinced that right lies at Craven Cottage and wrong at Stamford Bridge? Can the population explosion be halted? Are our beaches sufficiently protected from sewage? Is censorship bad? Should there be more stringent powers to prevent the creation of unsightly shop fronts? Is television the opium of the people? Is the sinking of underground wells the answer to the water shortage? Is opium the television of the Chinese? Are the penalties for defacing public bus shelters too lax? Is necessity the mother of invention? Should immature herring be landed by fishermen or will this lead to the gradual depopulation of the sea? Should dustbins be emptied once or twice a week? Under what circumstances should abortions be allowed? Is love more important than an efficient public transport system? Should people with council houses be allowed two garages? Are rent rebate schemes effective?

I don't know.

Dijon, Sept 31

Drove down past all the vineyards. Chambertin and Nuits St Georges and Vosne-Rosmanée and Chambolle-Musigny and old Uncle Tom Chablis and all. Not very exciting little places on the whole but I'm deeply moved by the thought of all that wonderful wine and its cultivation. Can't see myself getting the same effect with Coq au Mrs Roberts Cowslip Wine or Boeuf à la red barrel.

Dijon, Sept 32

Last night's dream was Frenchified, set in a future France consisting of vast cities with tracts of deserted countryside between them. The old parts of the cities were museums staffed by men and women who all smiled permanently in a meaningless way, as laid down by the Ministry of Internal Courtesy and Smiling. Around them were typical ugly white bleak French suburbs. Food con-

sisted of pills made to taste like the old French dishes. I was Chief
Three Star Pill and Luxury Globule Supervisor. We'd come
across a plot to poison the nation's brains through these pills. A
committee had been set up to fight the menace. It consisted of myself, Biggles and John Betjeman. Biggles and I believed that the
man behind the scheme was the dastardly Hong Kong double
agent and entrepreneur Ho Ling Fu. Betjeman seemed uninter-
ested. 'Is that man Betjeman trustworthy?' Biggles put in
shrewdly. And at that moment Betjeman rang up to say he'd got
Ho Ling Fu. He'd run him to earth behind a superb fourteenth-
century rood screen in a Suffolk wool church. Betjeman said: 'I
hit him over the head with the font cover. Fifteenth century.' We
asked what he looked like. 'His face has been heavily restored and
has no features of interest whatsoever.' Then the critics came on
and reviewed my dream, and I hated this as much if not more
than the dream. Very contradictory views. Biggles thought it was
'a rattling good yarn'.

Played billiards today with a nice man named Claude Pencillier.
He beat me 4-3, but I beat him 6-3, 11-9, 4-2 (unfinished) at
smiling.

Beaune, Sept 33

What an autumn. Day after glorious day.

Another nice town. Met Bowen in the main square. Said he was
enjoying the outing. He was wearing a funny cardboard hat and
seemed drunk.

Beaune, Sept 34

Had a shock when I read through yesterday's diary to see I'd
written about Bowen as if he existed. I honestly don't see how he
can exist, because I've met him doing a job that doesn't exist.

Getting very lazy, and just don't feel like going on. It's all this
food. Two huge meals a day — six courses both of them. But it's
an investment for the future. I've eaten three coq au vin, two coq
au chambertin, three boeuf bourgignonne, four lots of escargot,

and several different quenelles de brochet. I've made notes on each and in some cases I've been able to discuss the recipes with the chefs so I'll be able to introduce some more dishes to my menus. But I do feel a bit bloated.

Beaune, Sept 35

Still here. Can't get going at all. Venison, partridge, salmon, brains and blackberry flan all good. Clothes beginning not to fit. Kept going by the thought of my destiny. Seem to sense God now as something real, spirit watching over my progress, keeping me going.

Disappointed not to make more progress with my own master-pieces, but hardly any new thoughts at all. But I may be on the way towards a rather interesting parsnip soup. Only time will tell.

Beaune, Sept 36

If I turn back it will mean getting nearer to time of decision. Dread this.

Possible ways of deciding between Jane and Paula. Meeting families. Toss of coin. I.Q. tests. All disgusting. No way except the true way. Probably get easier as I get nearer home.

I could decide, I can't really love them absolutely equally, so I could decide, but for the fact that I don't want to. Who would?

No use letting it get me down. Have to wait till I get home.

Semur-En-Auxois, Sept 37

Skipped lunch today, ate only a slice of simple peasant sausage. Repulsive.

Nice quiet romantic and above all ordinary town.

Last night's dream was about disease. Disease had been abol-ished and the population was enormous, health no longer had any joy in it, and everyone was bored. I had patented a new game, which was sweeping the world. There was a pack of cards marked with various diseases, and you had to act out the disease you drew. It was all the rage. It gave people something to live for. Then I was persuaded to play for the first time. I drew a fatal heart attack. I died. The only people who came to my funeral were the critics. They panned it, saying it was the most derivative funeral they'd ever been to. Except Biggles, who thought it a rattling good yarn.

Excellent wild boar tonight.

Utter lassitude today, in the sun, and bloated with food. Wished all the world could be like this, but felt the nagging worry underneath. Almost home again now. Knew I had to face up to the problem somehow. Finally had a brainwave.

I've got a phrase book out here, full of the usual useless phrases of the 'excuse me, porter, your gaiters are on fire' type. It's got several characters, hypochondriac, xenophobe and so on. I thought maybe I could find Paula and Jane in it, and turn a few pages into a play. Might help me work out my responses to their character.

Found six characters altogether. Made two of them mother and father, cast the other two as Cousin Percy and Tarragon Clump. Added a few stage directions. Took most of the afternoon.

THE HOLIDAY

An hotel somewhere in Europe. Six guests are seated on the terrace. The MANAGER *of the hotel hovers in the background.*

FATHER: It will rain tomorrow.

TARRAGON: There will be mud on the roads.

FATHER: It did not rain today.

TARRAGON: The roads are pitted with large holes.

COUSIN PERCY: Wireless Telegraphy is a splendid invention, is it not?

(*An awkward pause.*)

PAULA: How beautiful the streets are.

JANE (*to the* MANAGER): Can you recommend me a pill which will dispel the effects of over-indulgence?

(*The* MANAGER *makes no reply. Perhaps he is dumb.*)

MOTHER: Are you thirsty?

JANE: I am extremely thirsty.

PAULA: I am not thirsty.

TARRAGON: We are all thirsty.

COUSIN PERCY (*to the* MANAGER): Pray, tell me, are there twenty-six letters in your alphabet also?

(*The* MANAGER *does not reply. Perhaps he is dumb.*)

JANE: My headache is too bad for me to visit the gallery.

PAULA: But the pictures are extremely beautiful. Everyone sings their praises.

TARRAGON: Those museums are dull, and that museum is draughty.

JANE: I do not want to go any further.

PAULA: But I want to see all the beautiful houses in the old quarter of the town.

FATHER: It will hail on Wednesday.

JANE: I shall have the backache on Thursday.

PAULA: We shall see the frescoes and the gardens on Friday.

TARRAGON: Our horses are larger than yours.

MOTHER (*to the* MANAGER): Are our rooms on the third floor?

(*The* MANAGER *looks at her as if she is stupid. After all, they have already been at the hotel for three days.*)

JANE: My room is noisy. I cannot sleep.

PAULA: I can see the bell-tower from my window. It is built in the Romanesque style.

TARRAGON: Have the goodness to give us fresh accommodation.

(*The* MANAGER *stares at them sullenly. He does not have the goodness to give them fresh accommodation.*)

COUSIN PERCY: The idle are seldom happy.

TARRAGON: I will thank you to direct me to the British Consul.

MOTHER (*to the* MANAGER): There was a mistake in the accounts you rendered to me.

PAULA: It is of no account.

TARRAGON: On the contrary it is of great importance.

MOTHER: Do not worry yourself about it.

FATHER: See to it instantly.

(*The* MANAGER *says nothing. Perhaps he is confused by these contradictory demands. Or perhaps he is dumb.*)

COUSIN PERCY: The next century will see many changes.

(*Exit* COUSIN PERCY.)

FATHER: It will freeze tonight.

(*Exit* FATHER.)

MOTHER: Let us hope we shall all have hot water bottles.

(*Exit* MOTHER.)

TARRAGON: All our boxes have been broken by the servants.

(*Exit* TARRAGON.

PAULA *and* JANE *are left alone on the terrace.*)

PAULA (*enthusiastically*): We shall see the cathedral tomorrow.

JANE: We shall all catch cold.

(*Exeunt* JANE *and* PAULA. *The* MANAGER *turns to the audience, and tries to speak. But no words emerge. Perhaps he is dumb, or perhaps he is merely dumbfounded.*)

CURTAIN

Jane's attitude is tiresome but I'm inclined to think that Paula is being just as tiresome in her different way. She is finding everything so wonderful in order to be provocative to Jane.

It hasn't helped at all, and it has made me feel rather lonely.

Paris, Sept 39

What a long and wonderful autumn. The city looks lovely, but I have almost no money left and so can't really carry on with my eating.

Met Bowen again today, in the Rue De Rivoli. Told him I was pretty sure he didn't exist. He said I must be pissed. If he does exist, I'll have to speak to him about it.

Paris, Sept 40

Back in London tomorrow afternoon. Beginning to feel very nervous.

Don't seem to have found out as much about myself as I'd hoped. Certainly haven't had any inspirations as regards food. Haven't sorted out Jane and Paula either. All rather disappointing.

Enjoyed it all though. Enjoy drifting anonymously, no responsibilities, yet always feeling that I'm getting somewhere.

Much more stylish city than London. Rather dread London. Dread stepping into own life again in case it doesn't fit.

But also feel excited. When I get home and see Paula and Jane again after not seeing either of them for a fortnight I know I shall suddenly realize which of them it's to be. I'll feel very sorry for the other one, but it will be an exciting moment.

26

Thin layers of high cloud were infiltrating slowly into the pale blue autumn sky as Paula made her way towards the seat. The trees were beginning to turn. Autumn is a beautiful and tragic time, thought Paula.

He was there. He was already sitting on the seat. Her heart crashed with sickening fear. She had a cold, she felt feverish and unattractive on this most important of all days, she felt that she was fated to lose.

He saw her. She hurried towards him. He stood up. They kissed, neutrally.

The frame seemed to Paula to have been frozen. All the other people in the park, did they but know it, were stricken into immobility. Then movement returned, and life went on.

'Well?' said Paula, as they began to walk towards the Albert Memorial.

'Well what?'

'What sort of a holiday did you have? Was it all lovely?'

'Very nice, thank you.'

'Good. That's nice.'

'You've got a cold.'

'Yes. I got it off Cousin Percy, damn him.'

The grotesque pile of the Albert Memorial loomed before them. Paula felt awful, felt she looked awful, felt she was doomed, so blew her nose angrily.

'Poor old Paula,' said Pegasus.

'Yes.'

He wasn't touching her. It looked like being poor old Paula all right.

'The trees have hardly started changing colour,' she said. 'I never realized they changed so late.'

'What?' asked Pegasus, and then when Paula didn't reply he said: 'No. They do change fairly late.'

'And what about Burgundy? You sounded as though it was marvellous.'

'It was nice.'

'I liked your cards.'

If only he would say something definite. She knew that she had lost him but until he told her so she would feel this awful futile hope.

But she mustn't get angry. If she hadn't gone off with Simon they wouldn't be in this position now. It wasn't altogether his fault.

'You're not very lively. I want to hear all about it,' she said.

He put an arm round her waist, but it just flopped there.

After a minute or two of flopped arm round waist, he moved on to finger tapping. His fingers tapped her waist and hips nervously. She waited for the shock, expecting it every second, knowing that even though she was expecting it it would be a shock.

'Do you believe in God?' Pegasus asked.

'What a funny time to ask.'

163

'Do you?'

'We've discussed all that hundreds of times. You know my attitude. I believe in the value of beauty and so . . .'

'What do you mean, the value of beauty?'

'Well, I mean, I assume that in finding certain things more beautiful than others we are making a value judgement which implies that those things are also better.'

'What do you mean, better?'

'Stop picking on me.'

'I'm trying to find out whether you believe in God?'

'I don't want to discuss it now. I've got a cold. I'm tired. You don't normally talk about things like that.'

'It's not important, I suppose.'

'Of course it's important. But it's not what I want to talk about just now.'

'What do you want to talk about?'

'Well, you know.'

Pegasus gave her a strange look, as if he was sizing her up. She intended to be furious about it, but then he grabbed her with both hands and she could feel his slender body pressing against her. He began to push her backwards.

'Don't. You'll break my back,' she said.

He let go and lay down on the grass.

'Come on,' he said, smiling up at her. 'I love you.'

She felt herself falling. She was on top of him. He was about to kiss her.

'Let's get married,' he said.

Their faces moved closer.

'You'll catch my cold,' she said.

'It'll be better by the time we're married.'

'Idiot.'

As their faces met Paula saw that his eyes were shut and his face was contorted.

'When?' she asked.

'Soon. Soon.'

One of his hands had found her stocking tops and was stroking her right thigh. It wasn't really the sort of thing that ought to happen in the Royal Parks, but this wasn't the time to protest. She didn't want to be cross-examined about her qualms.

'It's you I love, Paula. It always has been.'

She wanted to believe it.

'Then why all the doubt?' she said.

'I was frightened. It had gone wrong once. I didn't really want to get involved in it all again. That's fair enough, isn't it?'

'Seven out of ten.'

She saw him look at her sharply to see if there was any malice in her words. There wasn't, not really.

They lay side by side and stared at the sky.

'Why all this sudden interest in God?' Paula asked.

'We're all part of the grand design,' he said.

She sat up and began straightening her clothes.

'What do we do now?' she said.

'I'm going to have to go fairly soon,' he said. 'I've got to tell Jane. I want to get it over.'

She tried to get up, but he held her down.

'What's wrong?' he said.

'Nothing's wrong,' she said. 'The grass is damp, that's all.'

Jane felt curiously confident. During the last fortnight she had felt sick and empty, working until she almost dropped. Now, waiting in her green skirt and black sweater, she was ready. The bar was being taken care of, she had nothing to do but wait. Her nerves tingled, made her expectant and eager. She lived on her nerves. When they were tuning up she felt confident and proud. When they were going down again, that was when the troubles began.

At this moment she could even look at herself in the mirror and notice the lively alert movement of her nostrils, the colour in her cheeks, all the signs of life. Soon he would be here, and anything would be better than his absence.

There he was, at the door. She coursed through herself almost uncontrollably. Every inch of her body could be felt. And he was early. It was a good sign.

And then she saw his doom-laden face and she knew that she had been wrong. Here was the messenger announcing the total victory of the Persians. Here was her mother breaking the news of her granny's death to a young girl. Here was all bad news.

'Hullo,' she said.

'Hullo,' said the face of doom.

He kissed her, to a certain extent.

She could feel the smiling mobility of her face dying, the legs standing awkwardly a little apart, the body thin and angular, the indecency of her mistake. She was on the downward slope, at the bottom of which there was nothing.

'Did you have a good time?' she forced herself to say.

'Yes.'

'You've put on weight.'

'I've been very conscientious about my eating.'

'Did you get any new ideas?'

'One or two. I'll have to think about them.'

They were just standing there. Staring. It was terrible.

'Did you see Paula on your way through?'

'Yes, I – er – it seemed, you know, natural, while I was there.'

'Of course.'

His hand was shaking. He was staring at her. She found herself looking at his trousers. And slipping. Slipping.

He came towards her and put his arms round her. He was kissing her mouth. His right hand was stroking her left buttock. She could not respond. It was too late for that. But must respond. But must. Must.

'Let's get married,' he said.

'All right,' she said.

Later that night the wind began to get up and the doors and windows rattled. The Indian summer was over. But by that time all was well. She had responded. Her body was in one piece, and at rest on the sheets.

'How did Paula take it?' she asked, thinking of Paula less as a rival than as a fellow soldier in the Pegasus Campaign.

'I think she always knew, in a way, that it had, you know,' said Pegasus. 'Ended.'

'I didn't.'

'You can't bring back the past.'

'I don't suppose I'll ever meet her now,' said Jane.

'Who knows?'

27

Pegasus had no idea what to do next. He loved them both. He was overflowing with love. It seemed to be part of the Grand Design that he should love them both. And as to the future, he just didn't know. Besides, he had caught Paula's cold, and he couldn't think clearly, or at least it was an excuse for not thinking clearly.

He rang Paula up, which meant driving to Foxwick Cross-Roads. He was worried that he would be seen, or that Jane would notice his absence.

'I think I'd better write,' he said. 'It's cheaper than phoning. I'll write every day.'

'I can ring you.'

'It's awfully difficult. I'm right at the top and there's no public phone on that floor. But you can if you want to.'

She did, once, but luck was on his side, and Jane wasn't about. And he kept her waiting for several minutes, to prove how difficult it was to find him.

'You've got my cold,' she said.

'Yes.'

'Sorry.'

'It's an honour.'

'Look, I'm ringing to say I could come down this week-end.'

'That would be lovely. But I honestly don't think we ought to.'

'Why?'

'Well it'd be so embarrassing for Jane. I mean put yourself in her position. You wouldn't like her to come down, would you?'

'I suppose not. I don't know. I want to see you, that's all I know.'

'I'll get a day off soon, and I'm going to give in my notice in a couple of weeks.'

'Why not straightaway?'

'I don't like to the moment I come back off holiday.'

'I should have thought under the circumstances she would be glad to see you go.'

'Yes, but you see if I give it in now the chef will be on holiday when my replacement arrives.'

'Don't you want to see me?'

'Of course I do. I'll see you every day for the rest of my life in six weeks' time. Surely you can wait that long?'

'I suppose so.'

Always looking round, wondering if someone would overhear, or was listening in. He'd die if she rang again. And he must get her off the line.

'Look, darling, I'll have a new job and we'll get somewhere to live and it'll all be settled in no time. And I'll write every day. And I'll have a day off soon. And now I really must go. I'm in mid-cooking. I'll write later tonight.'

He put the phone down, feeling weak. He went upstairs and hurriedly wrote three letters to Paula, so as to have some in hand. It might not always be so easy to find the time without arousing suspicion.

And then Jane kept asking him if he had told his parents yet.

And he said he'd written and hadn't got the reply. So when she saw that the reply had come she'd want to see it. Oh, the problems. He lived in constant terror of being found out.

'Miss Paula is all ready,' said Bowen.

'Thank you, Bowen.'

Pegasus went into the great bulbous boiler. Bowen did it all so efficiently. He was a marvel, that man.

Paula lay reclining on gold cushions with black edges. She was naked, with her full, slightly low-slung body presenting a seductive invitation to him.

'This heat is wonderful,' she said.

'I want to take you away from all this,' he said.

They made love. Gorgeous love.

'You do love me, don't you?' said Paula anxiously.

'I adore you. I'd follow you to the ends of the earth. And now, darling, I really must go and see to the infra-red refraction spasms.'

'One of these days I want to be all yours, darling, and not to have to share you with your beastly infra-red refraction spasms.'

He gave her a last kiss – had there ever been such a kiss?

God, he felt tired.

'You wonderful hunk of man,' said Paula.

Pegasus stepped out of the boiler.

'Bowen?' he called.

Bowen seemed to appear from nowhere. They walked across the vast hall towards the other great bulbous boiler. Some of the men waved Union Jacks.

'Miss Jane is all ready, sir,' said Bowen.

'Thank you, Bowen. Give Miss Paula her clothes, will you?'

'Yes, sir.'

'Better lay her on again at 4.30, Bowen.'

'Yes, sir.'

'I hope this isn't causing you too much trouble, Bowen,' said Pegasus.

'Not at all, sir. It's an inspiring example to the men,' said Bowen.

'In what way, Bowen?'

'Your energy, sir. Your vitality. Your dynamism. Your productivity. Some of it's bound to rub off.'

'I'm glad to hear it, Bowen.'

'That's why they're waving their flags, sir.'

'Ah, that's the reason, is it?'

Bowen opened the door of the other huge bulbous boiler. Jane was reclining on a leopardskin rug, her slender, shapely legs crossed seductively, naked.

'It's funny,' she said. 'One always forgets just how handsome you are.'

They made love. It was excellent.

'You look a little tired,' she said.

'The prismatic polarization sluice has packed up.'

'I want all of you. I don't want the prismatic polarization sluice coming between us.'

'It won't be for long.'

She looked at him with her adoring eyes.

'Tea?' she said, in her best hostess voice.

'That would be delightful.'

She pressed a button. There was no reply.

'I'll go and stir them up,' said Pegasus.

Outside, in the huge hall, men were running in all directions. Pegasus saw Bowen in the distance. He seemed distraught.

'Bowen?' he called.

Bowen came rushing towards him.

'Who pressed that button?' he said.

'We did. We wanted some tea,' said Pegasus.

'Well you've destroyed Peking,' said Bowen.

Pegasus woke up. Jane was slapping his cheek.

'You were dreaming,' she said, 'and tossing and turning awfully.'

'Did I say anything?'

'No.'

'You destroyed Peking.'

'Oh.'

What with his dreams and his worries about the two women Pegasus was becoming increasingly nervy. But this gave him a renewed enthusiasm for his work, purely as a kind of sedative.

'You regain the enthusiasm for the ingredient,' said Alphonse. 'That is good. Always we are for respecting of the ingredient.'

Pegasus might have been always for respecting of the ingredient, but he was no longer for respecting of Alphonse.

'This week when I am during my home, you are still working so hard, I hope,' said Alphonse.

'You're going over to France again?'

'Yes. My mother, she has the, how you say, heart contrition.'

'Oh dear. I'm sorry.'

This time Tarragon will get you, thought Pegasus. All he need do is wait for you in Sheffield where he lost you last time.

Soon he would get promotion. This in itself would raise problems, because to stay at the hotel clearly meant to decide in favour of Jane, and he wasn't ready to decide yet.

It would all be revealed to him in due course.

Slice slice. Dice dice. Chop chop.

Smile on, Alphonse. You won't be smiling long.

28

Saturday. George Baines was in a good mood, almost perky, almost light-hearted, as he finished his breakfast in the kitchen before leaving for work.

'Just as we said. Brief sunny intervals, blustery showers and squally winds,' he said, looking out of the window.

'I heard it. I listened to the five to six,' said his wife Margaret.

'Look at them. If those showers aren't blustery I don't know what are.'

She didn't understand, of course. She didn't know what a pleasure it was to know exactly what the elements were going to do, and then to see them do it, to forecast a pattern and then to watch the pattern develop. Of course he was just a cog in the machine, but you felt that it was your forecast, that you'd done it on your own. It was just like that at a football match. When Jimmy Greaves scored a goal at Tottenham 39,467 people swelled with pride, 2,500 were comically deflated.

Women didn't understand these things, he thought, taking a luscious draught of tea and looking indulgently at his wife. They were different from men. They didn't understand the weather, they had no sense of direction, they had no real understanding of objects. Men understood that sportsmen were objects – you bought Pickering as you would buy a table. You said: 'He's over-rated, Venables' or 'I've no use for Bremner myself'. A woman couldn't see it like that. She would say: 'He looks shy, that goalkeeper' or 'Manchester United are all Roman Catholics, aren't they?' Women missed the point. Though of course George Baines was very happy with his wife, and loved her very much. They didn't talk a great deal – no need for that – but they were happy.

When the weather was going well, thoughts of that nature often passed pleasantly and undemandingly through George Baines's head.

'It's time we went and saw Pegasus,' said his wife. 'After all, it's a hotel. We can stay there.'

'True.'

'I'm going to write to him today and tell him we're coming down next week-end. You are off next week-end, aren't you?'

'Yes, but . . .'

'No buts.'

'That fence, it . . .'

'No fences.'

'Those bulbs . . .'

'No bulbs.'

'What about Diana?'

'She can come too.'

'I suppose it is about time we went. And speaking of time, I must be off.'

Mr Prestwick of Wine and Dine Ltd was ready to be off as well. He had taken a flat in town, and was selling the house with all its faded recriminations. He never saw his wife these days.

Mr Coggin had said 8.30 at the corner of Gloucester Road. It was ridiculous, going at the week-end like this, but Mr Coggin had insisted. 'Never get the desk work done if we start taking bites out of office hours,' he had said. Mr Prestwick didn't like Mr Coggin. Mr Coggin suspected the terrible truth.

The terrible truth about Mr Prestwick was that he was turning into a wireless set, a powerful wireless set capable of receiving all the foreign stations. Barely a day passed now without his getting Hilversum. Often he got Kalundborg and Stavanger as well. And his voice was liable to interference from crackle and whine. People noticed it – that was why they had transferred him from personnel to do a routine job in the hotels department.

The organization had become too large, too impersonal. It all led to efficiency, and benefited the few at the expense of the many. He would have moved, if he wasn't too old, and if it wasn't the same everywhere else.

Mr Prestwick was one of life's casualties. He knew that the older people become the more of them become casualties – and they are all casualties in the end. Mr Prestwick was therefore looking forward to his old age.

He had let his friends slip, as you did, and he had no particular assets to enable him to gain any new friends. No great wit, no riches.

You slip an inch at a time, never noticing it. The young grew to despise you. Mr Coggin despised him. One of these days Mr Coggin would become old and some junior executive yet unborn would despise him, and Mr Coggin would begin to go funny in the head. And we call ourselves a civilized society, thought Mr Prestwick, who had been blessed with health and a wife and a son and a good if not outstanding brain, and was now going funny in the head.

It was all implicit in his tired, creased suit, his odd bouncy walk, his constant slight facial movements as he waited for Mr Coggin at the corner of Gloucester Road.

Alphonse had set off two hours ago, accompanied by his attractive wife Lucienne. He was crawling slowly over England now.

Tarragon Clump had set off early too. He would be in position in good time. Each brief burst of sun brightened his spirits. This business had brought him to his senses. When he was free of this burden his whole personality would begin to breathe more freely. He would sweat less. His bouts of constipation would become a thing of the past. He would marry Jane Hassett.

With appalling slowness the bright pale green car rattled hesitantly across the crowded, messy, once lovely land of Britain.

Tarragon Clump parked on the main road just before the point where he had lost the bright pale green car, and waited.

Pegasus took it out on the carrots. Hateful stupid red objects. They were always the first to feel his bile, of all the vegetables. He peeled them viciously. Outside it rained for five minutes and then stopped. Even here, in the dry East Anglian bulge, it was wet.

Soon he would be at least assistant chef. Perhaps even now Tarragon Clump was bringing the culinary imposter to book.

Not yet. Soon. But first Mr Prestwick and Mr Coggin will drive into the yard of the Goat and Thistle.

'Posh this place up a bit, you could make something of it,' Mr Coggin will say.

They will meet Jane and they will be astounded that she knows nothing about it. Mr Hassett had given them no indication of the situation. He had told them that a Saturday visit would be quite convenient. Mr Hassett had sold them the hotel. He needed the capital to get married and start a new business. Oh, Jane was his wife, not yet divorced. They were sorry (especially Mr Prestwick), they apologized (especially Mr Prestwick), it was an awkward situation (especially to Mr Prestwick) but there it was (especially to Mr Coggin). After all, the hotel had been Mr Hassett's, had it not? Mr Hassett may have assured her of all sorts of things, but that was unfortunately no concern of Wine and Dine Ltd. Perhaps Mrs Hassett had been a little, shall we say (shall Mr Coggin say) naïve.

Wine and Dine Ltd's plans were not yet finalized, so was there any point in getting het up about it? Mrs Hassett mustn't think they were an inhuman organization (even if they were – thought Mr Prestwick). Mr Coggin and Mr Prestwick were merely having a look round. They would have to give advice on several matters as a result of which their superiors might take any one of several courses of action. In the meantime, they dared say, some kind of arrangement could be reached.

The bright pale green car appeared at last. In it were Alphonse and his attractive wife, Lucienne. Lucky they hadn't bought their new car yet, thought Tarragon, setting off in pursuit.

The bright pale green car turned left into Ponston Road, and Tarragon followed it up Ponston Road, followed it round the Tracton Corner Roundabout, followed it down the wide Cranston Road, turned left with it into the narrow but busy Poundsley Road, saw it turn right into Tadcaster Road, was about to follow it, noticed that Tadcaster Road was a cul-de-sac, drove on and turned right into the next street, Pontefract Road, also a cul-de-sac.

There he sat for a moment, gazing at these grimy brick terraces, the derelict canal, more terraced houses on the hill beyond, a new world. Tarragon's favourite author was Simenon. He loved those provincial towns where the doctor was such a valued member of the community, even when making love to all his maids. Tarragon didn't want to be a specialist. He wanted to draw on his well of frustrated kindliness. He wanted to work in a community. Here, in these streets, dealing with people and all their varied problems. Even though he knew that being a doctor wasn't like that any more.

He would never forget this scene, small men hurrying off to tiny crowded pubs, and the old terraces patiently waiting to die. Never. He knew nothing.

This wasn't the time to be thinking of all this. He must decide on his plan. Was he to be from the council or a sales representative? There were his samples on the back seat, but he decided that the council might be safer.

He locked the car, walked briskly down Pontefract Road and along Poundsley Road into Tadcaster Road. Right at the end, outside number 46, was the bright pale green car.

Tarragon knocked at the door of number 46, firmly but not arrogantly. He felt surprisingly confident in this the first acting role of his life.

An elderly woman came to the door.

'Oh good afternoon. I'm from the council,' said Tarragon.

'Oh aye.'

'We're doing a survey of this street.'

'Tha what?'

'We're doing a survey. Checking on how many people there are in the various houses in the street.'

'Oh aye. Why?'

'We're just checking on the – er – the zone density regulations.'

'Oh.'

She was guarding the door against him and he was careful not to seem to want to come in.

'Well there's just Tom and me.'

Tarragon took his carefully prepared official form from his inside pocket.

'Funny time to come, isn't it, Saturday dinner time?'

'Well, I'm rather new up here.'

'Aye, tha would be.'

'Yes, and I'm a little behind hand, so I'm having to work over-time a bit.'

He held out the form so that she could see its long list of names. This seemed to ease her suspicions.

'That's . . . ?'

'Tom and Annie Moob.'

'And there's no one else living here? I thought I saw someone from that car outside.'

'Oh, well, that's our son Fred, tha knows. He's come up to see us, wi' the old man being badly.'

'Oh, I'm sorry to hear about that.'

He was, too.

'Aye, well.'

'Anyway, it's nice to have your son with you.'

'Well, it is.' She was thawing fast. ' 'E's a good lad, though, is our Fred. 'E's one of these cooks down south.'

'It's nice to have your children with you.'

'That's just what I said to our Fred. Tha wants to get stuck in, I said. Excuse my bluntness. We're blunt folk hereabouts. Tha wants to get stuck in, I said. Tell 'im to get on wi' it, Agnes, I said. That's 'is wife, tha knows. Aye. Tha wants a son, doesn't tha, afore it's too late, I said, same as what we've got our Fred. Aye, she say, but . . .'

'I quite agree, yes.'

'Aye.'

'So anyway there's nothing for you to worry about. No over-crowding here.'

'Aye, well, there wouldn't be, would there? Our Tom's very well up in 'ygiene. 'E's made a big point of it.'

Someone, presumably Alphonse, called out.

'What's up, mother?' he said in his natural Yorkshire tones.

'Just a man from t' council.'

M 177

'Oh.'

'Well I'd better not be keeping you,' said Tarragon.

He drove happily back towards London, pleased with himself. He had performed his role well. On the Stamford By-Pass he realized that there was nothing to stop him going down to the Goat and Thistle there and then.

No. He might make a mess of things. Better bask in his new self-esteem a while longer first.

Yes. Take the bull by the horns.

Easy way to decide – ring up and see if there was a vacancy. A Saturday night, but in October. 50-50 chance.

Tarragon telephoned the hotel. There was a vacancy.

A heavy shower trapped him in the telephone box. The rain hammered furiously against the panes. But he didn't mind. Ten minutes either way made no difference now.

He began to sing – loudly, lustily, tunelessly. A great defiant bellow came from the red call box as the rain swept viciously down upon it.

Saturday evening. With the fading light the winds began to drop, just as George Baines had said they would.

'I wrote that letter,' said his wife.

'What letter?'

'To Pegasus. Saying we'd go down next week-end. He can book for us.'

'The weather won't be good.'

'Never mind. He's our son. That's what counts.'

'What on earth can have made him do a thing like that?' said Jane. 'I mean, it's not as if it was all my fault the marriage broke up.'

'He may think it was,' said Pegasus.

'You don't, do you?'

'No, of course I don't, but he may. People can deceive themselves completely about these things.'

178

'They'll turn me out,' said Jane.

'Why on earth should they?'

'They will. I know it.'

'We'll manage somehow, whatever happens,' he said, kissing the top of her head. 'I won't let you down. I won't ever let you down.'

He meant it with all his heart.

Dinner was almost over when Tarragon arrived. Pegasus offered to stay on and cook him his meal, but Tonio insisted that it was his duty. So Pegasus went into the bar and had a drink.

Mr Flitch was making caustic comments about the merchandising of seed. Mr Thomas was complaining about an own goal which had cost Brighton and Hove Albion two points and Mr Thomas a good pools win.

'It's Mrs Thomas I'm thinking of. She's had a hard life,' he said, speaking of Mrs Thomas's hard life as if it was an external phenomenon quite outside his control.

When Tarragon came in after his meal Pegasus bought him a brandy. He bought himself another pint.

'Good trip?' Pegasus asked.

'Very good, yes. I called on a couple I know in Sheffield. Name of Moob. Fred and Agnes Moob. His parents live at 46, Tadcaster Road, Sheffield.'

Tarragon drank his brandy in two gulps.

'Same again?'

'Thanks.'

Pegasus rapidly sank the remainder of his pint and handed the empty glass to Tarragon.

'This beer is wonderful tonight,' he said.

There was a touch of recklessness in the air, which made Pegasus drink very rapidly. Tarragon seemed to feel it too.

'Come up to my room and I'll tell you all about it. Bring your drink,' said Tarragon.

Pegasus bought another round, which they took upstairs. On

the first floor landing a guest – a Mrs Emily Pulstrom, did they but know it – looked at their drinks askance. They entered Tarragon's room and found there two chairs, one each, an arrangement that recommended itself to both parties.

Then Tarragon told Pegasus how he had discovered that Alphonse was really Fred Moob and his attractive wife Lucienne was really his frumpish wife Agnes.

Pegasus told him that Tony Hassett had sold the hotel behind Jane's back. Tarragon said it wouldn't make much difference to him, he would still have his hold over Alphonse, who wouldn't want his deception to be known to the new company.

'The bastard,' said Tarragon. 'Never marry a pilot.'

'I'll remember that,' said Pegasus.

'Will they keep on Mrs Hassett, do you suppose?' said Tarragon.

'Who knows?' said Pegasus.

'I ought to be at her side,' said Tarragon.

'Why?'

'Well as you know I'm – er – and I thought that now this blackmail affair is over . . .'

'I think I ought to tell you that I'm engaged to Mrs Hassett,' said Pegasus.

'Oh. I see.'

'I'm sorry.'

'Not your fault at all,' said Tarragon, staring sadly at his brandy. There was a long pause. 'I rather thought you were engaged to someone in London.'

Pegasus, who was in the act of removing his glass from his lips, spilt beer all down his trousers.

'What gave you that idea?' he asked.

'Our friend Percy. I had dinner with him last night. He seemed to be under the impression you were going to marry some girl called Paula.'

'He must have got the wrong end of the stick,' said Pegasus.

'Oh.'

'I do know this girl. I saw her on Sunday actually. That's where I got this cold. But it was all broken off, you see.'

'Yes, I see. Only Percy seemed to think it was on Sunday that she'd got engaged,' said Tarragon.

'Really? How odd.'

'It's all a bit odd really.'

'Yes, I suppose it is.'

'Odd's the operative word.'

'Yes.'

'Actually I think old Percy will be quite pleased when I tell him. I think he rather fancies the girl, between you and me.'

'Perhaps it would be better if I told him,' said Pegasus.

'Perhaps it would. Well, lucky old Percy, unlucky old Tarragon. Come on. I think we'd better finish off this business of getting drunk.'

29

'I've had a letter from my parents. They're coming down at the week-end.'

'Oh. Lovely. We'll give them number 12.'

'With Diana.'

'She can have 20. What do they say?'

'What do you mean?'

'About us.'

'What about us?'

'About our getting married.'

'Oh, that. Oh, they're simply thrilled. Can't wait to meet you.'

'We ought to have a ring, oughtn't we?'

'Of course.'

'Only I saw one in Ipswich which I liked. Unless fifteen pounds is too expensive. We could get it tomorrow morning if we started early enough.'

'Hullo, mother. Pegasus here.'

'Oh hullo dear. How are you?'

'I've got some surprising news for you. I – er – I'm engaged . . . are you still there?'

'Yes, I'm still here.'

'Well, why don't you say anything?'

'I was so surprised.'

'Aren't you pleased?'

'Of course I am. Delighted.'

'You don't sound it.'

'Our generation doesn't express its feelings, but of course I'm delighted. Who is it?'

'Jane Hassett. The manageress of the hotel here . . . are you still there?'

'Yes, I'm still here. I thought she was married.'

'I told you. She's getting a divorce. I told you . . . are you still there?'

'Yes, I'm still here.'

'What's wrong? Lots of people have divorces. Some people have lots. Oh, that's bloody marvellous. I give you my good news and all I get is disapproval.'

'I'm sorry, dear. It was just – I'm surprised, that's all.'

'You are pleased, really, aren't you?'

'Yes, of course I am. And so will your father and Diana be, when they come in. Have you told Morley?'

'Not yet.'

'He'll be pleased, too. Well, that is good news. Oh, I'm thrilled really, dear. It's just that it was such a surprise.'

'Why? Is it incredible that I should get married, or something?'

'No, of course not. But I mean you never told us.'

'I've just told you.'

'You never told us you were keen on her or anything. You kept it all so quiet . . . are you still there?'

'Yes, I'm still here, mother.'

'I've said the wrong thing, haven't I?'

'Yes. I mean I've just announced that I'm engaged and all you can do is rebuke me. It's a bit much, I must say . . . are you still there?'

'Yes, I'm still here.'

'See you at the week-end, mother. It's all fixed up. Good-bye.'

'Good-bye.'

'My parents are coming down at the week-end so I'll have to use up my day off then.'

'You're determined not to see me, aren't you?'

'That's not fair.'

'Well.'

'Well nothing. I can't help it.'

'Have you given in your notice yet?'

'I've told you, a fortnight. Besides, there's a complication. This place has been taken over by Wine and Dine Ltd.'

'What difference does that make?'

'Well it's possible that Jane might have to leave and of course I might have to leave or I might be able to stay. And you see Alphonse isn't really Alphonse, he's Fred Moob, so maybe he'll get the sack. It could mean promotion for me.'

'With Jane still there?'

'No. If she stays, I go. But if she goes and Alphonse goes, and I don't have to go, then I stay.'

'Supposing I don't want to live in the country?'

'You will.'

'I see. Oh, look, darling, I want to see you.'

'Well I want to see you too but things are happening pretty fast. We'll know for certain one way or the other in a week or two. And I'll come and see you as soon as I can. And I love you.'

'And I scored a goal.'

'What?'

'I didn't say anything.'

'Who were you playing?'

'Lousy old Nelson.'

'Will you get off the line?'

'What?'

'There's someone on the line.'

'What, mummy?'

'There's someone on the line.'

'There's someone on the line, darling.'

'You're on our line.'

'*You're* on *our* line.'

'We were here first.'

'*We* were *here* first.'

'I'm not getting off the line.'

'Nor are we.'

'I want to sleep with you.'

'What, mummy?'

'Take no notice of them, dear. What was the score?'

'Damn, there are the pips.'

'Those are your pips, not ours.'

'They're your pips, we've only just . . .'

Click.

'Is that you, Paula?'

'Biggs Minimus was sent off for fighting.'

'Is that you, Paula?'

'Yes.'

'Thank God.'

'Look, why can't I come down at the week-end and meet the family?'

'I've told you. I've caused Jane enough heartbreak without making her endure something as awkward as that.'

'I suppose you're right. Oh hell.'

'I know.'

'And Nelson had beaten Beatty two-one. So we did jolly well.'

'A very good choice, if I may say so. You can always tell a marriage from the ring, you know. Now you, you have chosen a ring I would choose myself, if ever I was getting married. Oh yes, my instinct tells me that you are both going to be very happy indeed.'

30

The Baines's car drew up at the Goat and Thistle at ten past one on the Saturday afternoon. Pegasus hurried out of the kitchen and found them already talking to Jane.

'So you've met,' he said.

'Yes,' said his mother. 'We've met.'

'Yes,' said his father. 'We're here.'

'The hotel does look lovely,' said his mother.

'Well I hope you'll be comfortable,' said Jane.

'I'm sure we will,' said his mother.

'It really is lovely to meet you. We've all heard such a lot about you,' said Diana sarcastically.

'I suppose we are being a bit formal,' said his mother.

Pegasus carried their luggage upstairs. Everyone else followed.

'I hope you'll be able to come out for a drive this afternoon,' said Mrs Baines to Jane.

'I'd love to. I'm sure the hotel won't miss me for a few hours.'

'All get to know each other,' said George Baines.

After lunch as they stood beside the car and waited for Jane his mother said: 'You look tired.' He said: 'I am tired.' He had slept badly. Dreams. A sense that things were coming to a head. This was something irrevocable, introducing Jane to his parents. She was now his fiancée. The fact was being ratified by social intercourse. He had taken the plunge, or rather he had had the plunge taken for him.

'There's not a lot of her,' said his mother.

'You don't get her by the yard,' said Diana.

'It's nice to know they think so much of her,' said Pegasus to Diana.

'I've said the wrong thing,' said their mother.

'I'm afraid so, Margaret,' said their father.

'I was only wondering how strong she was,' said their mother.

'She runs a hotel perfectly adequately but cuts a pretty poor figure at weight lifting,' said Pegasus.

'I think she's very pretty anyway,' said his mother.

'Seal of approval,' said Diana.

'Sorry,' said Jane. 'Have I kept you waiting?'

Everybody jumped, wondering how much she had heard.

They set off through the lanes of Suffolk, past churches and farms, aerodromes and secret research establishments. Conversation was sticky. Pegasus longed to get these preliminaries over. What could he say that would make them all like each other? What would Peter Ustinov . . .

'We thought we might go and see your Great Great Uncle Edgar,' said his mother.

'About time we did,' said his father.

'I don't think this is a very good time for that,' said Pegasus.

'We sent a card,' said his mother.

'I didn't know you had a Great Great Uncle Edgar,' said Jane.

'He's never been to see him once,' said his mother.

'Embarrassing,' said Pegasus.

'Nonsense,' said his mother.

The old man sat in a wheelchair at his broad french windows, which overlooked his idyllic lawns, his landscaped trees and shrubs. It was a white Regency house, not huge but very elegant. E. Newton Baines had lived there for forty-five years, never visiting London. He abhorred 'the Great Wen'. He was ninety-eight now, very frail, his skin drawn so tightly across his face that it seemed about to disintegrate. All around the room were shelves lined with books he had written – books about local place-names and customs, books about local birds and animals, books about local fungi and bees.

Miss Peck, his housekeeper-cum-nurse, showed them into the big shady drawing-room and then withdrew with the martyred air of one who knew her place.

'You remember me, don't you, Great Uncle? I'm George,' said George Baines in a loud, slow voice.

'In certain villages in mid-Suffolk the word George is used to mean a feast, though I think it has almost died out now.'

'This is our daughter Diana.'

'This may simply have been due to the presence in the area of some man named George who was renowned for the feasts he gave – or possibly merely attended.'

'And this is our son Pegasus.'

'How do you do, Great Great Uncle. This is Jane, my fiancée.'

'But it could possibly be derived from the word gorge. We're going to gorge. We're going to a gorge. We're going to a george. Peck.'

The last word was shouted with truly amazing force for one so old and frail. Miss Peck entered immediately.

'The lapsang souchong and the digestive biscuits, Peck.'

There was a pause. Jane clearly felt that she must say something to show that she wasn't uncomfortable among strangers.

'I run the Goat and Thistle, and Pegasus is one of the chefs there,' she said, as loudly and as slowly as she could.

'Or alternatively it could be a form of another rare and now almost obsolete mid-Suffolk word, jorage, a hut or low shed, totally unconnected incidentally with the word garage.'

Jane didn't seem too discomfited, but Pegasus felt awful. He willed his mother not to say anything, not to continue the futile attempt at communication. Thank goodness King . . .

'We saw some lovely villages today. There were some wonderful old houses with magnificent gardens, and some splendid churches. Really the whole thing was quite a picture,' shouted his mother, leaning across towards Great Great Uncle Edgar.

'One would of course find it difficult to give immediate credence to the idea of holding feasts in a hut or low shed. Some more substantial structure is normally selected.'

Miss Peck entered with the lapsang souchong and the digestive biscuits.

'But possibly there were no substantial structures, and the villagers may have said to themselves: "It's a hut or low shed, or it's nothing". And so, our ancestor being a great trencherman, he prepared the hut or low shed for the feast or george. But that is all very hypothetical indeed, and remains in the realm of total conjecture.'

Miss Peck handed round the lapsang souchong and the digestive biscuits.

'The name Diana figures in some Norfolk verses celebrating the safe return home of a missionary of that name.

> Let us raise the joyous banner,
> Welcoming our brave Diana,
> Who went to spread the Christian faith,
> And now returns to Wroxham Staithe.
> Let us lay the festive table,
> To reward as best we're able
> She who spread the Christian faith,
> And now returns to Wroxham Staithe.

'Pegasus, eh? An unusual name for a person. More usually given to horses.' The old man leant forward in his wheelchair and fixed a sparkling eye on Pegasus. 'Engaged eh? Very good. Very good. Never you forget this. Successful marriages are made in bed. One old boy in the village used to have a recipe for a successful marriage. Four times a week, and plenty of green vegetables. Our country folk know a thing or two, you know.'

The old man laughed wheezily. Diana grinned. Pegasus looked embarrassed. Miss Peck hurriedly gave everyone a second digestive biscuit.

The old man stopped wheezing and leant forward again, conspiratorially. 'You've made an excellent choice, young man. A lovely girl. Extremely beautiful.'

'Thank you,' said Jane.

'Oh, I meant her,' said the old man, pointing at Diana.

'Some more tea?' said Miss Peck.

'Thank you,' said Mrs Baines.

Diana blushed crimson. Jane took it well. His parents looked very embarrassed. Pegasus felt that it wasn't a good start. He concentrated on looking out of the window. Bowen was standing at the window making urgent signals to him to come outside. He made angry signs to Bowen to move away, and he did so. Everyone saw his signs and he tried to turn them into a shaking of his hand.

'Cramp,' he explained.

'It must be extremely convenient to have him working as one of the chefs in your hotel,' said Great Great Uncle Edgar.

'It is,' said Jane.

'I'm glad you saw some lovely villages today, and that there were some wonderful old houses, with magnificent gardens and some splendid churches, and that really the whole thing was quite a picture. Have another digestive biscuit, Diana.'

'Oh, thank you.'

All Pegasus wanted out of life was to leave.

'See the jackdaw on the roof of the summer house. I have heard this bird referred to as the devil, the old croaker, Jack-a-mischief, and the Skrank. This last word comes from the same root as the skrangle, or curved edible toadstool pan. I . . . I'm very tired. My strength is not what it was.'

'We must leave you.'

'That *is* a good idea. Good-bye. It was nice of you to call, and I was fascinated to hear your interesting news.'

'Good-bye, Great Uncle.'

'Good-bye, Great Great Uncle.'

'Good-bye.'

Miss Peck saw them out.

'What a grand old man,' said Diana.

'Isn't he? Everyone is very attached to him,' said Miss Peck. 'He's a little tiring, of course, because he talks so much. He's afraid he'll go senile, you see, but he never will. He thinks his memory is going, but it isn't. In fact I'm afraid it's improving.'

'I'm sure he's very glad to have someone as thoughtful as you looking after him,' said Mrs Baines.

'It's a vocation,' said Miss Peck, 'like any other. Some people are schoolteachers. Others are farmers. I look after Mr Baines. I think he enjoyed your visit. There aren't many callers these days, except the vicar for his halma.'

'Well he was,' said Diana as they drove back. 'He was a grand old man.'

'Nobody said he wasn't,' said Pegasus.

Pegasus was very anxious to find out about Bowen, and to ring Paula and tell her it was all off. After work he slipped out the back way, drove down to the power station, and asked to see Mr Bowen. He was told that his shift wouldn't be on until eight o'clock the following morning.

On his way home he went to the phone box at Foxwick Cross Roads and rang Paula. His heart was thumping. He didn't know how to tell her. His legs were weak. But there was no reply. They were both out, Paula and Sue. Or she was in, ignoring the ringing of the phone. He felt a pang of jealousy.

That night, in his own bed for propriety's sake, he slept fitfully. In the middle of the night he was sent before the escape committee in Hut 14. They read his plans – the North Easterly tunnel, the sand disposal scheme, the impersonation of the Wesleyan chaplain, the escape route by barge. He glanced anxiously at their faces, the Shah of Persia (Chairman), The Nawab of Pataudi, Tom Graveney, Kings Hussein and Feisal, Peter Ustinov, Escoffier, Prince Rainier and Princess Grace. They asked why he wanted to escape. He made a slashing indictment of the whole sordid impersonal place, drab, standardized, bureaucratic, timid, dominated by usury, without values, without spirit, without hope, moving forward blindly, relentlessly, suicidally, towards nowhere. To his astonishment they didn't seem impressed. They told him he was imagining things. He mustn't take things to heart. You couldn't put back the clock. You couldn't bury your head in the sand. They treated him as if he was a child, as if he knew nothing. And they rejected his escape plans. He left the room proudly, haughtily even, and tried to work off his anger in a brisk walk round the perimeter. Light snow was falling. Over the tannoy came the critics, condemning his dream. There was no escape. He was freezing. He woke up.

His day off. A blue sky. Aching legs. A bath. Breakfast. It must be Tonio on because the toast was leathery. He excused himself after breakfast and went down to the power station.

He told the man in the guard room that he was an old friend of Mr Bowen. The man looked doubtful but Pegasus was insistent.

Mr Bowen arrived, the same man as before, a stranger, not his Bowen.

'It's you again. What the bloody hell do you think you're playing at?' said someone else's Mr Bowen.

'Are you still the only Mr Bowen working here?' said Pegasus.

'I bloody am.'

'There's been a mistake.'

'There bloody has.'

He dialled Paula's number in the phone box at the Foxwick Cross Roads. He heard it ring twice with thumping heart and then rapidly put the phone down before she answered. It was only half past ten and she found it difficult to get up in the mornings, so it would be better to try later.

191

He rejoined the family and they went out to lunch at a place recommended in the *Good Food Guide* by Elizabeth and Humphrey Penwether; Professor E. B. Blackstock; Christina Fang; Sir Roland and Lady Knightly; Monseigneur F. Branzano; F.Q. St.J.Z.; Lt.-Col. A. Whiston-Dodds; T. F. Palfrey-Underwood; and others. Pegasus felt that the Baines's were very 'and others'. As he looked round the correct, upper-crust gormandizers with their foghorn voices and complacent taste buds he felt that it was not for him. He wanted to cook wonderful food for ordinary people whose one aim in going to a restaurant was to enjoy some wonderful food.

After lunch they went back to the hotel, picked up Jane, and took her out to tea. They admired a lovely country house. They gazed at a handsome old church. They were impressed by some fine rolling parkland. Not a dovecot or gypsy caravan escaped their eyes. Nothing untoward occurred. Everything had been decided. He must get to a phone and ring Paula before she went out for the evening. He wondered who she would be going out with.

Over tea they discussed future plans.

'You'll live in the hotel, I presume,' said Mrs Baines.

They explained about Wine and Dine Ltd.

'We've got to go and see them next Wednesday, both of us,' said Pegasus.

'So we're rather in the dark,' said Jane.

Jane had been summoned for an interview at twelve and Pegasus at three. When the letters had come Jane had said: 'I don't seem to mind what happens now I've got you.'

Pegasus looked across at her, halfway through the éclair. The family had pressed her to take the éclair, and so she had, although he knew it wasn't what she wanted. That was what marriage and children and fiancées and families and middle-class English society was all about. Taking the éclair when you didn't want it. Pegasus was now a fiancé. Tired, nervy, anxious to get to a phone, but above all a fiancé. He wanted to run his hands up Jane's legs and roll her stockings down to the ankles and kiss the beautiful slender legs above the knees, slowly moving his mouth up the widening warm legs . . . he took the macaroon.

Then they drove back to the Goat and Thistle and the family set off for home. 'You'll think us very dull, but we don't keep late hours,' said George Baines.

Diana looked so reluctant to leave and be counted among the dull ones that it made Pegasus feel sad for her.

Jane and Pegasus lay side by side on her bed, their hands just touching.

'I feel done in,' she said.

'It's with nobody making a *faux pas*,' said Pegasus. 'The longer they don't make one the worse the tension gets as you wait for the first one.'

'Anyway, I liked them,' said Jane.

'Good.'

'Mine next.'

'Yes.'

She talked a little about her home. Loving, affectionate, but with a permanent hush. Never feeling quite lived in. Always tidy. Dinner at seven-thirty each evening. Tennis in the summer. Always tennis. Unable to sleep in the hot, acutely sexy youthful summers. Mental illness. Analysis. In bed with and married to Tony before you could say: 'Fifteen-love.'

She asked why he was so exceptionally tired. He told her about his dreams but not about Bowen appearing by day. This would have been a delicious moment, together on the early evening bed, if he hadn't been so eager to get away and ring Paula, and end all this anxiety once for all.

He began to undo Jane's stockings and roll them down to the ankles. There was a knock on the door.

'Who is it?'

'It's me. It's Mr and Mrs Baines.'

'What about them, Patsy?'

'There's been an accident.'

George Baines had punctured. He had swerved, hit a car which was overtaking them, and slewed to a messy halt in the hedge. Diana, sitting in the front seat, had been cut and needed six stitches. She was being detained in hospital overnight, but his mother and father were released after treatment for slight cuts and shock. A nail had been found in the punctured wheel.

31

There were 200,000 people in the huge head office of the Ministry of Exports.

'Baines,' said his individual tannoy. 'Cousin Percy wishes to speak to you.'

This was it. The moment of truth. Pegasus was head foodstuffs export co-ordinator. Under the new National Plan exports of foodstuffs were to rise by 12.3/8ths per cent per year. He had failed to achieve his target.

He set off across the huge room, past the rows upon rows of workers busy at their audioputers, laser dirigitators, sonic beam writers, directo-psychico-inventicles, extra sensory perceptiphones, and multi-lingual portable permutoscopes. But however fast he walked he seemed to get no nearer to the end of the room, where Cousin Percy sat at his controls in the little soundproof box with the glass panel.

He broke into a run. Time could be vital. As he ran he saw as if in a dream the strained white faces of the workers, Jane, Paula, Miss Besant, Mother, Tarragon, Father, Morley, Diana, Miss Besant, Brenda, Bill, Patsy, Miss Besant and thousands of others, intent upon their machines, deaf to the world. He saw their faces relax for a moment as the mid-morning subliminal coffee break was beamed to them, that voice of which they were not aware whispering suprasonically: 'You are enjoying a cup of coffee, with milk and two lumps. Gosh, you needed that. You are enjoying a cup of . . .'

He thought about the P.M.'s speech last night. It had been magnificent, his most effective yet according to the impactometer. He had said: 'Good evening. Our policy is this. More. Good night.'

Only last week Mervyn had been liquidated for failing to achieve his gherkin import target. Now it was Pegasus's turn.

His feet were unbearably heavy. They seemed to be stuck to the ground. He was running as fast as he could and getting nowhere.

On on on. He must get there quicker. His heart was hurting, jabbing him rhythmically. There was blood in his mouth. But life was good. So much to be grateful for. So many unproductive classes had been wiped out – buskers, librarians, artists, acrobats, monks . . . Twenty per cent of the population were now employed on production and forty-two per cent on planning production and eight per cent on telling everybody about production and ten per cent on telling everybody about planning production. Only twenty per cent wore the shaven heads of the unproductive, and the vast majority of them were babies and old people, who were all bald anyway. And he was letting them down. He ran on, terrified. Above him the great paper rafters passed by all too slowly. And there was blood in his mouth. Hot sweet blood.

'I do have ideas, Cousin Percy. I do have plans. Just give me one more day. Just one more day.'

He realized that he was shouting the words out loud. But no one was listening. They were all too busy.

Cousin Percy came forward towards him. He had a gun in his hand.

Pegasus closed his eyes and waited for the bullet to scud savagely into him.

'One last chance,' he murmured desperately.

He felt the gun sticking into his back.

'Move,' said Cousin Percy.

Pegasus moved. He opened his eyes, cautiously. They were walking straight towards Cousin Percy's little box.

Pegasus entered the box. There were six chairs. Five of them were occupied. Cousin Percy pushed Pegasus roughly into the sixth chair.

'Read,' said Cousin Percy.

The red light went on. Pegasus began to read what was on the paper in front of him.

'Welcome to another edition of *The Critics*. We've been to see a dream by Pegasus Baines, showing at the single bed, the third room on the right down the second floor corridor, the Goat and Thistle. This is one of a series of futuristic dreams which have obsessed this brilliant, highly perceptive and deeply sensitive young man during the last year. It is set in a huge office at the Ministry of Exports, at some unspecified future time, and deals with the modern obsession with productivity and trade figures and industrial effectiveness generally. Did you find this dream productive and effective, E. V. Aitcheson?'

'No, I didn't. I found it shallow and banal, typical of the absurdly snobbish attitude of Britain towards the realities of the industrial age. And in any case why should life become like this rather than like anything else? I don't believe it will. What for instance were those machines all those typists were using? We were just fobbed off with pseudo-scientific mish-mash. No, I'm afraid I didn't like this dream at all,' said E. V. Aitcheson.

'The question isn't "does Aitcheson believe life will become like this?" but "does Baines?"' said Terence Lister. 'Clearly at some level of unconsciousness he does. And as to being fobbed off with pseudo-scientific mish-mash, I thought that was exactly the point Baines was trying to dream – that that is just what we always are fobbed off with. This dream was surely an attempt to come to terms in his sleep with observable reality, with the collective conscious. It reminded me of some of the dreams of the avant-garde Finnish insomniacs. It really is incredibly naïve of Aitcheson to worry about whether this sort of thing will ever happen. I myself believe it will, because already we tend to regard productivity as an end in itself rather than a means of enabling more people to lead a better life. But, you know, all that is basically irrelevant. We are talking about creative truth, dream truth. We don't have to say whether this dream worked qua prediction, but whether it worked qua dream.'

'Did this work for you qua dream, Bigglesworth?' said Pegasus.

'A rattling good yarn,' said Biggles.

Pegasus woke to find himself saying out loud, 'Did you find it a rattling good yarn, Margaret Garden?'

He stretched, tried to relax his limbs, began to remember where he was. It was Wednesday morning. He was in his bedroom where he was sleeping all alone.

Jane had gone down with 'flu on Monday and so he would have to go to London alone for his interview. In a way this was convenient. It meant that he would be able to see Paula and break it off. He had telephoned her yesterday. She had been so pleased that she was going to see him.

He took a bath. It wasn't likely that they would start sniffing at him at the interview, but it was as well to take no chances.

He loved the Goat and Thistle. He hoped he wasn't destined to leave it.

'Come in.'

Pegasus entered the large, impressive, calculatedly forbidding room, designed by London's leading man at large, impressive, calculated forbiddingness.

'Sit down,' said the new personnel manager, Mr McNab, a florid Scotsman in his late fifties, with large, wasteful feet.

Pegasus sat down. On Mr McNab's left sat Mr Coggin and on his right sat Mr Prestwick.

'I'm the personnel manager,' said Mr McNab, 'and these are my two colleagues, Mr Coggin and – er – Mr Coggin.'

'Mr Prestwick,' said Mr Prestwick.

'I'm so sorry,' said Mr McNab. 'Mr Prestwick and Mr Prestwick.'

'Mr Coggin,' said Mr Coggin.

'I'm so sorry,' said Mr McNab.

'Mr Prestwick and Mr Coggin,' said Pegasus.

'Well done,' said Mr McNab. 'It's a point in your favour. I shan't forget that. I'm afraid my memory for names is not what it was. Well now, McNab, you have already been offered a job with our organization, and you have said in effect, stick it up your arse. That's not a very polite thing to say. However, we are prepared to overlook it, if in other respects . . . Perhaps you could carry on from there, Mr Baines.'

'Certainly,' said Mr Coggin.

'After all, you know more about the hotel than I do. You've been there,' said Mr McNab.

'What is your view of the gastronomic future of the Goat and Thistle, Baines?' said Mr Coggin.

'Well,' said Mr McNab, 'I suppose first of all . . .'

'Not you. Him,' said Mr Coggin.

'Well, sir, I think it could be improved,' said Pegasus. 'The menu seems to me to be very conventional, and I should have thought . . .'

'Yes. Good. Let me put an idea to you,' said Mr Coggin, leaning forward dynamically and abrasively. 'Seaside, lonely coast, what does that spell? Smuggling. Yes? Good. So we do the menu in the form of a customs declaration. Read this carefully and declare everything you intend to have. Starters. Avocado pear. Duty 6s. 6d. Does that say anything to you?'

'No.'

'Oh. Then there'd be your duty free allowance – roll and butter. A gimmick, you ask? Certainly, but an effective one. Then there'd be all sorts of special dishes – the Smuggler's Haul, the Fisherman's Catch, the Yachtsman's . . .'

'Rig.'

'I beg your pardon?'

'The Yachtsman's Rig,' said Pegasus.

'Not bad at all. Not quite right, but not bad. You've picked up the general idea. The wine would be served concealed in suitcases with false bottoms. We'd build fifteenth-century underground passages leading to the dive bars. The map of the hotel would be called "The Chart". The rooms would have some kind of nautical names, "The Sunk", "The Goodwins", I don't know, off the top of the head. But you get my drift.'

'A thought has occurred to me,' said Mr McNab. 'It may not be of any use. The word bird applies to creatures of the feathered variety, but it can also be used colloquially to refer to creatures of the human variety. But as I say it may not be of any use.'

'So there it is. Got any thoughts?' said Mr Coggin.

'No,' said Pegasus, looking fixedly at Mr Prestwick, who was screwing his face up into strange contortions and appeared to be tapping his feet in time with some music.

'Do you feel you could make a contribution to a hotel run on those lines?' said Mr McNab.

'No,' said Pegasus.

'Oh,' said Mr McNab.

'Do you intend to keep your chef Alphonse?' said Pegasus.

'Yes, we do. We're seeing him tomorrow,' said Mr McNab.

'I think you ought to know,' said Pegasus icily, 'that the man is an impostor. He's no more French than I am.'

'Just how French are you?' said Mr McNab.

'His real name is Fred Moob, he comes from Sheffield, and his references and qualifications are all forgeries.'

'What do you think of that, Prestwick?' said Mr McNab.

'People seem to take him for French, which is the main point,' said Mr Coggin. 'And as to cooking, all he'll have to do is to stick what we send down on to a hotplate and serve it up. On the whole I think it's a good thing he isn't French. He won't start having ideas above his station.'

'I agree,' said Mr McNab.

'That's all we've got time for from the Jubilee Ballroom, Amersfoort, for tonight,' said Mr Prestwick.

'But I thought your organization believed in good food,' said Pegasus.

'You want bouillabaise in Barnsley?' said Mr Coggin.

'You want moussaka in Macclesfield?' said Mr McNab.

'You want lasagne in Letchworth Garden City?' said Mr Prestwick without conviction.

'Then dine and wine at your nearest Wine and Dine house,' said all three.

'I needed that,' said Mr McNab contentedly.

'One dish at all our hotels and restaurants, selected for its alliterative quality,' said Mr Coggin. 'The rest of our menu is entirely standardized. Believe me, it pays.'

'Mr Prestwick is right,' said Mr McNab.

'The point is this, Baines,' said Mr Coggin. 'I don't myself feel, from what we've heard from you today, that there is a place for you at the new Goat and Thistle.'

'Sorry to interrupt,' said Mr McNab. 'But wasn't there something I wasn't going to forget?'

'Baines got our names right,' said Mr Coggin.

'Oh yes. So he did. It's a point in his favour. I don't want to feel that there's no place at all for him in the organization,' said Mr McNab.

'No, I agree. In fact I would have thought he'd be ideal for our research department,' said Mr Coggin.

'I don't . . .'

'Could we use him on artificial colouring research?' said Mr McNab.

'I don't . . .'

'The day is dawning when food will be coloured like clothes,' said Mr Coggin.

'Purple steaks will be "in" one year, green another,' said Mr McNab.

'I suppose you'll have fashion shows,' said Pegasus. 'Judith is eating a divine spring Wimpy in yellow and mauve stripes.'

'Might be a bit over the top,' said Mr Coggin thoughtfully. 'Good thinking, though.'

'Excellent thinking,' said Mr McNab.

'I'm afraid all this is a waste of time,' said Pegasus. 'I'm destined to be a great chef. I could never forgive myself if I failed to fulfil my destiny.'

'You can have a month's notice, McNab,' said Mr McNab.

He rang Paula. Yes, she could get off early. Everyone was in Dubrovnik. It was drizzling, he was not so far from her office, so he suggested that it wasn't worth going down to the seat.

It was a symbol of their impending separation.

They arranged to meet in a little Italian coffee bar instead. Pegasus arrived first, and ordered an espresso. It was strong and acrid and good for his nerves. He dreaded this meeting.

'I'm awfully sorry, Paula. I can't marry you after all. I've only – only got six months to live. The quack told me last night. No, they've tried that. And that. It's no use. I know you would, but I can't let you waste your youth on me. Look, Paula, I've inherited an estate in Brazil. A complete surprise. And a – a girl goes with it. I have a photograph of her. Rather blurred, I'm afraid. I – I had an accident in the kitchens yesterday, Paula. I'm afraid I wouldn't be much use to you any more. I've never told you this before, Paula old thing, but I'm involved in the secret service. They're parachuting me into China tomorrow night. I think you feel the same way about England as I do, Paula, and – Paula, I've been a bastard and I've been lying to you and I've been engaged to Jane all along and I'm sorry, Paula, and good-bye. God bless you, my love.'

I must tell the truth.

Dimly Pegasus recognized that his hold on the truth was weakening. He was worried not only about Paula. Somewhere in the back of his mind he knew that it wasn't going to be easy to persuade other people of his tremendous talents. He could see into his own mind and the superb banquets that were stored there in their full potential. All they would be able to see was the competent but inexperienced vegetable chef of a modest country hotel. They had no vision.

And then Paula was there, sitting beside him, kissing him, saying: 'Shall I take you to the Fellini? I'd like to see it with you,' and she was in no way huge and bloated, just a full-figured young woman in the first years of her juicy prime. Pegasus recalled in a great yelp of memory their many moments of pleasure together, in Italy, bed, and the National Film Theatre. He remembered the heartache of separation, the sleepless nights of jealousy and Simon hatred, the empty days, the grovelling letters, the desperate parties in the cellars of cellar-racked Hampstead, the disastrous blind-drunk dates that resulted from them, the gradual recovery, the slow fading of the all-powerful desire for such a moment as this. He remembered their mutual dislike of Visconti's films, their love of the immaculate vulgarities and baking decay of Venice, how they ate veal despite the cruelty that went into producing it, but drew the line at sucking pig because it seemed cruel to eat something so young. How they agreed on so many matters that Mervyn used to call them Paulasus. He remembered all the arguments, sudden and surprising at first, almost a new game, a variant in their love-play, how the arguments began to home on to possessiveness, how they spawned doubts and tensions, so that they suddenly realized when it was too late that what they took to be a great love affair was a maelstrom of petty hostilities, how Paula realized this first and dived frantically for calmer waters, only to be utterly becalmed in the Simon doldrums.

Paula smiled at him with her strong white teeth and he thought of Jane lying in a sick bed and he thought, I want to be out here with the strong white teeth.

'What's wrong with you?' said Paula.

'I've got to leave the job.'

'I thought that was what we wanted.'

'I was wondering how I'll go about getting another one. I haven't got the qualifications, Paula.'

'You'll be all right,' she said.

'Two espressos,' he said.

'Your hand's shaking,' she said.

He put it where it wanted to go and where it wouldn't shake.

'Not here,' she said.

He moved the hand a little further up her leg by way of protest.

'You can be quite puritanical at times,' he said.

'It's all hypocrisy anyway.'

He removed his hand from her leg.

'Why is it all hypocrisy?' he said.

'You feel free to do it because it's Italian. You wouldn't do it in the Chicken Inn.'

'I wouldn't do it in Italy either.'

'Well there you are then.'

The espressos arrived. Pick me ups on a drizzly afternoon in damp, exotic Soho, grey and impotent.

'By the way, oughtn't we to be getting a ring?' said Paula.

'I suppose we ought. I'm afraid I'm not very good at things like that.'

'I saw one I liked, actually, just round the corner. Fifteen pounds. Is that too much?'

The financial position was getting a bit desperate but what could he do? After all, fair's fair.

'Let's go and get it,' he said.

32

The next day Pegasus went round to Rose Lodge to see Brenda. She seemed quite calm, but the blotchiness around her neck was well pronounced.

'I've just heard,' he said.

'Come in,' said Brenda.

The cottage was oppressive with sadness. Pegasus had forgotten how small it was, and just how oppressive it had always been, behind all those roses.

'There's some brandy,' said Brenda. 'It's for medicinal purposes. I've had some already.'

Pegasus fetched the brandy. There wasn't much left. He poured some for Brenda.

'You have some too.'

'No, thanks.'

'I'd rather you had some as well. It'll make it more sort of normal.'

'All right.'

He poured himself a small amount of brandy.

'Thank you for coming,' said Brenda.

'Jane would have come but she's got the 'flu.'

'You love her, don't you?'

'Yes, I do.'

He felt a little ashamed of it. He always felt ashamed of telling a pretty woman that he loved another.

He almost said 'cheers' which would have been a bit of a faux pas. He didn't know how to begin.

'Are you cold?' she asked.

'A little.'

'Let's have the electric fire.'

The room was a fraction less depressing with the fire on.

'I knew he was up to something,' said Brenda, and it was as if she was helping him out of his quandary, when it should have been he helping her out of hers. 'He was often out late. I don't know how, but I could always tell when Bill was lying. There was something sort of furtive.'

He nodded, waiting, not wanting to seem to encourage or discourage.

She saw this and said: 'I want to tell you all about it. It'll do me good.'

'If you're sure.'

'It was on Saturday night. Bill was out and I was listening to the play, and I got restless. I thought of popping over to the bar or to the Magnet and Cowslip. But Bill used to see red if I went out like that when he was out, and he disapproved of drinking. And he'd been almost impossible since Johnny died. I was terrified of him.'

'I, you know, never realized.'

'So anyway I thought it had better be just a walk. I walked up Bassett's Lane alongside the estate. Then I heard Bill's car and I don't know why, but I didn't want to be seen, so I went down this track there is there. He went on past and then I heard him stop. I knew where it must be. There's an old hut up there that they use, they keep a lot of broody hens up there and put pheasants' eggs under them in the summer. So I thought, what's he doing there at this time of night. Anyway I went straight off home because I thought it would be better if I got home before he did. I was definitely sort of suspicious. I knew it was to do with those late nights of his.'

She paused, with a sigh. Pegasus poured out the remainder of the brandy for her and this time she didn't notice that he wasn't giving himself any.

'Bill soon came back. I said: "Where've you been?" He said:

"Saxmundham. There's a chap over there has these films about hawking. Very interesting." I kept quiet. Well then yesterday Bill had to go to Ipswich, and I knew he'd be gone most of the day, so I went up to the hut. It was locked. Anyway I was sort of sure there was something wrong, and there was no one about, so I broke the window and climbed in. There was this box of nails but it didn't seem to click at first because I mean it wasn't so impossible that there should be nails there. Then of course I realized what a lot of nails there were and they were really the only things it could have been. And I thought, my God, the punctures. The police had called everywhere, you know, asking had anybody seen anything.'

'Yes.'

'I think perhaps I half knew already without realizing it, and that was why I went to such lengths as breaking the window. Anyway I went home and I waited for him. He didn't get back till about half past seven. He said: "What's for supper?" I said: "Nothing." I said: "I've been too worried, Bill. I saw those nails." I said: "It was you, wasn't it, with all those punctures?" He said: "Yes." There was a sort of look in his eyes. I just froze when I saw it. He got quite angry. They killed our child, and didn't stop. He would revenge himself. A life for a life. He stood there with that strange look. He looked half smug and he said it again: "A life for a life." I said, that's no way to go on, we're Christians. It sounded silly. We haven't been to church for two years, except for the funeral. But I meant it. I mean you go on being a Christian underneath and then it comes to the surface and you realize you just are one. He said the child had been his life and he wouldn't rest until justice had been done. I said, how was it justice when it might be a complete stranger who died? He said it would be justice, whoever died would be guilty, of something else if not of that. I said he must stop. "I'm still your wife, Bill," I said, "and I won't ever tell if you stop. It'll be past history." He refused. "A life for a life," he kept saying. He said he would go out then and there. He worked himself up into a state. So I said: "Well, Bill, I'll have to tell the police. It's my duty." '

'You were very brave.'

'I was frightened. But he was very calm and said I was quite right, he could see that from my point of view it was my duty just as from his point of view it was his to do what he was doing. So I went to the police and they thanked me, they were very nice, gave me a cup of tea, and took down everything I said. They knew it had started again but this time they were keeping it quiet. Lulling the suspicions. He must have been pretty careful, never to have been caught. Anyway eventually we got back home, I don't know what charge they could have brought in a case like that, but there he was. He'd shot himself through the head and he'd left a note saying: "A life for a life". That's all there is to it.'

'I'm sorry,' he said, inadequately.

'Did I do enough for him? Could I have prevented it after Johnny died?' she asked.

'I don't see how. It wouldn't have been easy.'

'No. To be honest, the boy had been an obsession all along. Bill was very proud. I think he saw himself in the boy, which seemed all wrong to me. And then he was killed and then when you came along, well, I don't need to tell you. And then you left and I was left alone with him. You didn't even come back to see us once.'

'No. I know.'

'I quite understand. You were glad to be out of this madhouse. It was nothing to do with you.'

'I wish I had, though.'

'The real sadness for me is in the past. I lived through it slowly, day by day. In a way it's a relief to me that it's over. I'll go away and begin again. I've still got most of my looks. I'm not the sort that goes to seed.'

'Poor old Brenda.'

Pegasus saw himself in a flash, sitting on the edge of women's lives, saying 'poor old . . .', and most of the time he himself responsible, but not this time, not very, just thoughtless and unobservant and stupid.

'Will you help me, Pegasus?'

'Of course. What?'

'Help me move those books and toys.'

'Yes, of course.'

'The past is the past.'

They worked quickly. It only took a few minutes. Brenda was obviously glad not to have to do it alone. Pegasus was careful not to let their bodies touch. In a few minutes the room was stripped of its personal effects and several years of intense living were as if they had never been.

Then it was done. Brenda held out her hand and said: 'Thank you for coming.'

'Will you be all right?'

'Yes.'

He squeezed her hand and then let the hand drop.

'I'm not coming any more to work at the hotel. They'll understand,' said Brenda.

Later Pegasus rang Paula and he told her about it all and he told her how you thought of yourself sitting there listening sympathetically, even as the story was told you were conscious of your own sympathy.

'You can't be anyone but you,' said Paula.

'Even now I'm thinking and talking about myself,' said Pegasus.

'Then shut up,' said Paula. So he did, and they talked of other things.

Later he went to see Jane. The room smelt of minor illness, he found himself lacking in sympathy. He thought, but did not say, some people have real troubles, all you have is 'flu, but we're expected to treat you like an invalid. He was uneasy in the presence of illness. Sometimes it brought out his affection, to protect someone with his strength. Sometimes as now it made him feel a little contemptuous. He wanted to be with Paula. He told

Jane the full details of Brenda's story and also of his disastrous interview with Wine and Dine, which he had intended to keep from her so that she wouldn't worry too much about her own interview.

Then he went into the dark wet autumn night and told himself that he didn't like himself. But he couldn't summon up the intensity of self-disgust that he wanted.

He walked towards Rose Lodge, thinking about Brenda, alone, the house dark, the roses tapping, the radio droning on irrelevantly, the disc jockeys obscenely cheerful. He turned back before Rose Lodge.

He couldn't get to sleep for quite a while that night. He thought of Brenda lying there, he could remember the individual tap of every rose against every window on a night like this.

A few yards away Jane was sweating the germs out. Up in London Paula was asleep.

I saw it all from my angle, of course. He thought back over his stay at Rose Lodge, trying to remember how it had been between Brenda and Bill. But then he had been behind a Biggles book, shutting them out. There had been the forced gaiety. Mervyn, even more peripheral, being himself. Then he had had lunch with Brenda, and afterwards she had said it was nice of him to have pretended. Then he had gone and he had never returned to see them.

Then he fell asleep. They droned on at a height of 30,000 feet, and he was comforted to see the planes of Biggles and Algy to the right of him.

It was only six days since the P.M. had told a grave and expectant nation: 'We are at war.'

There had been a moment's silence. Algy had been the first to speak.

'At last,' he had blurted out impulsively.

'It's difficult to feel hatred. They're ordinary chaps just like us,' Biggles had mused quietly.

A grin had spread over Ginger's face.

'I can't wait to have another crack at the Boche,' he had averred avidly.

'The Boche are on our side this time,' Biggles had returned evenly.

Pegasus had felt only a sense of tragic futility.

He had been impressed, like everyone else, when man had controlled the weather. No more floods, no more savage gales. A few clashes between minor bodies like the water board and the M.C.C. but nothing more. Tremendous prospects for international co-operation. And then the triumph at Geneva. World disarmament at last. Commemorative disarmament stamps, designed by a chimpanzee. Jumbo-sized steaks at the Royal Aero Club, fireworks over the river, huge crowds all down the Mall, boisterous but good-humoured, happy and delirious in the balmy London night.

And now here they were, in the thick of the First World Weather War. Already Coventry and Plymouth had been badly flooded, Swansea wiped out by a freak tornado. The Low Countries were in the grip of a freeze more savage than anything in their long history. People were dying in their thousands, ships wouldn't move, birds froze to death on the open sea.

Pegasus had seen it coming and had joined 266 Blizzard Squadron four days before the outbreak of war. Now he was a veteran already.

500 planes were going in that night. The aim – to cripple China with the biggest snowfall in her history, to sweep the snow into huge drifts in the streets and villages, to smother the paddy fields and destroy the livelihood of millions.

He saw Biggles gesture towards the earth. He looked down. There far below them were the angry rain clouds, in a long line as far as the eye could see, pouring forth their vicious cargo on to the sodden fields of Europe.

The warm front!

The clouds parted for a moment, to reveal the muddy fields and swollen rivers of no-man's-land. Those tiny specks standing out of the flood waters must be towns and villages, deserted and lifeless now.

Then the clouds rolled back again, the plane was buffeted in savage pockets of air, they were over the cold front.

Enemy territory! The very air seemed colder, the very vapours more hostile, the very clouds more threatening.

The headwinds were getting stronger, slowing them down to a mere 2,400 m.p.h. The turbulence was increasing all the time. Pegasus had never known such a storm. The enemy had clearly flung all their resources into it.

'Climb. 50,000 feet.'

The enemy would be waiting, in the clear air beyond the clouds, ready to pounce on the 500 British planes. Could they climb above the cloud ceiling in time? It would be touch and go.

He turned to see how 'Smiler' Cheeseman was getting on, but he had disappeared. That was odd.

Now they were at 50,000 feet and still in thick cloud. God, what a storm.

'70,000.'

She would climb all right on the automatic pilot. He struggled through the bucking, tossing cockpit. Outside the wind was howling, fierce, man-made, a terrifying sound. The plane seemed a mere toy in its hands. It was inconceivable that it could survive.

A flash of lightning lit up the whole cabin and shone on the body of 'Smiler' Cheeseman, swinging gently on a rope in the middle of the room, a ghastly grimace on his naturally cheerful Cockney face.

Darkness again. Pegasus stumbled forward. The plane seemed to fall bodily, slap into an open fist, and then be tossed up into the storm again like a frail racing pigeon.

By the next flash of lightning Pegasus saw a note on the floor below 'Smiler'. He bent down to read it.

The writing was shaky but the words could be made out quite clearly.

'A life for a life,' they said.

33

Pegasus walked down towards the marsh in the early morning and sat on the edge of the heath looking out over the reeds and mud. Out there, one day was very much like another, and he was envious of that.

Yesterday he had hated working in the kitchens, seeing Alphonse so smug after his interview, so Gallic and courteous to him although he must have known that it was Pegasus who had told Wine and Dine that he was really Fred Moob. He hadn't said anything. What good would it do?

That night alone, wanting to sleep with Jane, 'flu or no 'flu, he had lain between sleep and wakefulness, visited by Bowen, either in sleep or wakefulness. Frightened. Now he had to start being a great chef – and he didn't know how to take the first steps.

The sun was rising. It seemed to Pegasus to be without warmth, but the earth was steaming. Under its thin crust it was boiling. He couldn't help wanting to move to a firmer piece of ground, although he knew it was ridiculous.

The power station was very three-dimensional, very stark, very disturbing, its edges so sharp it almost cut the eyes to look at them. Pegasus wanted to see Mr Bowen and say: 'You have told me twice that you're the only Mr Bowen here, haven't you?' but it would be no use, he'd only want to go back and say: 'You have told me three times that you're the only Mr Bowen here, haven't you?'

It was eleven years since he had last prayed and he hadn't any very clear idea how to go about it.

He knelt carefully on the earth's fragile crust.

'Oh God,' he said, 'whatever my humble part in your Grand Design, show me how to find it. I know you want me to be a chef, but how should I begin? And is it to be Jane or Paula? Amen. Oh, and please stop the Vietnam War.'

He walked on across the dykes, more confident now that he had prayed. And he decided what he must do. He must give a dinner party of his own. A showcase for the trade. When? As soon as possible. Where? At home. It was the only kitchen he had access to.

He drove into Aldeburgh and walked on the beach until the shops opened. Then he bought the invitation cards. He ordered an enormous breakfast in an hotel and began to write the cards.

After breakfast he rang his mother. Oh dear, what a shame. Still, he wasn't the first person ever to lose his job. To have resigned, then. No, of course there was a difference. Was he still sure he was doing the right thing? There was no need to raise his voice. What? Yes, it was a very good idea. Well, what about next Saturday? Morley might be able to come as well if he made it a Saturday. No, no, if he wanted to invite one or two members of the catering trade, that was up to him. It was his party, after all, although it would have been nice if it had just been the family.

He felt impatient all day at work, impatient in the evening visiting Jane, who was on the mend. He didn't tell her about the dinner party, as he wasn't quite sure whether to invite her.

At last he was free to finish off the invitations. He invited all the leading culinary journalists, a representative of Trust Houses, the managers of the Mirabelle, the Caprice and the Savoy, representatives of every other hotel group and catering organization he could think of, and Mr Prestwick, Mr McNab and Mr Coggin.

It would be embarrassing if every single one of them accepted, but on the law of averages he thought this unlikely.

Sunday
Sunday in the Cotswolds. A large gathering for lunch. At one end of the table, his father, deaf and withdrawn. At the other end

his mother, talkative and dominant. Between them the family. Parsley, pregnant already and feeling sick; her husband, unnerved by this, as if no one had ever felt sick in pregnancy before; Basil, who never changed; Basil's angular wife, ditto; Basil's five children, noisy, hungry, with their arms in splints. Family jokes. Tarragon didn't feel in the mood for family jokes.

He had begun to write a letter to Alphonse. It began: 'The game is up, Moob.' After that he had got stuck. He wasn't used to writing to blackmailers.

Trying to write the letter depressed him. He didn't want to think about the Goat and Thistle any more. He loved that woman more than he had ever loved anyone, even the woman who walked down Wimpole Street and lived in Ongar with nice legs. It was proving to be a depressing week-end.

The Stilton dragged on and on. The children were excused. Parsley was excused. Her husband fluttered after her, an anxious butterfly. Lunch was being whittled down. It was over.

Tarragon went for a brief walk round the garden, but there were children everywhere. He decided that as soon as his meal had been worked off he would have a bath. You could see the horse chestnuts dimly through the frosted glass, and listen to the birds singing. He liked afternoon baths at the Clumpery.

'The game is up, Moob. Cease your . . .' Jane. At the window. Shaven armpits. Black stubble. Nuthatches nesting in the copse. 'The game is up, Moob. There is no further use . . .' Perhaps he didn't really want any more than to hide in copses and watch. Perhaps marriage would only have been a substitute for the real thing.

He climbed the stairs, looking forward to his bath. It was no use worrying over what might have been. He should be thankful at least that he was no longer in Alphonse's clutches. 'The game is up, Moob. You . . .'

He went into the bathroom eagerly. It was full of one of Basil's children. He had cut his knee open. There was blood all over the bath.

Monday

Shortly after nine in the evening Pegasus had a phone call, which he was forced to take in the lobby.

'Hullo, Pegasus. It's Cousin Percy here.'

'Oh, hullo.'

'My old friend Tarragon Clump rang me today.'

'Oh.'

'You may well say "oh". He told me rather an interesting story, which he seemed to think you had promised to tell me. He seemed to think you were engaged to a Mrs Jane Hassett, land-lady of the Goat and Thistle.'

'Well?'

'Well are you?'

'Er – no.'

'That's a relief. Because I talked to a Miss Paula Bancroft last week, and she seemed to think you were engaged to her.'

'She's right.'

'You're not engaged to this Hassett woman?'

'No.'

'Then I wonder why Tarragon thought you were.'

'He's got hold of the wrong end of the stick.'

'I rang your family, because I was a little bit confused. I didn't ask anything directly, but I did gather that they thought you were engaged to this Hassett woman too. Have they got hold of the wrong end of the stick as well?'

'It seems like it.'

'I suppose they rashly deduced this, simply because you intro-duced her to them as your fiancée, did they?'

'Well, the thing is, I – I was engaged to Jane, and then I broke it off and got engaged to Paula instead. Only I didn't tell Jane. I funked it. You know how these things are.'

'No, I don't.'

'Anyway I have explained it to Jane now. It's all sorted out.'

'I see. Why are you talking so quietly? Are you afraid of being overheard?'

'I'm not talking quietly.'

'You sound as if you are to me.'

'There must be something wrong with the line.'

What Pegasus had dreaded happened. Jane came through the lobby on her way upstairs to bed. She made 'Who is it?' signs. She looked pale and delectable. Pegasus smiled at her. She waited for him. He was terrified.

'Well I'm very relieved to hear all this,' said Cousin Percy.

'I love her very, very much,' said Pegasus. He blew Jane a kiss. She responded in like manner. If only she'd go away. 'We've got a very nice ring. Fifteen pounds.'

'Good. By the way, I understand from your parents that you're giving a little dinner party on Saturday night. Your début as a chef.'

'Yes.'

'Am I invited?'

'Of course. I'll be very offended if you don't come.'

He smiled at Jane. She smiled back. If only she'd go away.

'I presume you've invited Paula?'

'I haven't actually yet. I will do of course.'

'Of course. Well, I'm reassured by all this, Pegasus.'

'Good.'

'Good-bye, then, till Saturday.'

'Good-bye.'

Pegasus put the phone down with a feeling of vast relief. Which he mustn't show.

'Who was that?' said Jane.

'Cousin Percy.'

'Oh, the horoscope man.'

'Yes.'

They were on their way upstairs to her room.

'He asked me if he could come to our wedding. I said I'd be very offended if he didn't. I hope you don't mind.'

'Of course not.'

Pegasus kissed her on her cold cheek.

216

'How are you feeling?'

'All right. A bit tired.'

He helped her to take off her dress. She looked childlike without it.

'I rang Wine and Dine this afternoon. I'm going up on Thursday,' she said.

'I wish you luck.'

He helped her with the difficult task of taking off her stockings.

'You must conserve your strength,' he said. Then he went on: 'By the way, the real reason why Cousin Percy rang was because he wants me to go up and see him at the week-end. He'd heard about my leaving the job and he said he had an idea that might help.'

'That sounds promising.'

'He wants me to meet a friend of his for lunch on Saturday. I'll probably go home afterwards if that's all right and then come down on Sunday morning. It's not really my day off, but does it matter?'

'I suppose not, now.'

'Are you sure you don't mind not coming? I mean I thought it would be best if I went alone to discuss this business. And it'll all be very boring.'

'You don't have to apologize.'

'I mean you're most welcome to come if you want to.'

Jane laughed. Pegasus continued to help her undress. The aftereffects of 'flu are notorious.

Tuesday

'I'm giving a little dinner party at home on Saturday. It's my début as a chef. Can you come?' said Pegasus.

'I'd love to. And it's about time I met your parents,' said Paula.

Wednesday

'Paula seems quite a nice girl,' said Cousin Percy over the brandy. 'I'd hate to see her hurt.'

'Mrs Hassett has always seemed perfectly pleasant to me,' said Tarragon.

'I'm going to have dinner at the Uxbridge residence of the Baines family on Saturday, and I have reason to believe that Paula will be there.'

'You sound like a policeman,' said Tarragon.

'I feel like a policeman,' said Cousin Percy. 'Now Pegasus will presumably present Paula as his fiancée. What we really need to know is whether at that time Mrs Hassett, serving beer in the Goat and Thistle, also believes herself to be his fiancée. I suppose you couldn't go down there, Tarragon?'

'I suppose I could. It's a long way, but . . . Why are you smiling?'

'Was I?'

'I could go down there and . . .'

'And say "Excuse me, Mrs Hassett, but are you still engaged to Pegasus Baines?"'

'I could easily find out.'

'If she's no longer engaged to Pegasus, that's the end of the matter. But if she is then something has to be done,' said Cousin Percy. 'We can't let those two poor girls be fooled any longer.'

'No. It would be unthinkable.'

'I would have thought the obvious thing to do, if it was possible, would be to get Mrs Hassett up to London on Saturday night on some pretext or other. Bring them face to face and let them find out for themselves. Are you any good at pretexts?'

'I tried my first one the other day, in Sheffield. It was a success.'

'Good. Well, let's hope that if needed you succeed again.'

'It's odd. He seems quite a nice chap.'

'I'd always thought he was.'

'Can't you tell what's going to happen, Percy?'

'The stars aren't strong enough.'

Cousin Percy raised his glass.

'To your second pretext.'

'To my second pretext.'

'Are you feeling better, Mrs Coggin?' said Mr McNab.

'Yes, I'm much better thank you,' said Jane.

'Have you lost any weight?' said Mr McNab.

'No, I don't think so.'

'So by nature you're on the slim side?' said Mr Coggin.

'I suppose so.'

'We don't mean anything personal,' said Mr Prestwick.

'Far from it,' said Mr McNab.

'Nobody looking at you would say: "Good God, that woman is as thin as a rake",' said Mr Coggin.

'You're nothing like as thin as a rake,' said Mr McNab.

'I wouldn't even dream of calling you thin, except in so far as I'd be even less likely to dream of calling you fat,' said Mr Coggin.

'Exactly,' said Mr McNab.

'It's just that for the Goat and Thistle we had something altogether fatter in mind,' said Mr Coggin.

'We regard you as efficient and capable,' said Mr Prestwick.

'But thin,' said Mr Coggin.

'Slender,' said Mr McNab.

'Thin for our purposes,' said Mr Coggin. 'The point is . . .' But at that moment he was interrupted by a stupendous burst of sneezing from Mr McNab. 'Damn. Three o'clock.'

They waited. At last the sneezes died down.

'Mr McNab is allergic to the closing of the National Provincial Bank in Bury St Edmunds,' said Mr Coggin. 'Look, Mrs Hassett, to be brutally frank, I'm afraid you aren't the sort of person we see as the landlady of one of our hotels.' He leant forward abrasively, dynamically. 'We're going to play up the smuggling angle. Give it a bit of style. What we need is someone fat with three chins and a great booming voice, and a parrot, and a monocle. A personality. We could fix you up with the parrot and the monocle, but not with bulk.'

'Character, A.1. Bulk, not quite so satisfactory,' said Mr. McNab with a kindly smile.

'We're awfully sorry,' said Mr Prestwick.

Friday

Tarragon stood under a plane tree in the dark unlighted side-road, waiting to intercept Alphonse on his way home from the hotel. He had no intention of depositing two hundred pounds in an old Peak Frean biscuit tin buried in the sand two feet below a tuft of marram grass three quarters of the way down the western slope of the eleventh sand dune south of the south-eastern corner of the bird sanctuary.

Shortly before nine-thirty Alphonse turned the corner and walked briskly up the road towards his house. Tarragon accosted him.

'The game is up, Moob,' he said.

Alphonse shrank away, startled, but soon regained his composure.

'What do you mean? Which game?' he said.

'Your name is Fred Moob.'

'What is this foul incinerations? Am I taking leave of your senses?' said Alphonse.

'You live at 46, Tadcaster Road, Sheffield.'

Alphonse turned away from Tarragon to walk on towards his house. Tarragon held him firmly with his right arm.

'The game is up, Moob,' he said.

Alphonse stared at Tarragon coldly for a few moments.

'Piss off,' he said.

'If you don't cease your demands this instant, Moob, I shall tell your employers of your deception,' said Tarragon.

'They already know.'

'What?'

'Some bastard told them. It wasn't you, was it?'

'No, it wasn't.'

'Just as well for you. Now get out of t'bloody road.'

Alphonse tried to shake himself free, but Tarragon held on.

'I can still make you look pretty foolish. This makes no difference. The game is up, Moob,' he said.

Alphonse brought his free right hand down on Tarragon's arm with a fierce blow that almost paralysed it. Tarragon let go. Alphonse pushed him backwards and he fell awkwardly against the plane tree.

Alphonse walked on to his front gate. Then he turned and spoke quietly, in his French accent.

'The eleventh sand dune,' he said. 'Do not forget.'

Tarragon walked slowly back to the hotel, surprised to find how confident he felt. After a humiliating encounter with one's blackmailer under a plane tree, a saloon bar holds no terrors.

The bar was crowded, but he found a seat which gave him a good view of Jane. He felt as if he had returned from the dead, never having expected to see the Goat and Thistle again, or Jane's green eyes and curved nostrils and straight, black hair. He was only there in spirit, and he was seeing for the first time what she was like when he wasn't watching her. Perhaps there was an evil side to her nature which she had previously hidden, perhaps her conversation consisted entirely of cruel jokes about him, or perhaps she didn't exist except in his desire.

He saw enough to reassure himself on that score. He loved her. If Pegasus had broken it off with her, he would marry her, and tell her all about the blackmail, and be free.

After closing time he stayed on until they were alone.

'I was sorry to hear of your bad news,' he said.

'Oh, thank you. Yes, it was a bit of a blow,' she said.

Pegasus had broken off the engagement. She was free. She was his.

'He seemed so nice, too.'

'Who?'

'Well, er, Pegasus.'

She seemed perplexed by this remark. 'We're going to be married, you know,' she said.

'No, I didn't, er, you know, know. No. Well, congratulations. Jolly good. Yes. Well, here's to you.'

He drank to their future happiness, wondering now what her bad news was.

'When you spoke about my bad news, you meant Pegasus having to leave, did you?'

'Yes, that's right.' Goodness knows what she's talking about.

'I thought you meant me.'

'You?'

'I went to see Wine and Dine yesterday. I've got to leave as well.'

'Oh, I'm sorry.'

She told him about the plans for the Goat and Thistle. He grimaced and offered her a drink, but she said: 'No, please, have one on Wine and Dine.'

They sat over their brandies, one each side of the wet beery counter.

'I was making a success of this place. I'd built up goodwill. Hadn't I?'

'I'm sure you had. With me, at any rate.'

She put her hand in his, in thanks. He thought, please, Tarragon, don't explode, but at the same time he saw how distant he was from her, that she could unselfconsciously put her hand in his with no thought of anything but thanks.

She made him drink more brandy. He was a volcano full of love and brandy. He hoped he wouldn't erupt.

'Where's Pegasus now?' he asked.

'Oh, he's gone home. He's got an important interview tomorrow with some people who may be able to help us.'

She was being deceived. He began to prepare his pretext. Nothing violent. No unnecessary pain.

'Oh, there you are. Pegasus rang earlier but I couldn't find you,' he would begin. 'They're having a party tonight, and he'd love you to go. He asked me as well. I could drive you there. Do let's go. This place can look after itself. And Pegasus will be awfully disappointed if you don't go.'

She would think for a moment and then she would say: 'All right. I'll come.'

'Good.'

'What?' she said.

'I didn't say anything,' he said.

'You said "good",' she said.

'Did I? How odd. Yes, odd's the . . .'

He had stopped himself in time!

'Odd's the . . .' he said to himself experimentally and again he was able to stop himself in time.

'Could I have another brandy?' he said.

34

In the train Morley Baines was trying to catch up with his work. He was a slow worker, and he was behind hand. This trip to London was a nuisance, but although they had become so distant he was still very fond of Pegasus. And admiring, too, because Morley had an inferiority complex where his brother was concerned, believing Pegasus to be made of lighter, more delicate material altogether.

'Come off it, Alderman Pooley. That is my honest advice to this self-appointed keeper of the city's morals.'

Pegasus would be in a bit of a stew about this dinner. Morley himself was beginning to feel the tension as the train wriggled between the wet Midland towns.

'No decent citizen can fail to be appalled by the revelations that have come to light in the Plugden Street Orgy Case. It is disgraceful that these drug-taking sex orgies should be allowed to take place in our city. It is intolerable that members of a women's institute returning from an angling expedition should be molested by so-called students and publicly subjected to an indecent psychedelic happening in a corporation bus station.'

He should have visited Pegasus. It was an awkward journey without a car – Pegasus thought him a dullard not to have bought a car – but he should have gone.

'But – and it is an enormous but – no good can come out of exaggeration. Alderman Pooley blames our schools, our repertory theatre, our cinemas, even this newspaper, for their part in encouraging a decline in youthful morals.'

Perhaps Pegasus really was a good cook. He hoped so. My God, he hoped so.

'What dangerous rubbish! Less than 200 young people have been involved in these "goings-on", yet Alderman Pooley tars every young person in the city with the same self-righteous brush.'

Of course in theory one had to oppose anyone's decision to opt out of a scientific career for one of less value to the nation in an increasingly competitive age. But how did you apply this in an individual case? Pegasus was blatantly unsuited temperamentally – and he hadn't chosen his temperament, remember – to a life of biological research. In theory you had to oppose, but in fact Morley envied Pegasus.

'The truth is that the vast majority of our young people are better citizens than their parents ever were. A new frank, unhypocritical generation has sprung up – and their elders and so-called betters are jealous of them.'

Morley would make up for his recent neglect. Their youthful love and understanding would be reborn.

At 23, Grimsdike Crescent, all was bustle. Pegasus had been extremely disappointed at the response to his invitations. It seemed that he had chosen a particularly inconvenient evening for the Mirabelle, the Caprice, the Savoy, Trust Houses and culinary journalists. The acceptances consisted only of Mr Prestwick and Mr McNab, and a Miss Murchison, the representative of Gourmet Guest Houses, Ltd, a sedate organization devoted to providing good food in an atmosphere of the utmost gentility. But he was getting over these disappointments as the day wore on and the big occasion drew near.

The table was laid for nine – his mother and father, Morley, Diana, Cousin Percy, Paula (Oh God), Mr Prestwick, Mr McNab and Miss Murchison. Pegasus himself would not eat at the table. This was his début not as a host but as a professional chef. The table seemed slightly on the small side for nine even when the extra wing had been brought into play, so that perhaps it was just as well that there had been a few refusals.

Dinner was timed for 8 p.m. Place cards had been arranged by Diana, who with Mrs Baines would assume responsibility for the serving. George Baines had prepared a list of conversational gambits to be kept in reserve in case of need. Cutlery was of the Scandinavian style and place mats depicted country scenes of exceptional loveliness. Correct glasses for the Berncasteler Doktor and the Chassagne Montrachet had been hired.

In the centre of the table there was a menu card. On it was typed:

Menu
Soup Baines
Hake Baines
Hare Baines
Apple Baines

In the kitchen the ingredients were piled up on all sides and attractively laid out charts aided Pegasus in the complicated business of timing his first ever meal. The soup and the hare were already in the process of creation, and all was going well. What should bubble had bubbled. Where a certain light browning had been expected, a certain light browning had occurred. This was his vocation. This was the sort of work for which human beings had been made.

Morley arrived at 5.43 and George Baines returned from the office at 6.20. The immediate family was complete.

At 6.40 George Baines broached a bottle of sherry, to calm everyone's nerves. This was the moment that Pegasus had dreaded, the moment of explanation. He joined them in the lounge.

'Have a drink, old chap,' said his father.

'Well, just one,' said Pegasus. 'I don't want to blunt my faculties.'

'Quite right,' said his father.

'I've something to tell you all,' said Pegasus.

Morley smiled encouragingly, warmly, with good resolution.

'The thing is,' said Pegasus, 'that I've broken it off with Jane.'

George Baines, caught in mid-sip, spilt some of his sherry on to the carpet.

'Oh dear, I am sorry,' said Margaret Baines.

'But what happened?' said Morley.

'You seemed so happy,' said his mother.

'You looked a perfect couple,' said Diana.

'This is no time for sarcasm,' said Morley.

'I wasn't being sarcastic. I meant it. But every time I say anything that isn't typical of mindless decadent youth I get accused of being sarcastic. You people force teenagers into becoming what they are,' said Diana.

'May I resume?' said Pegasus.

'Sorry,' said Diana.

'How did it happen?' said their father.

'I – after you'd gone I got to, you know, thinking. You seemed a little upset about my marrying a divorcee.'

'Rubbish,' said his father.

'That was before we met her,' said his mother. 'We thought she'd be somebody flashy and flighty.'

'We rather took to her,' said his father.

'It's not you who'd be marrying her,' said Pegasus.

'But you were so happy,' said Diana.

'I thought so, but I wasn't really,' said Pegasus. 'I thought afterwards, do I really love her? Isn't there a risk of what happened once happening again? After all, I never heard the other side of the story.'

'I don't believe you'd ever think like that,' said Morley.

'I'm telling you what I thought,' said Pegasus. 'I just didn't feel I could go through with it any more.'

'This is what comes of meddling. You should have let him lead his own life,' said Morley to his parents.

'It's none of your business, Morley,' said Pegasus.

'I'm your brother. If I think people are poking their noses into your private life, that's my business.'

'What did they say, anyway?' said Diana.

'They didn't say anything. I just gathered their attitude from mother's voice over the phone,' said Pegasus.

'I really am awfully sorry,' said their mother. 'I never meant . . .'

'It wasn't you. It was me,' said Pegasus. 'Honestly. You set me thinking, that was all.'

'Better have another drink, old chap,' said their father.

Pegasus accepted the offer.

'I've something else to tell you,' he said. 'You know this girl Paula that Cousin Percy's bringing. Well . . .'

'I was very glad he was bringing someone. I've wondered about him sometimes,' said their mother.

'She's my fiancée,' he said.

George Baines spilt some more of his sherry on to the carpet.

'You seem to be becoming quite a lad,' said Diana.

'Congratulations,' said Morley with a show of warmth which reminded Pegasus of something which he decided later in the kitchen was a man who refused to admit that he was about to be seasick.

'I don't like to seem a wet blanket, but isn't it rather sudden?' said their father.

'Not really. She's a girl I've known for some time,' said Pegasus.

'Oh, is she the one . . .' Morley stopped abruptly, remembering that the incident he was about to describe was not known by the rest of the family.

'Yes,' said Pegasus.

'I feel awful about this,' said their mother.

'Please, mother, there's no need to. This would have happened anyway,' said Pegasus.

'I hope so,' said their mother.

'I've known Paula for years. I'd, you know, taken her for granted, I suppose.'

'She'd become part of the scenery,' said Diana.

'Shut up,' said Morley.

'She'd become part of the scenery,' said Pegasus.

'Well, I just hope it works out, and . . .' Pegasus knew that if his father had continued the sentence he would have said 'that you'll both be very happy'.

'That goes for me too,' said their mother.

'Paula doesn't know about this other engagement,' said Pegasus.

'Well, here's to you,' said Morley.

They drank to him, fervently, with good resolution.

'I'd better be getting back to my kitchen,' said Pegasus, and he did so.

'*His* kitchen,' said George Baines.

'I hope those stains come out,' said his wife Margaret.

Shortly before half past seven Cousin Percy arrived with Paula.

'We're very pleased to meet you, Paula,' said George Baines.

'We hope you'll both be very happy,' said his wife Margaret.

Pegasus came out of the kitchen to greet the new arrivals. He kissed Paula on her bright red lipsticked lips. Her fair hair burnt brightly in that otherwise dark assembly.

'How's it going?' said Paula.

'It'll be all right on the night,' said Pegasus.

Nobody else was allowed in the kitchen. It was a secret place. Pegasus was now forecasting a twelve minute delay but apart from that all was well.

Miss Murchison arrived at 7.40. She was a quiet middle-aged Scotswoman with grey hair. She looked as if she owned and was wearing a small wool shop.

Over their sherry Cousin Percy and George Baines chatted.

'Well, Percy, how's the world?'

'Not so bad, George. How's the weather business?'

'Mustn't grumble, Percy. Any ideas about next year?'

'A natural disaster in central France.'

'Below average temperatures.'

'A rail accident in Scotland.'

'Severe spring frosts.'

Morley was left with the women.

'I'm surrounded by women. Lucky old me,' he said, and to his utter astonishment everybody laughed. In fact they laughed at everything he said, so to save everybody embarrassment he went on talking, and he thought, if I live to be a hundred I may never again get the laughs as easily as this.

At five past eight Mr McNab's car arrived, bringing Mr McNab and Mr Prestwick. They were late due to Mr McNab's insistence that they were aiming for 23, Tadcaster Road, West Drayton, an address which luckily did not exist.

At 8.23 the company sat down to dinner in a state of considerable tension. Pegasus entered with a handsome tureen of steaming soup. He was wearing a chef's hat and was smiling confidently.

'What a handsome tureen,' said Miss Murchison.

'Of steaming soup,' said Mr Prestwick.

'Soup Baines,' announced George Baines, reading from the menu card.

'What exactly is Soup Baines?' asked Cousin Percy.

'Parsnip soup,' said Pegasus.

'I once had an excellent parsnip soup in Berwickshire,' said Miss Murchison.

'Let's hope this one is as good,' said Cousin Percy.

'But that was before the war,' said Miss Murchison.

Pegasus returned to the kitchen to complete the next course. The soup was handed round and everyone began eating.

'Jolly hot,' said Diana.

'Isn't it?' said Paula.

'Jolly hot,' said George Baines.

'I like my soup to be hot, I must say,' said Margaret Baines.

There was a rhythmic consumption of soup.

'I must congratulate you on your table mats,' said Mr Prestwick.

'Salt, please,' said Mr McNab.

'Cotswold scene on mine. Chipping Camden unless I'm very much mistaken,' said Mr Prestwick.

'Could I have the salt, please?' said Cousin Percy.

'Mine is of the Cheddar Gorge.'

'Thank you.'

'It's become very touristy, the Cheddar Gorge.'

'The only other time I've had parsnip soup was in Berwickshire.'

'So many places have.'

'Could I have the pepper please?'

'But that was before the war.'

'We like Winchcombe as much as anywhere.'

'The North Wales Coast has been ruined.'

'So many places have.'

'It's an overpopulated island, after all.'

'That's just the trouble,' said Diana. 'But nobody does anything about it. They're all so greedy, *they* can have babies but nobody else should.'

'There are certain religious views which make matters more complicated than that,' said Cousin Percy.

'That's stupid. Religion's for solving things, not making them worse,' said Diana.

'Diana does have a point. An important issue like that, without solving which none of the world's problems can be solved, and on which we certainly ought to give a lead if we have any real claim to be a moral leader, stands no chance of being officially considered in this country because it's not a political issue. That's the great weakness of democracy. It is geared to producing entirely political measures, which are just the kind of measures this country almost invariably doesn't want,' said Morley.

'You can't change human nature,' said Margaret Baines.

'Pepper, please,' said Mr McNab.

'Would anybody like any more?' said Margaret Baines.

'I'd love some,' said Miss Murchison. 'But I don't think I could finish it. I'm not used to big meals.'

'Delicious, but I'm going to keep room for what's to come,' said Mr Prestwick.

'Me too,' said Paula.

'Good idea,' said George Baines.

Diana and Margaret Baines cleared away the things.

'You could tell it was made with real parsnips,' said George Baines.

In the kitchen Pegasus said: 'But there's half of it left.'

'We all want to leave room for what's to come,' said Diana.

'We aren't used to big meals,' said their mother.

'But I'm not ready yet.'

'We can work up an appetite.'

'Wasn't it nice?' said Pegasus.

'Lovely,' said Diana and Margaret Baines.

There followed a ten minute delay, during which the Berncasteler Doktor was sampled and pronounced excellent.

'What do you think of the political situation?' said George Baines.

'What do you think of this Frank Sinatra fellow?' said Mr McNab.

'He's a wonderful singer,' said Paula.

'I didn't know he sang,' said Mr McNab.

'Well of course he does.'

'He may be a good singer, but he's a very bad president,' said Mr McNab.

'My mat's nice,' said Paula. 'Salisbury Cathedral.'

'We love Salisbury,' said Margaret Baines.

'I must confess a preference, rather a heretical one perhaps, for Exeter,' said Miss Murchison.

'Who was it who said "the taboos of yesterday are the banalities of tomorrow"?' said George Baines.

'Ely takes some beating,' said Mr McNab.

'Prophesy something, Cousin Percy,' said Morley.

'Yes, tell our fortunes,' said Diana.

'I don't want to know mine,' said Miss Murchison.

'I don't mix business with pleasure,' said Cousin Percy.

'Ah!' said George Baines.

The cause of this interjection was the arrival of Pegasus, bearing a large dish piled high with food.

'Hake Baines,' said Miss Murchison, reading the menu.

'What exactly is Hake Baines?' said Mr Prestwick.

'Hake with rhubarb,' said Pegasus.

Margaret Baines divided out the Hake Baines as fairly as she could. Glasses were topped up where necessary. Pegasus returned to the kitchen. Another bout of eating began.

'Do you think some form of censorship is inevitable?' said George Baines.

'No,' said Diana.

'Yes,' said Morley.

'Salt, please,' said Mr McNab.

'I do like your cutlery,' said Paula.

'Yes, isn't it nice? The Scandinavians have such a flair where knives and forks are concerned,' said Miss Murchison.

'What charming curtains,' said Cousin Percy.

'Oh, do you like them?'

'Very much.'

'I wonder if the Common Market will be a success.'

'We need a political union and economic freedom. So we get an economic union and political freedom.'

'Oh come come.'

'We must function in ever larger units if we're to survive.'

'The continental Sunday would be a good thing.'

'In Europe they go to church and then behave all day as if they hadn't. In England we don't go to church and then behave all day as if we had.'

'I forget. Is it hypocrisy, homosexuality or bronchitis that is called the English vice?'

'This is Wensleydale on my mat, unless I'm very much mistaken.'

'Wensleydale is our favourite of all the dales.'

'I don't think I can finish this,' said Mr McNab.

'Not if there's more to come,' said George Baines.

'We'd better leave a bit of room,' said Paula.

'I'm not used to large meals.'

This time Paula helped Diana and Margaret Baines to clear away the things.

In the kitchen Pegasus said: 'But they've hardly touched it. Wasn't it all right?'

'You gave us rather a lot,' said his mother.

'We want to be able to enjoy the next course,' said Paula.

'It was nice, wasn't it?'

'Delicious,' said Paula, and Diana, and Margaret Baines.

'I don't think the Hare Baines is quite ready,' said Pegasus. 'I thought you'd be longer.'

'That's all right. We're having a simply lovely conversation, and the wine is absolutely super,' said his mother.

'Paula?'

At his request Paula remained in the kitchen when the others left.

'Aren't they enjoying it?'

'Of course they are.'

'Are you?'

'Of course I am.'

'I had some. It was delicious.'

'Of course it was.'

'Kiss me.'

233

They kissed.

'Thank you.'

'I'd better go back.'

'I love you.'

'I love you too.'

Paula rejoined the company, where the Burgundy was now being served.

'This wine is lovely,' said Mrs Baines. 'Can I have some more?'

'I think we ought to wait for the food,' said Morley.

'Absolute rubbish,' said Mrs Baines. 'I want some more.'

'All these discoveries of scrolls and things are really a bit of a poser for the church,' said George Baines.

'I want some more wine.'

'Later, mother, later.'

'Mother's tight. She's pissed,' said Diana.

'Is your school interesting?' said Paula.

'No,' said Diana.

'My job is to make sure we don't employ any Jews,' said Mr McNab.

'I didn't think you got that sort of prejudice in your line of country,' said Morley.

'The Jews are very nice people,' said Mr McNab 'Some of my best friends are Jews, present company excepted. But we just can't employ them. It's not prejudice. It's just that they might refuse to cook the pork chops, and then we'd be up the spout.'

'I want some more wine.'

Mr Prestwick leant across the table to Diana.

'What do you think of the band?' he said.

'I don't get you,' said Diana.

'Not with it enough for you, eh?'

'I'm not with you.'

'I say!'

The reason for this exclamation was the arrival of Pegasus with a huge silver casserole containing the steaming Hare Baines. Mrs

Baines began to serve it out in a rather glazed kind of way while Pegasus fetched the accompanying vegetables.

When Pegasus returned Cousin Percy leant forward to read the menu.

'Hare Baines,' he said.

'What exactly is Hare Murchison?' said Mr McNab.

'Hare braised in honey and grated chocolate, stuffed with oysters wrapped in seaweed, and served on a bed of bananas and pimentos, with boiled potatoes and curried pumpkin,' said Pegasus.

Silence fell on the assembly. The meat and its contents were divided, the accompaniments added, the plates passed round. The whole company watched as if mesmerized.

When everyone had been served there was a moment's delay. Pegasus was standing by the door, watching them.

At last George Baines took up his knife and fork and cut himself a portion of the hare. Everyone else did the same. Nine forks rose slowly towards nine mouths, nine mouths opened reluctantly, nine hands hesitated involuntarily and then moved on. Nine portions of Hare Baines were chewed in nine mouths, were swallowed down nine throats. No one spoke. The first two courses seemed, on reflection, to have belonged to an Arcadian age. Pegasus watched them, hope dying, his lower lip quivering, his eyes expressing his astonishment.

'I must see to my Apple Baines,' he mumbled.

Paula half rose to follow him, but didn't.

'I don't know if any of you have much to do with computers,' said George Baines. 'They're pretty useful instruments.'

It was a shame that most of his family were too drunk to appreciate his courage.

'Very useful,' said Paula.

Nine forks rose towards nine mouths, nine mouths came down to meet them, nine sets of jaws chewed, nine people swallowed.

'It could be pretty awful if one of them broke down,' said George Baines.

Mr McNab pushed his plate away.

'Full up,' he said.

'I think I'd better stop too if I'm to leave room for what's to come,' said Miss Murchison.

'My appetite isn't what it was,' said George Baines.

'I think we ought to clear the air and admit that this thing is totally and utterly inedible,' said Cousin Percy.

'I'm afraid so,' said Paula.

'Poor old Pegasus,' said Diana.

The tension slipped away from them, and with it went life. They flopped in their places like a beaten boat race crew. Intoxication was a muzzy, swirling, bloated sickness. Conversation was inconceivable. And there was still Apple Baines to come.

'Excuse me,' said George Baines, rushing from the room, and despite closed doors the distant sound of retching could be clearly heard. Margaret Baines turned green and left the room also, muttering something about seeing how her husband was.

Paula and Diana began to clear the things away.

Mr Prestwick turned towards Cousin Percy and whispered: 'I like these old songs.'

'What old songs?'

'These ones.'

'Have some more wine. We may as well enjoy something.'

Mr McNab fell asleep and began to snore very loudly. Miss Murchison sat still and hunched-up in her warm clothes like a petrified rabbit.

When he saw how little Hare Baines people had eaten Pegasus turned quite white.

'I'm afraid the Hare Baines didn't really work,' said Diana.

'It's not everyone likes oysters,' said Paula.

'Or grated chocolate,' said Diana.

'Or seaweed,' said Paula.

'The soup and the hake were fine,' said Diana.

'I think you've been a little over-ambitious for a first time,' said Paula.

'I'm ahead of my time. People aren't ready for me yet. They don't understand what I'm trying to do,' said Pegasus.

Paula and Diana began to pile up the uneaten portions of Hare Baines and wrap them in pages of the *Sunday Times* Colour Supplement. Some of the pages were about the Russian Revolution, and the others told you how to make and decorate your own patio. They worked rhythmically, mechanically, without spirit. Pegasus watched them without seeming to see them.

'I'd better get on with the Apple Baines,' said Pegasus.

Paula and Diana looked at each other.

'I'm sorry, but I think we ought to scrub the Apple Baines,' said Diana.

'But . . .'

'It'd be best.'

'I'm no good. No good at all,' said Pegasus.

The doorbell rang.

'I'll go,' shouted George Baines, who was coming downstairs, feeling slightly better now.

He went to the door. Pegasus came from the kitchen to see who it was. Cousin Percy came to the door of the dining-room. Through the open door Mr McNab's snores could be heard. Miss Murchison sat with a fixed smile on her face and Mr Prestwick's feet were faintly tapping, tapping.

George Baines opened the door. Tarragon and Jane were standing in the porch. Jane was smiling but Tarragon looked acutely uncomfortable. Tarragon had a bottle of Spanish Burgundy and Jane was wearing a mauve trouser suit with bell-bottoms. As soon as the door was opened her smile began to look a little uneasy.

If turning white had been a little more spectacular to watch Pegasus would have been assured of a career in a circus.

'We've brought a bottle,' said Jane uncertainly.

Behind Pegasus Diana closed her eyes in horror and Paula looked at her in surprise.

'Well, er, come in,' said George Baines, regaining his powers of speech.

'Didn't Pegasus tell you we were coming?' said Jane.

'Er . . .'

'What are you doing here?' said Pegasus.

'You invited us,' said Jane.

'Oh no. It can't be,' said Paula.

Margaret Baines came down the stairs looking white now rather than green. When she saw Jane she stumbled and almost fell. George Baines rushed to the stairs to support her and she finished the journey safely. She was staring at Jane as if in a dream.

Tarragon, looking foolish, stepped forward and handed her the bottle of Spanish Burgundy. She gazed at it without comprehension and said, 'Thank you. Very nice.'

'You invited us to a party,' said Jane.

'What party? There is no party,' said Pegasus.

'Good pretext,' said Cousin Percy.

'I hope you haven't come to make a scene,' said Mrs Baines.

'We sympathize, but there's nothing we can do,' said George Baines.

'Will someone tell me what's happened?' said Jane. 'Can you explain?' she said to Tarragon, who looked at Pegasus. Jane, following his gaze, noticed Paula properly for the first time. 'Who are you?' she asked.

Pegasus, who had been leaning against the wall, slid slowly down it on to the floor. Jane rushed forward towards him. So did Paula.

The two women stood over the body of Pegasus and looked at each other.

'You're Jane?' said Paula.

'Yes. Are you . . . ?'

'Yes. I'm Paula.'

'Why are you here?'

'I'm his fiancée.'

'I rather thought I was.'

They looked down at the inert body of Pegasus. The others

went back into the dining-room at the frantic instigation of Cousin Percy. All except Diana.

'Come on, Diana,' said Cousin Percy.

Diana looked at Jane and Paula in astonishment.

'Aren't you going to scratch each other's eyes out?' she said.

'Come on, Diana,' said Cousin Percy.

Paula and Jane began to slap Pegasus lightly on the cheeks.

'Well, we've met,' said Paula.

'Yes,' said Jane.

'Trust him to faint and leave it all to us,' said Paula.

Pegasus moaned and began to come round. He looked up at them, and memory came flooding back. He sat up against the wall.

'Where's everybody?' he asked.

Paula's eyes filled with tears. Jane's did not.

'What's that awful smell?' said Jane.

'Apple Baines,' said Paula.

Pegasus slid slowly down the wall again and collapsed inert on the floor. Paula hurried upstairs, where she could break down unobserved. Jane stood looking at Pegasus, her legs apart, her shoulders hunched awkwardly.

She turned towards the front door and walked over towards it. She paused to tap the barometer. She went over to the umbrella stand and picked up an umbrella.

Cousin Percy, peering discreetly round the dining-room door, saw Jane swinging the umbrella lazily, even elegantly, in a seemingly idle manner.

'Where's Paula?' he asked.

'Upstairs.'

Cousin Percy went upstairs. Half-way up he stopped.

'Tarragon's in there,' he said, pointing towards the dining-room. Jane shrugged.

Soon everyone began to depart. Paula, the worst of her facial damage repaired, went off with Cousin Percy. Tarragon and Jane set off on the long trek back to Suffolk. Miss Murchison disappeared off the face of the earth whence she had come, and Mr McNab and Mr Prestwick returned to their empty flats. Only the immediate family remained.

'God, that smell,' said Diana.

Margaret Baines switched off the oven in which lay the charred remains of the Apple Baines.

'Poor old Pegasus,' said Diana.

'He carried out his instructions very efficiently,' said George Baines, looking at the charts. 'It's just that he gave himself such bad instructions in the first place.'

'Where is he?' said Morley.

He had been so central to everyone's thoughts that none of them had realized that he had gone.

'His car's gone,' said Diana.

There was nothing they could do. They washed up and disposed of the enormous pile of left-overs. Pegasus did not return.

'He's probably just gone back to the hotel,' said Diana.

'I expect he wants to be alone,' said Morley.

It was one o'clock before they went to bed. And even then none of them slept at first, although there had been a special issue of sleeping pills.

Diana was the first to drop off, round about two.

'Get some sleep, dear,' said George Baines. 'There's nothing we can do.'

'I suppose he can look after himself.'

'Darling,' said George Baines's voice in the dark with a kind of wonder at the sentiments it was expressing, 'I love you.'

'Oh, I love you too, George.'

And all that had been over long ago, thought George Baines.

Shortly before three George Baines began to snore. Margaret Baines listened to the snoring hypnotically, and then could hear it no more.

By 3.30 Grimsdike Crescent was quiet and dark, except for one light, in an upstairs room at number 23. There a solemn young man sat up in his dressing gown, writing.

'Well spoken, Alderman Pooley,' wrote that solemn young man. 'How refreshing it is to find someone who is not blinded to the truth about our city's young people.

'The Plugden Street Orgy Case is merely the repulsive tip of a huge iceberg of youthful decadence. It is good to know that some at least of the City Councillors are not blinded by the half-baked theories of the pseudo-humanists.

'What our city's children need is not greater freedom, and a more liberal atmosphere, but a harsh municipal smack on their spoilt, over-affluent bottoms.'

'Bottoms,' said the solemn young man out loud.

35

Four cars drove away from 23, Grimsdike Crescent. In all four cars there were long periods of silence, broken only by the swishing hum of the wipers on the wet windscreen.

Pegasus drove fast, but with care. He drove straight through the centre of London. A confusion of thoughts passed through his head. Sometimes he thought, the meal was terrific, they have no appreciation of originality, I am years ahead of my time. Sometimes he thought the meal was awful, he had no ability whatsoever. He felt angry and from time to time he muttered to himself. Once or twice he shouted angrily, but his language moderate even then : 'Blast you all.' At times there were tears close to the surface, hard to tell whether it was tears in his eyes or rain on the windscreen. Sometimes he was apologetic and ashamed, sometimes proud and defiant.

He thought of Jane and Paula. They both knew now. Perhaps

one of them would forgive, and he would marry her. It didn't in the slightest matter which one. Or perhaps they would both forgive, and what would he do then? Perhaps neither would forgive. And then he would think, whether they forgive or not, it makes no difference. All that had reached its resolution, had been worked to its end. What came next would have to be something fresh. Very fresh. And anyway there was nothing to forgive. He had done nothing wrong. It was no sin to be teeming with love.

Anyway it was out of his hands now.

'God, thank you for making me teeming with love. Help me to place that love at the disposal of thy Grand Design. Show me how to use it,' he said.

'God, I have done nothing wrong, so why haven't things worked out? Show me my path,' he said, and: 'Oh God, forgive me. Help me.'

He was on the A.12, never having decided on such a course. He was being directed, increasingly, and at speeds of sixty-five, seventy, seventy-five, rather excessive for his old car. He was vaguely conscious of his surprise at finding that the Almighty did not observe the speed limit. But there were no police cars around, the Almighty knew that, that was where the advantage of being omniscient came in. Seventy-five, eighty, eighty-five.

Mr McNab drove slowly, carefully, as he always did when he had had too much to drink.

'I think we were right not to give him a job as a chef,' he said.

Mr Prestwick made no reply. His feet were tapping gently, tap tap tapping, in time to the music of Stig Aggersund and the Malmo String Octet.

Cousin Percy drove with refined expertise towards Paula's flat.

'Your little plan has worked out fine, hasn't it?' said Paula.

'What do you mean?'

'You and that doctor, you had it all worked out.'

'For your own good, Paula. You were being deceived.'

'Well it was my fault, wasn't it, for trying to go back to him? But you can't make allowances, can you? Oh no, you have to blow the whole thing sky high. I suppose you have a nice warm feeling of moral justification.'

'That doesn't come into it.'

'He might have made his mind up in the end, mightn't he? And in my favour. Who can tell?'

'I was just thinking of you, Paula.'

'Or can't you tell? I thought you were supposed to be able to see into the future.'

'I couldn't just stand by and see you hurt.'

'So you joined in and saw me hurt instead.'

'You're being very unfair, Paula.'

'Please. Do you mind if we just drive on in silence, Cousin Percy?'

Tarragon Clump drove fast, but without any greater recklessness than usual. Jane Hassett asked him why he had done it, why he had bothered, why all the lies. He said: 'We were cruel only to be kind.' She snorted and said no more. She remained unnaturally still, staring straight ahead at the line of the wet road.

Shortly after Ingatestone Tarragon Clump said tremulously: 'I did it because I love you.'

She said: 'Please.'

Tarragon said: 'Ever since I first came to the hotel . . .'

She said: 'Don't.'

He said: 'But I must . . .'

She said: 'Please, Mr Clump, be quiet.'

The rain poured down steadily, the noise of the engine purred on, time stood still, but space didn't.

Paula began to sob. The tears streamed down her face. Cousin Percy put an arm across towards her and then withdrew it again. It might be thought of not as a gesture of sympathy but as an attempt to take advantage of her in a moment of weakness. Indeed he himself didn't know which it was.

'We're here,' he said, pulling up outside Paula's flat.

'I'm sorry,' said Paula.

'Are you sure you'll be all right?'

'Yes. Don't come in.'

'Good night, then, Paula.'

'Good night, Percy.'

Mr McNab refused to come in for a cup of coffee and when Mr Prestwick saw the dirty uncleared mess of his flat, he was glad.

He undressed and went to bed, trying to get comfortable in the lumpy, badly-made bed. He could hear the sweet tones of Jan Mortensen and his Stavanger Players. The music was pleasant, relaxing, refreshing. He was on the verge of falling asleep, drowsy, warm, a cave of rhythmic warmth easing the tension and dropping dropping dropping warmly into the bowels of sleep, and then the music was interrupted by a road works report. 'Here is a warning for motorists in the Stavanger area. Due to a collapsed trench on the road between Stavanger and Haugesund . . .'

He sat upright and switched on the light. He put his hands to his ears and told himself : 'You are not a wireless set. You are not a wireless set. You are not a wireless set.'

And because he wasn't a wireless set he found it impossible to switch himself off.

Pegasus was directed to Rose Lodge. The rain had stopped, there were glimpses of the moon between the swift clouds. Trees stood out jagged and disturbing. As he passed through the gate, he felt that his toes would be spreadeagled on the gate, his skin would be torn as two of the toes went to the wrong side of the gate, but this didn't happen.

He banged hard on the door. Nothing happened. He banged again. Brenda opened her bedroom window and called down : 'Who's there?'

'It's me – Pegasus.'

'What on earth are you doing?'

'Can I come in?'

A few moments later the door was opened.

'Are you all right?' said Brenda.

'Yes, I'm all right. Are you?'

'Yes, I am.'

'Good.'

'Why on earth did you call at this hour?' said Brenda. 'It's three o'clock.'

'I didn't know,' said Pegasus.

'Has something happened?'

'You look beautiful, Brenda.'

'Are you drunk? You don't look it.'

'I'm not drunk.'

'Would you like some coffee?'

'Will you marry me, Brenda?'

Brenda stared at him in astonishment.

'Me? Why? Is this a joke?'

'Of course it isn't,' he said angrily.

'Do you love me?' said Brenda.

'Well, it isn't exactly that.'

'You pity me, is that it?'

'No, it's not that either.'

'Well what is it, then?'

'It's our destiny, Brenda.'

Brenda gave him a questioning glance.

'I'm in God's hands, Brenda. He steered me here. I gave myself to him, and I was pulled here. He wants us to get married, Brenda.'

'You're serious, aren't you?'

'Of course I am. A lot of things have happened, Brenda. Some of them may have seemed just chance at the time. It's hard to say this, but even your son's death, even Bill's suicide, they were meant to happen. What we've got to do is to learn from them, Brenda.'

'I'll get you a cup of coffee.'

'I would like some coffee actually.'

Brenda busied herself at the stove. Pegasus, worn out after the events of the day, fell asleep.

'Ah, there you are, sir,' said Bowen.

'It's you, Bowen,' said Pegasus.

'I know that, sir.'

'Good. Good. Was there anything else, Bowen?'

'Yes, sir. The Supremo wants to see you. He's in the fragmentation chamber.'

Pegasus hurried. You didn't keep the Supremo waiting.

Sir Percy Baines sat at a makeshift desk which had been erected for him in the middle of the circular steel fragmentation chamber.

'Sit down, Baines,' said Sir Percy.

Pegasus sat down. You didn't disobey the Supremo.

'I've studied your record,' said Sir Percy, 'and I'm afraid I can't give you permission to die.'

'Oh, but sir . . .'

'Why exactly are you so anxious to die?'

'It's all this eternal life, sir. I've had enough of it.'

'But eternal life is man's greatest achievement, the perpetuation not only of the species, which any wretched animal can do, but of himself.'

'Perhaps it would be different if we grew old, sir. I've been in my prime now for a hundred and thirty years, and it's wearing me out,' said Pegasus.

'Why haven't you had yourself murdered, then?'

'I can't make enemies, sir.'

'It's not always easy to face the truth about oneself, Baines. But I have to say this. You're a good worker. A fine patriot. A model husband. I'm afraid we shall need you for ever. The week-end is a very good time for sporting activities and you should consider a business proposition very seriously. Next, please.'

Pegasus hurried from the power station, passing through the bar on his way.

'A dull first act,' commented E. V. Aitcheson.

So, there was more to come. Well, thought Pegasus, I'll give them something to make them sit up. Something in the Supremo's words had given him an idea.

He walked purposefully up the drive of Pegasus Towers. Flack opened the door.

'Morning, Flack,' he said.

He went into his study, selected his favourite gun, patted his favourite retriever on the head, admired with proprietary satisfaction his famed collection of antlers, and summoned up his resolution.

He entered the small drawing-room.

'Hullo, dear,' said Jane and Paula. 'Did you have a good day at the office?'

They came forward to embrace him. He was conscious of the warmth of their affections and the depth of his love. But he must do what he had set out to do. He fired five times. There were two shrieks, two gasps, their bodies fell all over him, blood was everywhere, his clothes were covered in sweet, sticky blood. He looked down at his wives with love, pity, sorrow, remorse, cool resolution and horror. He took the gun back to his study, patted his favourite retriever on the head, and walked out through the hall of Pegasus Towers, down the avenue of limes, through the wrought iron gates, over the hump bridge, and into the nuclear power station. His way led through the bar.

'Needless sensationalism,' said E. V. Aitcheson.

He knocked on the door of the fragmentation chamber.

'Come in,' said Sir Percy.

He went in. You didn't disobey the Supremo.

'Sit down,' said Sir Percy.

He sat down.

'I've killed my wives. I'm no longer a good citizen, sir,' he said. 'Please may I die now?'

'No.'

'But sir, I'm base and wicked.'

247

'We aren't so easily fooled, Baines. You're a brilliant, public-spirited citizen. You wouldn't harm a fly,' said Sir Percy.

Pegasus was almost blinded by the fierce light on the desk, which was shining straight into his eyes – a typical ploy of the Supremo. But he wasn't going to be put off.

'It's just as base and wicked to kill people in order to seem base and wicked as it is to kill them because one actually is base and wicked,' he said.

Sir Percy pushed the light further over towards Pegasus. 'Good point,' he said. He stared at Pegasus sternly. 'You have committed a vicious and appalling crime. I sentence you to live for ever, as a deterrent to others,' he said.

Pegasus woke up, to find that the sun was pouring in on his face. He leapt to his feet.

'Where am I?' he said.

'Rose Lodge,' said Brenda. 'I'm making some breakfast.'

There was indeed a succulent smell of bacon and eggs.

'That smells good,' he said.

Brenda smiled.

In the bathroom he washed his face and his hands, and rubbed the water into his eyes with his fingers. It took him back, the bathroom. It brought on a pang of inexplicable nostalgia.

He went downstairs again. Brenda smiled at him, a little anxiously.

'Better?' she asked.

'Than what?'

'Than nothing,' she said.

'My word, I'm hungry,' he said.

Over a huge plate of bacon and eggs Pegasus said: 'You refused to marry me last night.'

Brenda looked serious.

'I know,' she said.

Pegasus told her the whole story of Jane and Paula.

'I've caused a great deal of misery, whether I was to blame for it or not. Atonement comes next.'

'So you want to marry me, in atonement?'

'Not exactly. I mean that sounds as though I wouldn't enjoy it.'

'Have some more toast.'

'Thank you. I'd enjoy it very much, Brenda. It's too soon to say that I love you. That will come. Love is something that ripens slowly. Our love will ripen slowly. All I can say at the moment is that I like you, and you need me.'

'Why do I need you?' said Brenda.

'Because of what's happened.'

'But I don't love you.'

'Not yet, no. You couldn't be expected to,' said Pegasus. 'You don't have to decide on the spot, you know. Could I have some more coffee?'

'Of course. I have decided. I could never love you.'

'You can never say that, until you try.'

'It isn't something you try.'

'But you like me, don't you?'

'Quite. Only quite. You're selfish and inconsiderate,' said Brenda.

'Yes, but . . .'

'I'm going home. I'm going to start a new life,' said Brenda, handing him his coffee.

'Yes, but . . .'

'I'm still quite young. I carry my years fairly well. I'm not a hopeless case.'

'But, damn it, Brenda, I've driven all the way down here in the pouring rain to get married to you.'

'Then you can drive all the way back again. That'll be your atonement,' said Brenda.

'What the hell's the use of a Grand Design if people won't co-operate in it?'

'Have some more toast.'

'Thank you. This is a terrific breakfast, Brenda.'

'It's partly my fault. I made that suggestion to you once.'

'That's got nothing to do with it.'

'I was desperate. You don't realize at the time what things are going to mean later on,' said Brenda.

Pegasus ate in silence for a moment. Then he spoke again.

'All right. Let's accept that you don't need me. Let's look at it from my point of view. I need you,' he said.

'You don't need me. You need a doctor,' said Brenda.

36

Paula married Cousin Percy on February 16th. They had the reception at a hotel just outside Loughborough. They were quite surprised that Pegasus accepted the invitation. They hadn't known whether they ought to invite him, but in the end they had decided to ask all the family, and they had all come.

Pegasus was looking thinner and paler. He drank only orange juice.

'Are you sure you won't have any champagne, love?' Paula asked him.

'Honestly, I'd rather not,' he said.

'How are you?' she said.

'I'm all right,' he said.

The room was crowded. Jane and Tarragon were there too, somewhere. Pegasus hadn't managed to talk to them yet. He had heard his father say: 'It's not a very nice day for it, and the shame of it is that tomorrow is going to be lovely.'

'Tell me what happened,' he said.

'There isn't really anything to tell. I was very fed up, sitting there all on my own in Punic Films, moping. Percy rang me up and asked me out to dinner. I thought, there's no harm in that. Over dinner he said I ought to go away somewhere for a few days.

A change of environment will bring new business and personal interests, he said. The week-end is a good time for travel, and a chance meeting will bring social opportunities which you would do well not to neglect. So I invented an illness, everyone was in Stockholm anyway, took a few days off, and went to Venice. I met Percy in St Mark's Square.'

'It was all a fiddle,' said Pegasus.

'How could I have known she was going to Venice?' said Cousin Percy, appearing out of nowhere.

'You are aware of her love for Venice. Where else would she go?'

'I love all sorts of places,' said Paula.

'You love Venice above all.'

'How was I to know she'd be in St Mark's Square?' said Cousin Percy.

'Everyone in Venice goes to St Mark's Square sooner or later,' said Pegasus. 'Anyway, what were you doing in Venice?'

'My horoscope persuaded me to go.'

'What did it say?'

'A change of environment will bring new business and personal interests. The week-end is a good time for travel, and a chance meeting will bring social opportunities which you would do well not to neglect,' said Cousin Percy.

'But why Venice?'

'I had a commission to do some Venetian scenery some time, so it was the obvious place to go.'

That was true, and Pegasus knew it.

'Where do the new business interests come in?' said Pegasus.

'I'm his secretary,' said Paula.

'I give up,' said Pegasus.

'Are you sure you won't have some champagne?' said Cousin Percy.

'I'd rather not,' said Pegasus. 'By the way, thank you very much for inviting me. It's a lovely wedding, absolutely lovely.'

'Thank you.'

Cousin Percy was dragged off by a Paula relative.

'I just want to say how sorry I am,' said Pegasus.

'What about?' said Paula.

'Everything,' said Pegasus.

His father passed by.

'Bearing up, old chap?' he said.

'Thanks.'

'There are Jane and Tarragon,' said Pegasus. 'I must say hullo.'

He wandered across to them.

'Hullo,' he said.

'Hullo,' said Jane.

'Congratulations,' he said.

They murmured their thanks.

'I hope you'll come to the wedding,' said Jane.

'I'd love to,' he said.

'We went down to the Goat and Thistle,' said Tarragon.

'Ghastly,' said Jane. 'It made me very sad.'

'I can't say I'm surprised,' said Pegasus, and to Tarragon he said: 'Your fiancée looks exceptionally beautiful today.'

Jane smiled, with wide eyes.

'Excuse me a moment,' said Tarragon.

Jane touched Pegasus lightly on the hand.

'Well?' she asked.

'I'm all right.'

'What are you doing?' she asked.

'I've got a typing job.'

'Oh.'

Paula joined them.

'Hullo again. You really are looking exceptionally beautiful today,' said Pegasus.

'It's good to see him again, isn't it?' said Paula.

'Very,' said Jane.

'I'd just like to say how very very sorry I am about everything,' said Pegasus.

'Pegasus has got a typing job,' said Jane.

'Are you enjoying it?' said Paula.

'I can't say I am,' said Pegasus.

'What do you think you'll do after that?'

'I think I'll carry on with it,' said Pegasus.

'He's looking very well, isn't he?' said Paula.

'Yes,' said Jane.

'I mean it. I really am deeply sorry.'

'I wish you weren't,' said Jane.

'The past is the past,' said Jane.

'Paula,' called Cousin Percy. She obeyed his command.

'And how are you,' said Jane, 'in yourself?'

'All right. So what are you doing now?'

'We're going to get a hotel. Tarragon's giving up his work.'

'Oh.'

'You don't approve?'

'I didn't say that.'

'So you really are all right?'

'Yes.'

'And you don't have those dreams any more?'

'What dreams?'

'Jane,' called Tarragon, and she obeyed his command.

As she walked away Pegasus said: 'Honestly, I mean it. I am very very sorry. About everything.'

Diana, bursting into womanhood, was a centre of attraction. Morley and Pegasus had a brief chat, across their negotiated frontier. Pegasus met his father again, and his father said: 'Doing all right?' and Pegasus said: 'Yes. Doing all right.' He discussed the wedding with his mother, and they agreed it was delightful. The other guests did not talk to Pegasus. In a gathering where there is champagne nobody makes a beeline for the one person who is drinking orange squash.

Pegasus didn't really talk to Jane or Paula again. They were kept very busy by Percy and Tarragon. This might have been by chance or design. It might have been out of consideration for their wives or out of jealousy. Pegasus didn't speculate.

There were telegrams, of a rib-tickling nature. And there were speeches.

Cousin Percy made a speech.

'I owe my good fortune today to the stars,' he said, 'I have won the most splendid and shining star in the whole firmament. I am a very lucky, very happy man. People often ask me at parties and dinners to make prophecies about them. I usually refuse. I don't mix business with pleasure. But this is an exception. I feel that I should pay the stars back in some way, and how better can I do that than by expressing my faith in them on your behalf? In other words by making a prediction for each and every one of you here today.'

Cousin Percy gazed sternly at the gathering, and despite the occasion they all seemed to feel a touch of solemnity. Pegasus, thin, pale, an untasted canapé in one hand, a full glass of orange squash in the other, saw that despite themselves they were becoming tense. Even his father was afraid, even Morley. Jane and Paula seemed almost petrified. The mood ran through the gathering, communicating itself even to the waiters, to everyone except Pegasus. Cousin Percy waited, letting the mood build up, holding them all in the palm of his hand, enjoying his power and their fear.

'You will all live happily ever after,' he said.